THE Quiet PART OUT LOUD

THE Quiet PART OUT LOUD

Deborah Crossland

SIMON & SCHUSTER BFYR

NEW YORK | LONDON | TORONTO | SYDNEY | NEW DELHI

SIMON & SCHUSTER BFYR

An imprint of Simon & Schuster Children's Publishing Division

1230 Avenue of the Americas, New York, New York 10020

Text © 2023 by Deborah Crossland

Jacket illustration © 2023 by Jessica Cruickshank

Jacket design by Lucy Ruth Cummins © 2023 by Simon & Schuster, Inc.

SIMON & SCHUSTER BOOKS FOR YOUNG READERS

and related marks are trademarks of Simon & Schuster, Inc.

For information about special discounts for bulk purchases, please contact Simon & Schuster Special Sales at 1-866-506-1949 or business@simonandschuster.com.

The Simon & Schuster Speakers Bureau can bring authors to your live event. For more information or to book an event, contact the Simon & Schuster Speakers Bureau at 1-866-248-3049 or visit our website at www.simonspeakers.com.

Interior design by Hilary Zarycky

The text for this book was set in New Caledonia.

Manufactured in the United States of America

First Edition

2 4 6 8 10 9 7 5 3 1

Library of Congress Cataloging-in-Publication Data

Names: Crossland, Deborah, author.

Title: The quiet part out loud / Deborah Crossland.

Description: First edition. | New York : Simon & Schuster Books for Young Readers, [2023] | Audience: Ages 12 up. | Audience: Grades 7–9. |

Summary: Told in two voices, Mia must fight to reunite with her ex-boyfriend Alfie, whom she still loves, before the aftershocks of a devastating earthquake separate them forever.

Identifiers: LCCN 2022026185 (print) | LCCN 2022026186 (ebook) | ISBN 9781665927123 (hardcover) | ISBN 9781665927147 (ebook)

Subjects: CYAC: Love—Fiction. | Earthquakes—Fiction. | Survival—Fiction. | San Francisco (Calif.)—Fiction.

Classification: LCC PZ7.1.C756 Qu 2023 (print) | LCC PZ7.1.C756 (ebook) | DDC [Fic]—dc23

LC record available at https://lccn.loc.gov/2022026185

LC ebook record available at https://lccn.loc.gov/2022026186

For my family,
those I carry,
and those who will carry me

THE Quiet PART OUT LOUD

Alfie

I DON'T KNOW WHY YOU'RE HERE IN SAN FRANCISCO AND NOT in New York like you planned, or why it hurts so much that you didn't tell me.

After last summer, I don't know a lot of things.

I can't tell you what the weather was like that day when I first noticed you in sophomore gym. I can't remember everything about the way you made the required uniform shorts and T-shirt your own or exactly how you wore your brown curls. But I do know how brave you were when you helped that girl. Everyone laughed and pointed as she stood there frozen. Then you ripped off your hoodie and wrapped it around her waist, covering the back of her shorts. The whole time, you kept your expression so deliberate and your voice so matter-of-fact.

"Girls bleed. Get over yourself."

If I say the way you looked at me as you ushered her into the locker room—daring me to laugh or feel sorry—caused tiny electric shocks to prickle my cheeks and shoulders and arms, you'd roll your eyes and tell me to quit being so dramatic.

You never saw it, but you were always so fierce, bearing witness to everyone and everything around you—everyone but yourself. You buried everything. Your emotions twisted so deep, they made a tornado of intentions. For me, it was always easy to get lost in the storm.

I'd hoped maybe after all this time, that would have changed.

But you brushed past me at the coffee shop today, as easily as you brushed aside everything we'd become. Seeing you after so long—feeling the electricity that tingled on my skin when your eyes met mine—I realized I would still happily weather all of it for you.

Your only-child life seemed so sterile next to my big, messy family, yet you carried so much more around. I never understood how you could live with all that noise in your head.

The entire year we were together, we were sprinting toward an end, never realizing what existed beyond the finish line.

But even then, we both knew we couldn't keep up the race forever.

And if seeing you today in that crowded coffee shop is the last time, it'll be enough to know you've found another path to explore.

Mia

MY CHEEKS BURN THE ENTIRE WAY BACK FROM THE INTERVIEW.
Cheeks, neck, pretty much my entire upper body. I'm afraid if I exhale, flames will escape my throat. I can't believe after all this time, I ran into Alfie in a San Francisco coffee shop. I can't believe he got a front row seat to the crap show that has become my life.

Actually, I can.

I race up the stairs to Simi's dorm, where I've been crashing these last few weeks. She'll know what to do.

Flinging open her door, I let the the city's chill barrel in with me. Before I can say anything, Simi motions behind her back for me to duck, so I do—straight to the floor. It's later than I thought.

She's on her nightly FaceTime call with her parents and, as far as they know, I'm not supposed to be anywhere near this side of the country. To avoid getting caught, I inch myself inside as quietly as I can and keep out of the camera's eye.

"What was that light, Simi? Is someone there with you?" Her father's heavy accent drones through the air. Simi cuts her eyes across the floor, telling me to stay put.

If her mom thought for a second I was taking time away from Simi's studies, she'd have us both back at home before Simi could end the call.

Simi doesn't want to go home, and I can't. I don't have one anymore. Which is why I crouch and she angles the camera away from where her roommate—and all her stuff—is supposed to be.

I mouth "Sorry" and motion for her to hurry up. When she waves her hand behind her chair, I army crawl across the linoleum floor to the empty bed on the other side of the room. Leaning against the bare mattress and metal frame, I draw my knees to my chest and focus on the twinkle lights and vanilla spice candles on her side of the room. And wait.

"No, Papa, nobody's here. Just my resident advisor dropping off a flyer. It's nothing." She holds up a random paper from her desk. "See?"

"Don't let strangers into your room. And you don't need to be going to any extracurricular activities. You are there to learn." I can practically hear her mom shaking her finger into the camera.

"Hanji, Momma, I'll be careful." She narrows her eyes at me, but only long enough for me to catch it.

"And complete all your studies. We aren't paying for you to party all night over there," her dad adds.

Simi jerks away from the screen and covers her face with her hands. "Oh my god, Papa, please stop doing that."

I break my knee hug and crane my neck just enough to get a look. Her dad is wiggling in his chair doing the "Staying Alive" one-armed dance while her mom's dark eyes glare into the camera. I bite my lips to smother a smile.

"We want straight As, Simi," she says.

"Hanji, Momma, I know. Okay, I gotta go study now." Simi waves to her screen then ends the call. She face-plants onto her desk and lets out a frustrated groan. "These nightly check-ins are going to kill me, I know it."

"Sorry." I cringe apologetically before I bounce onto the opposite bed covered only with my sleeping bag and borrowed pillow. "You will not believe what happened."

The rustle of Simi skirting her chair across the floor fills the small space. Instinctively I wonder if the floor below can hear, and I cringe. Growing up, I was taught that girls shouldn't make noise—no yelling or boisterous play, and only soft padding when shoes connect with floors, no matter if in heels or flats. I remind myself those days are over and bounce again, just because.

Let them know we're here. Who cares, right?

"Did you get the job?" Her eyebrows lift as I figure out how to form the words I'm going to need.

I fold my five-foot-seven-inch frame and cross my legs.

"About that." I bury my face in my hands, trying to hold back the flood of emotion a little longer. A year ago, I was on my way to my dream school. Now I can't even land a job pouring coffee. "Pretty sure it's a no, but technically, I left before I found out." I peek to see Simi's brows come together.

"How come?" She stares at the water brimming in my eyes. "Are you okay?"

"I . . ." Tears well in the back of my throat, too, but I swallow them. I'm not okay, but I gave up the right to be anything like okay last summer. And getting lost in emotion isn't going to help anything. I close my eyes.

The mattress sinks as Simi sits next to me. She wraps her arm around my shoulder and pulls me into her.

"Why are you so good to me?" I ask.

"Stop."

"No, really. I don't know what I'd do without you. I also don't know why you're letting me stay here."

"You're my best friend."

"But after . . ."

"After nothing. It's in the past. Let's just forget it and move on. We're here now and that's all that matters." Her voice echoes the same warning tones her mother used on her just a few minutes ago, so I don't push.

"I saw him."

"Who?" she asks.

I stay quiet, let her figure it out.

"Alfie?" She inhales sharply.

I nod into her shoulder as she squeezes me tight. I let her hold me like that while I count to five. That's all the pity I'll allow myself. With a deep inhale, I sit up and wipe my face.

"It's okay to be sad, you know. He broke up with you, and you won't even let yourself talk about it. In fact, I'm kind of surprised you're acknowledging it now."

"I acknowledge it."

She takes a long breath, then nods. "Okay."

"I do. I mean, he broke up with me, but I made him. I messed up everything." It's a talent, honestly.

Like today. I stood at the counter of the coffee shop, all fake smiles and noble intentions as the manager flipped through his preplanned interview questions. Alfie glided through the door, his brown curls tucked into a beanie, a few pieces perfectly framing his cheekbones and strong jaw. His arm and attention draped over the blonde standing next to him. A shudder rips through my core.

Before today, it's like everything we used to be existed in some alternate timeline. Keeping him as a memory of another life made this one feel like less of a failure. But the image of him walking into the café, so happy living the life exactly how he dreamt it would be, might as well have been a match. Because, instantly, my reality—the one where I chose to leave and live a happy life without him—went up in flames.

"How did he look?"

Like a Greek god?

But how do I tell Simi any of that? Especially after everything that happened. When I was the one who refused to talk about him for months. A band squeezes around my chest.

"Well, his hair is way longer than normal, and his arm was around another girl. So that's fun." My voice is sharper than I want, but I can't help wondering if he looked like that when he used to stand next to me.

"Ouch." Simi's face scrunches into a tight ball. "Well, we did know it was a possibility you'd run into him here. San Francisco isn't as big as you think."

Of course she says it more like *We should've made a plan* than *I told you so.* I don't deserve her grace, especially after I wrecked what was going to be her first official date last summer, even if it was 85 percent an accident. I exhale and try not to melt into a puddle of grateful tears. I will forever live in the shadow of my best friend.

"I thought that since you're at a different school, it might not happen," I say. "At least not this fast."

She bites at the corner of her thumbnail. After she makes sure I get her telepathic *duh*, she asks, "What did you do?"

"Oh, you know." I swallow, pushing away the memory of how his eyes crinkled at the edges when he looked at her. "Not only did I forget that the manager had asked a question, but I was staring at Alfie so hard that when the manager put his hand on my shoulder and asked if I was okay, I jumped a million feet into the air, and my complimentary iced coffee went flying."

Simi pushes her lips toward her nose.

"Exactly." I gesture to her expression. "When I tried picking up my mess, I knocked my stool over and made a ton of noise. Of course, everyone in the place turned and gawked as I stood there soaked in coffee and picking ice cubes out of my hair."

Simi shoots me a *You're being dramatic* look, but I don't stop. I can't. My chest tightens even more and my lungs shrink. I gasp for a full breath. It doesn't come. My hands squeeze around handfuls of sleeping bag underneath me. I push down. Inhale and keep talking. I have to. Because if I quit now, I'm going to lose it.

"I look up and Alfie's staring at me. Naturally, I freeze. Me, deer. Him, headlights." And the look on his face was the two tons of metal and glass about to crush me.

"It couldn't have been that bad."

"I'm going to smell like dark roast for days." I inhale, like maybe I could suck the coffee scent from the air if I try hard enough.

"What did you do?"

"What any ex faced with their replacement would do. I ran."

"Ran . . . where?" Simi crosses to her desk and shoves a book into her backpack.

"Out the door. Pushed right past him and . . . his friend."

She stops packing and arches an eyebrow.

"Sorry, I know. It's not her fault." I pick at the little balls of fabric beaded on my ancient sleeping bag as frustrated tears plop into my lap. Wiping them away with the back of my hand, I exhale hard enough to blow out any remnant of my heartbreak. I was the one who caused it; I shouldn't get to be sad about it. I paste on my best *whatever* face and nod. "So, yeah. I did the professional thing. Stayed super calm and totally impressed the manager. Expecting a call any day. End sarcasm font."

Despite my efforts, Simi knows better. She hands me a roll of toilet paper. I tear some off and wipe at my nose.

Normally, when I think of Alfie and the way everything blew up last summer, I bury everything somewhere I can't feel it. But today, standing close enough to him that I could see he hadn't shaved in a day or two, I can't shove anything else down. Those places are full, so all the hurt and regret—and shame—overflows. When Simi sits beside me again and rests her head on my shoulder, the dam I'd been trying to build shatters.

"He looked happy. Maybe confused about why I wasn't in New York, but happy. He's here, doing exactly what he wants." Without me and all my baggage, the way I thought I wanted. My chest shrinks in on itself, and I welcome the pain. I let myself lean into her.

Simi doesn't move or make a sound. Leaning against her is like resting against the tree in my backyard when I was little—the one place that was all mine—sitting in the warmth of the sun and reading until it was too dark to see. I realize she is my home now. My tree and my warmth.

"He chased after me when I ran past him." My voice is almost a whisper. "Halfway down the block. But I kept running. I couldn't bear to stand there doing that weird smiling and head nodding at each other, waiting for him to offer to catch up sometime." Because *that* would be humiliating. A sob escapes my throat. This time I want to give in. I shift away from Simi and curl into the mattress. I'm tired of fighting it.

Tired of fighting everything.

"No, don't do that." Simi stands and tightens the long, dark braid hanging down her back. "Okay, you panicked. But you've come this far. You'll figure this out. We're going to get through this."

"Maybe," I say, grateful for the *we*.

I never wanted any of this. Couch surfing in Simi's dorm, trekking around a city I don't understand, begging for minimum-wage jobs. And especially giving Alfie a first-class view of it all. My whole body feels like it's being forced into latex gloves that are two sizes too small.

Simi shoots awkward glances until I reluctantly force myself back into a sitting position. I tuck my knees into my chest and wrap my arms around them and watch her pack her bag. When she's done, she turns to me with a strange expression on her face. "Why are you looking at me like that?"

"I have something you need to see." She opens her tiny dorm-room closet.

"What?" I ask as her color pales. "If it's something from my mother, I don't want it."

She stops digging through a box and stares at me—a classic Simi move. "Why would I have anything from your mom in my closet? Does she even know you're here?"

"Probably—I don't know." I resume picking fabric balls off my sleeping bag.

Simi continues digging and pulls out a blue envelope. The same kind Alfie used to send thank-you notes after his birthday. Definitely not from Mom. My heart pounds in my throat.

"What is that?" I point to her hand.

"He gave it to me the day he left for school. Don't be mad."

I want to be exactly that. Yeah, I made a spectacle of myself that night at the bonfire and did what I did, but it was only so he could see how much better off he'd be without me. But even after that, he left me a letter? With Simi? And she's had it this entire time? Something heavy and sharp inside my chest drives me to my feet. I reach for the envelope, but she moves it behind her back.

"Simi." My voice is low, and I hardly recognize it belongs to me.

"Listen, please?" She lifts her brows and pleads with her large, dark brown eyes. It's not like her to hide things, so I have to believe she had good reason. I take in a jerky breath and force myself back onto the bed.

"He left me a letter?"

"Yes, it's from him." She holds the envelope so I see my name written in his handwriting on the front. A knife plunges into my chest as I remember all the little notes he used to leave for me on my car and in my locker. "He asked me to give it to you when you were ready to read it. I know I should've handed it over immediately, but after what happened"—she clears her throat—"and the way you shut down when anyone brought him up, I honestly didn't think you'd want it. I didn't know you still felt like this. I'm so, so sorry."

The flurry of tension slips from my shoulders. I'm the one who should be sorry. I'm the one who blocked all pathways to Alfie, even with my best friend. As always, she's looking out for what I need, not just what I want. I collapse against the wall behind me.

"I get it. It's all good."

I hold out my open palm, and she passes the letter to me.

I stare at my name written with his hand. The slightly tilted *a* and the crooked dot so it's almost over the *M* more than the *i*. Closing my eyes, I can almost feel him here in this pint-sized room with us. Smell the lemon and wood tones that hover around his warm, olive skin. But instead of his mouth sliding into a half-moon when he sees me, he's smiling at the girl by his side at the coffee shop.

I turn the envelope over and rip the flap. Taking out the binder paper stuffed inside, I unfold it.

Across the top of the page, tiny, fluffy sheep drawn in his hand set the mood for his words. He put them on every note he gave me. Normally, they're smiling with the words *I love ewe* bubbled over their heads. Sometimes they hold bunches of flowers. Other times, balloons. This time, the sheep sit in a pool of tears. Their mouths turned down, they slump as they cry.

I used to love those sheep. Now they make me burn with guilt.

His voice floats off the page, every syllable its own verse.

I glance at Simi, and her image dissolves into a watery picture. She clasps her hands under her chin and waits.

"He said he still loves me." I choke out the words that, even as I speak them, can't be true. Judging from what I saw this afternoon, he's already moved on in every way—a new city, new habits, and even a new someone to drape his arm around. "He wrote this months ago, Simi. How can he possibly still feel this way?" I think back to the shock and questions on his face as I bolted by him at the coffee shop.

Maybe?

Simi flings her arms around my neck, her weight forcing me backward on the mattress. She squeezes tight, then rolls to the foot of the bed. "This is so great! I knew it wasn't over for you two."

"I don't know—that was a long time ago."

"It's been five months." Her practicality loosens the uncertainty that lingers on my tongue. "You should find out." She eyes the phone sticking out of my pocket, the one thing I couldn't bear to leave behind when I left home.

Ran away? Can you do that at eighteen, or is it simply moving out?

"I don't know," I say. She glances at the clock on her laptop, and not for the first time. I clear my throat, glad to finally be the

one to give what's needed. "Okay, enough about me. You're meeting your library group to study for that awful advanced calculus
test. I have a busy night planned, overthinking the last few hours
and contemplating every scenario where I could've avoided seeing Alfie's arm around someone else."

She shoots me a half-concerned, half-testing-my-BS face
before resigning to pack her gigantic textbook and notes into her
backpack. "Only if you're sure."

"Of course. When I illegally took over the empty half of your
room, I promised my drama wouldn't interfere with the insanity
that is your schedule." The ease between us that we've worked so
hard to maintain returns.

"Hashtag premed life." She twists her lips into a sly grin, and
I return one the best I can. "It was either that or work in my parents' tire store until I marry a 'nice boy.'" She air-quotes and adds
her dad's accent to the last two words. "This seemed the easy way
out. See you in a couple hours?"

"Unless they need me for an immediate barista shift, I'll be
here." I wave her off as she tosses one of her decorative pillows at
me, then quietly closes the door behind her.

I stretch out my cramped legs. No one warned me about all
the walking San Franciscans do. I thought I was in shape, but
small-town cheering has nothing on these Bay Area hills.

Pulling out my phone, I notice the battery is low and make a
note to charge it as soon as I'm done. I swipe through my contacts
until his name appears. When we broke up—when I made him
break up with me—I wanted to delete it. Get rid of every picture
and every moment from every timeline, but Simi wouldn't let me.

"Give it a month and see if you feel the same way. Then do
it," she'd said. After the thirty days, I couldn't bring myself to even

look, so I left everything the way it was. And I haven't posted anything since.

Now instead of my social media chronicling my way to the future, it's become a relic of the past. A museum of heartbreak.

His name, Alfie Thanasis, stares at me from my screen along with his number and email. My insides feel like they're being twisted into weird balloon animals. Just seeing his name brings him closer. I take a deep breath and imagine his warm scent wrapping me in a hug.

I could've done that earlier, at the coffee shop, but instead, I ran. What I always do.

His number may not even work anymore. He might have a brand-new one to go with his brand-new life.

My finger hovers over the call button. Before I can press it, the memory of the last time I saw him floods my mind. The way his eyes scratched over me, like I was some stranger who bumped into him on the street. The hurt in every pore of my skin reflected in his twisted expression.

I drop my phone onto the mattress and step back. Pacing, I take several deep breaths. I cross the room to the window and peer out. Students are milling around. Some have their heads down, some keeping pace with whatever music is playing through their headphones.

That could've been me, three thousand miles and a lifetime away. It could've been us, if I hadn't messed everything up. I lost it all in the span of a few weeks.

But Alfie.

His letter makes it sound like maybe I don't have to lose him with everything else. That he's still willing to see what's left. After everything.

Maybe that's the one thing that could go right.

One after the other, I wipe my palms against my jeans. I have to try. If there's a small chance, I need to know.

With a steadying breath, I press dial.

The phone rings and I almost hang up. What do I even say? *Hey Alfie, long time, no humiliation.* But then he answers, and it's too late. He knows it's me.

"Mia?"

My finger hovers over the end button anyway.

"Are you there?"

The crust of his voice sounds like the lazy nights we spent together at the lake with nothing between us and the stars except an old blanket. The air in his words breathes worry and curiosity. It's the worry that makes me stay on the line.

"Hey, Alfie." Just saying his name out loud, to him, makes me want to crawl through the invisible wires linking our voices together. I close my eyes and press my free hand to my mouth.

"Mi." He says my name the way only he said it, and I want to burst. "You were at the coffee place. I couldn't believe my eyes."

"Yeah." I want to ask about the letter, his words. *I need to let you go because that's what you said you wanted.*

What do *you* want, Alfie? Are you content with your arms around your new girl, or is there still space for me?

"But why? I mean, why aren't you in New York? What about Sarah Lawrence?" His voice cracks a little on his last word.

"Sort of blew a job interview there. The coffee place, not New York. Never actually made it that far." I attempt to laugh, but it comes out more of a reverse hiccup. I stare at the letter spread open on the bed. *You're the love of my life.*

Am I still? Or have you forgotten all about the letter you left for me?

"Oh."

Oh. That's all he says. But what else could he say, really?

That letter says I'm the love of his life. That I deserve good things, even after all that happened.

I need to know if he still means what he said, if he feels the same.

"Alfie?"

"Yeah?" His words are close, breathy. If I shut my eyes, it'd almost be like he's standing next to me. Like I could reach out and he'd be there, the way we used to be. Easy and solid and strong. I try to be strong too.

"Simi gave me your letter."

He says nothing. I close my eyes.

"I mean today, just now. I didn't know."

He takes in a breath and lets it out slow, the way he does when he's trying to figure out what to feel.

You're the love of my life.

"Do you—are you sorry she did?" My voice is a whisper.

"No, of course not. It's just, things are different now."

I try to hear the reason in his tone—why things have changed—but I already know. Of course they have. He's moved on. Of course he has.

"Maybe not different completely. Just updated."

"Updated?" I'm surprised at the hope in my own question.

"Like, if I could write the letter today, I might add something."

"Add something?" Great, I'm an echo now.

"Mi . . ."

I beam into the phone. It's the way only he says my name. The way he used to when it was just us. But then he takes in a quick breath, and my smile falters. Did he mean to say it that way, or was it drudged up from some old habit that people who used to love each other have? I open my mouth to ask, but a deep, hollow rumble groans from the floors beneath, stopping me.

"What is that?" As soon as the words leave my mouth, my knees buckle and the world rolls off its axis.

Then three beeps end my connection to Alfie.

Before I can redial, the rumbling invades every crevice in the room. Metal grinds on metal within the walls—underwater echoes of a ship grating against rocks. The taste of iron fills my mouth, its metallic smell stinging my nose. I touch my finger to my tongue. I pull it back, its tip covered with blood.

Simi's blue-and-yellow curtains sway. Framed posters dance in an odd rhythm against sterile, white paint. Twin bookshelves crash against their respective walls like whitecaps in a storm. The light bulb in Simi's lamp explodes as it hits the floor. The overhead fluorescents flicker. They bend in on themselves, then shatter.

I whip around and snag Alfie's words from the mattress, shoving them into my pocket. Then I'm prostrate on the floor, one arm instinctively covering my head, as the room gyrates in waves. Desks grate against bed frames. Simi's chair rolls serpentine-like, smashing the broken lamp pieces littered on the linoleum. The sound of glass crunching underneath turns my stomach.

Everything is loud and quiet at the same time.

Elementary school emergency drills take over. I roll under my bed and hold on to its legs.

Thinking better of it, I cross both arms over the back of my head and squeeze my eyes shut and pray nothing falls on me. The room comes apart in sounds—the whine of steel peeling away from wood, the thud of bricks crashing into earth, toppling over each other like bowling pins smacking against alley walls.

Frames fall from the bookshelf, their glass smashing into a thousand pieces. Every muscle in my body begs me to run. Get away. Instead, I make myself as small as possible against the wall, my heart thumping as adrenaline floods my body.

I close my eyes, and images of Alfie flash in my mind. His open smile. His arm draped so casually over the girl's shoulders like it's always belonged there. I squeeze my eyes closed tighter, forcing away the mental pictures of how happy he looked without me. Drawing my knees to my chest, I hug them tight and wish his arms were around me. Protecting me the way he used to.

An eternity later, the room is still.

It's a weird feeling, after an earthquake. All movement stops, but the memory of lights swaying and books falling exists in the corners of your vision, ghosts of destruction. The creaking goes on, an ethereal reminder of aftershocks to come.

Floodlights scream awake and cast red and blue shadows over the room—a traumatic still life in emergency colors.

I fumble for my phone. When I find it, my trembling fingers press the only button I can think of. Redial. Nothing. No service.

From underneath me, the earth draws in an angry yawn, hard and fast. The whole building shifts like a kid jumping rope. Then the windows explode as it exhales.

In the hall, students yell names and scream for help. If our room looks like this, what about the rest of the building? I suck in a breath.

Simi.

Alfie

I WANT TO SCREAM.

You were here, just a second ago. On the phone. My Mia. Mi.

Now you're gone. Your voice cut off and disappeared into the chill and fog winding its way through the city. I will find you again, even if I have to search every inch of the mist-covered streets between us.

Please let there be an us.

You must be so confused. I wish I could've told you why things have changed. Of course, I will. As soon as I dig myself out of whatever this is.

The more I think about you and me, the way we used to be, the more I remember. Like the time when our orbits finally crashed into one another. Since that day sophomore year, we danced around each other in our circles, but never more than that. Cheerleaders and baseball players gravitate in different orbits, but I'd always hoped ours would collide.

I'm so glad that day you finally noticed me, too.

Even though it was November, summer lingered like old friends over coffee. At our usual table, Chuck and I shared the pool of food we'd scavenged from our parents' pantries. He pilfered the leftover cheeses and grapes from his mom's Bunco night, and I managed breadsticks and four single-serving peanut butter dips.

We talked about spring training and how this would be our

last year of high school baseball. How we couldn't wait to get out of our tiny town filled with small jobs and dead-end dreams. For me, I didn't want to be stuck working in my family's restaurant forever, even if it might break Baba's heart. Mama was helping convince him it would be better for me to go to college, learn what I could.

Be something more.

Chuck said he wanted out from under his brother's shadow. As hard as he tried, he never felt like his life was entirely his own.

Then Josuè showed up with one of his schemes that always landed us in hot water. Remember Coach's pimped-out golf cart? Purple and gold paint splashed all over the flatbed he built on the back? That purple fur steering wheel cover he'd clutch while he chased after us on our runs? He'd left his keys in it when he parked it by the storeroom, and Josuè wanted to take it for a joy-ride.

Of course, Chuck immediately said no, but Josuè knew exactly what to say to get me to play along.

"Alfie, come on, bud. You got me on this, right?" he asked.

"I like being the starting pitcher. No thanks." I stood to leave and he followed.

"Come on, man. This is a once-in-a-lifetime chance." He stared at me with his puppy dog eyes—the ones he used to get all the teachers to let him make up late work and all those girls to, well, you know. After about thirty seconds of that, I couldn't take it anymore.

"I'll go with you, but I'm not touching Coach's pimp cart."

"This is about to be epic." Josuè fist pumped the air and told Chuck to get a good seat.

When he crept close enough, he started rubbing the back of

his neck, looking everywhere but at Coach's crazy ride, the way he always did when he tried looking innocent.

I knew I should be back at the table sitting with Chuck, doing the thing we'd done every day since third grade. But this was Josuè, and I was always in between the two of them.

When Baba met him, he put his arm around my shoulder and whispered, "Every guy who plays third base is a little crazy, and this guy is the same."

But that's why we worked. Why we took the team all the way to second place. Chuck was our catcher on and off the field. Josuè took all the risks. I pitched and got out of the way.

And it was the same that day in the cafeteria when he convinced me we were just going to sit in the cart. See what Coach sees.

"You're not really going to drive it, right?" I asked.

"I'd never."

And that's when everything moved slow and fast at once.

Across the room, Chuck's mouth flattened into a line and he shook his head.

Keys jingled and the battery clicked to life.

Josuè pounded the accelerator, and we lurched into the walkway between the tables and the doors. He hooted and hollered like a cowboy riding a bull. Everyone in the cafeteria joined.

Then you walked in. With Simi. You stopped in Josuè's path—in my path. Simi's dark hair tangled in your long auburn curls—heads together in your secret world.

I shoved his foot off the pedal, and we jerked to a stop inches away from you.

I still remember the way you studied me. Your brown eyes shadowed in dark clouds. Eyebrows knitted together. You could've yelled. Told us what jerks we were for almost hitting you.

In fact, I would've preferred it.

But you just stood there—that same look in your eye—while Simi went off on Josuè as he tried defending himself. Your jaw clenched and your nostrils flared, but you stayed silent.

There's always been something more to you, especially when you're as still as you were in that moment, when you think no one is watching. Deep waters rippled across your eyes. You seemed like you were everything I wasn't, and I wanted so much to be the stone that curved under that current.

If I'd known then the kind of storm you had brewing inside of you, I would've scooped you into my arms. Held you tight so you knew you were safe from the thunder and lightning ravaging its way through you.

But it was lunch on a random day during senior year. And those things don't really happen in front of the milk line on pizza day.

Mia

I HOVER MY SHAKING HAND OVER ALFIE'S NAME ON THE SCREEN,
the rest of me frozen after everything that's happened. He'd been
right there, after all this time. And the way he'd said my name, like
it was just me and him the way it'd been before.

And then the world split in half.

Did he feel it where he was? He had to—this afternoon
proved we aren't that far apart. My heart pounds faster. He has to
be somewhere safe. But what about Simi? She could be trapped
on the stairs, or worse. As much as I want to try to call him back, I
force myself to shove my phone into my back pocket. Alfie has to
be okay. Right now, I need to find Simi.

I'll call him back after.

All I can see are images of her under a mass of people and collapsed industrial ceiling tile or lying under a big chunk of building
on the ground outside. I squeeze my eyes shut as if that can stop
my brain from picturing every way Simi might not be okay.

I need to find her. I need to find out what's going on.

I push aside last night's pizza box and random fruit that'd
tumbled out of the wrecked fridge. Sliding my shaking body from
under the bed, I shiver as cold air slinks through the places where
the windows bellowed and burst.

Sound comes from three places. The outside fog tampers the
noise coming through the window, a blanket of heavy silence. In
the room, the walls and floor creak and moan, and I imagine the

lower decks of the *Titanic* must've sounded the same way. On the other side of the door, panicked voices call out while others bark orders. None of the voices sound like hers, which only makes me shake harder.

If she's not in the panic, she's in the quiet. And I can't lose her. I can't lose one more person.

I'm aware enough to know I shouldn't be walking without shoes with the landmines of broken shards and ceiling tiles everywhere. Using the pillow that Simi had tossed at me minutes ago, I sweep what glass I can find under her bed and search for my shoes.

I find my Uggs under the desk and shake them out, just in case. Sliding them on, I find the doorknob and rip open the door.

More red and blue lights bounce off the walls. The volume of yelling and crying floods my eardrums. Autumn decorations made from construction paper—animals and trees—droop off the walls in pieces as bodies pack the ruined hall. People race to knock on doors, begging their occupants to move down the stairs immediately. I push against the throng to get to the bathroom in case she stopped in there before leaving. A girl with bleary eyes and a clipboard points to me.

"You. Follow everyone downstairs. Now." She moves to the next person, points, and repeats her command. I don't listen.

"Have you seen Simi?" I ask the boy in front of me. "Do you know her? She was just here."

When he doesn't reply, I slip into the bathroom, cup my mouth, and shout into the stalls.

"Simi! Can you hear me?"

But it's too loud; too many other people are shouting names and directions. I check under the doors—all empty. Metal grinds against stone in the walls like nails on a chalkboard, sending nauseating chills up my spine. The shaking returns, and I can't tell if it's me or the ground. I try to brace myself against one of the sinks, but it cracks off the wall and shatters into porcelain chunks at my feet. I jump out of the way just in time.

What sounds like peeling away layers of cardboard quickly evolves into stone tumbling over stone, echoing through the tiled room. When I make it to the door, people scream louder and push harder toward the stairs. There's too much cold air. I look behind me and see half the wall torn away—a perfect view of the dorm next door framed by what's left. Gulping the frigid evening air, I let myself get swallowed in the mass of people like salmon swimming upstream.

Halfway down, I tuck myself into the corner of the landing and check my phone. I click on Safari, but it never loads. I try calling Simi's number, but there's only a busy signal and recorded message. Circuits overloaded, check back soon.

Something quiet takes over the panic in my brain. Every nerve ending comes alive at once.

Working my way back into the masses descending the stairs, I allow them to carry my hollowed-out body into the open air. Two security officers direct people to a space in the nearby parking lot. I trace the way to the library in my mind. She can't be that far away.

"Simi!" I summon all the diaphragm training my three years on varsity afforded me. "Simi, where are you?" My eyes scan the crowd for a Simi-shaped person.

"Mia!" Her voice ricochets off the group of people gathered on the asphalt. "I'm over here!"

I follow her cries until I find her long braid and backpack.

Relief replaces all the air in my body. Hurried, I push past offended people on the path and bear-hug my best friend from behind. When I let go, she turns around and hugs me back just as hard.

At least one person I love is here. Alfie's voice whispering my name echoes in my memory, making my heart hiccup. First, I have to make sure Simi is all right.

"Are you okay?" I search her face for scratches and cuts. She nods. She's okay. I mentally snap a thousand pictures of her perfect face and use them to drown out the images of her from earlier I can't quite get over. "What the hell was that?"

"People are saying earthquake. Over 7.0. Maybe 8. Worse than the one in the eighties." Her wild eyes dart from the gaping hole in her building and back to me. "They're scared more buildings will collapse."

"Holy shit." I cross my arms over my chest and squeeze. "Everything went crazy. And the wall . . . Were you on the stairs?"

"No, I was already out here, but just barely. Just fell to the ground like my legs were nothing." She blinks back the water collecting in the corners of her eyes.

"Yeah, I crashed too." A flash of terror jolts through me. "Simi, your room." We trade wide-eyed expressions. It dawns on me that there's no way we'll be let back into Simi's room. All I have is what's on my body. And my phone is already almost dead, not that I could use it anyway.

My mind races with the idea of no place to sleep. Owning nothing but what we carry—warm boots and an old letter for me, a backpack with an industrial-sized calculus book for Simi.

An overwhelming wave of defeat washes over me. I miss home, but it doesn't exist anymore either.

"What do we do now?" I ask.

"I don't know. Those guys are trying to get everyone out of the way in case stuff starts coming down. I'm sure they're going to make us shelter somewhere else tonight." Her eyes trail up to where her room is supposed to be. "My parents are going to flip out."

"We're going to be okay." My voice surges with confidence, even if it's propped up on empty hope. I put my arms around her and smooth the top of her hair.

Around us, trees rest at forty-five-degree angles, like they can't make up their mind to fight or give in to the earth's rumbles. Nearly every window in Simi's building is blown out, glass still falling in the aftershocks. But the building next to it looks the same as it always did—maybe a little quieter now that everyone stands outside.

It's like that all around. Some spaces are in complete ruin. Others, business as usual. But who knows what might collapse next? Every new shake poses a potential threat.

I close my eyes and imagine the way things were only a little while ago. Me on Simi's bed. Alfie's voice a hug around my heart. He has to be okay. Please let him be safe.

More than anything, I want to go back to the way it was before everything changed. Before I was about to be homeless in a strange town with no way for anyone from home to get to us. At least Simi has the safety of her student status to keep her sheltered and fed. I'm a squatter with no way to keep warm or get food. I don't even have a debit card.

Alfie's words come flooding back. *Things are different now.*

The trees, dorm, being safe. Alfie.

My entire body trembles as the layers of regret, denial, and if

I'm being honest, the rage I've been ignoring peel away from my heart—the one thing that hasn't changed.

I still love him.

The realization explodes inside me. My own personal earthquake, knocking down all the walls I've so carefully built over the last five months.

I'm so stupid for having pushed him away like I did.

I open my eyes and pull out my phone. I have to try.

"Who are you calling?" Simi asks. "Is it going through?"

Nothing but *All circuits are busy, try again later.* I swallow hard.

The idea that *later* might not exist starts my body trembling all over again.

"I was talking to Alfie when the earthquake hit. We got disconnected."

"What?" She pulls back. "What did he say? What did you say?"

"Not much, really. We didn't have time. Everything happened and the phone went dead."

"Mia." She shrieks my name as she grasps my shoulders. "If the dorms at State aren't safe, what about USF? They have way older buildings than we do." The blood drains from her cheeks.

"I know." Mine pools in my feet. My knees lose any hope of keeping me upright, and we both topple onto the cold tarmac. I land on some guy's shoes. He throws me a dirty look before he scuttles away.

The images of Simi hurt after the earthquake come roaring back, only this time, it's Alfie. Phone in hand, blood and brick—I shut my eyes, too afraid to see him broken, even if it's only in my imagination.

A wave of shame washes over me.

The last time I saw him, I ran away, too afraid he'd see exactly how much of a failure I am. Even though I found the courage to call him, he said everything's changed. And then the world turned upside down before I could ask what he meant. And most important, if what he said in the letter was still true.

My heart rises to my throat and I have to swallow to keep it—and the tears—inside.

The words forming in my mouth are an apology. But not to the guy with the shoes.

Since summer, that apology took up residence in my core and has played over and over in my head. Silently, in the background of everything else. I drop something in the kitchen? *I'm so sorry, Alfie.* I leave the door unlocked? *Alfie, I didn't mean it.* I get an email from a school across the country my dad "forgot" to pay for? *Alfie, you didn't do anything wrong. It was all me.*

It's stupid, but even though I did what I did, I always knew he was out there, only out of reach because I pushed him away. More than stupid—arrogant. Now he might be gone for real.

The idea is like a knife ripping through the fabric I'd used to hide how much I missed him.

A world without Alfie is more terrifying than going through it alone. At least knowing he was in it somewhere, making the world a better place with his pretty words, I could always hope.

He did send that letter. He wanted me to know he was still here. For me. When I was ready.

Now it might be too late.

I need to see him. Touch his face and hold his body against mine, just to know he's here. Because I know I won't be able to breathe until I do. In my bones, I know I need to find him. Look him in the eyes and tell him how thoughtless I've been these last five months—the contrived fights, me pushing him away, needing to be free of someone who could still look at me like he did today, even after everything.

I search Simi's face for the words I can't say out loud.

"Do you think he's okay?" Her eyes fill with tears. She nods over and over as if her insistence could override any other outcome.

"I need to find him." Tiny aftershocks strike my bloodstream like Pop Rocks exploding on my tongue and spread outward through my limbs.

"Did he say where he was?"

I shake my head.

"He was at that coffee place earlier." She raises an eyebrow. I answer her unasked query.

"She doesn't matter." I take in a breath to calm my voice that's shaking as much as the rest of me. "I have to know he's all right."

If he still feels the same way I do about him. *Things are different now.*

"Of course." Simi squeezes my hand as I set my expression. She squares her shoulders with the fact that nothing is going to convince me not to, but her eyes keep darting to her own ruined dorm.

"Everything's shut down, though. How will we get all the way across town?"

We?

"No way." I stand and she follows. "You need to stay here, safe. I'm sure they'll have shelter for you and a way to contact your mom and dad before long. I'm not really here, right? I can't stay."

I look around at all the faceless students standing in groups, their clustered bodies creating boundaries into their own worlds.

Simi should easily be able to find refuge in one of them.

"I'm not letting you go alone." Her hand slides into mine.

I open my mouth to argue, but her jaw is resolute. No use. Despite the chill, a warmth flickers in my chest.

"Well, like you said, this place isn't as big as everyone thinks. We can probably walk there." I attempt a smile.

"Hang on." She throws her backpack onto the ground between us. After some rummaging, she pulls out a laminated map of the San Francisco city proper.

"Why do you have a map of the city in your backpack? Not that I'm not grateful. I just . . ."

"My parents made me promise to carry it in case I got lost." She rolls her eyes, but there is still worry behind them.

"They do know cell phones and Google Maps exist, right?"

"Of course they do. They're just extra careful." A small sob escapes her lips. "Do you think they're okay?"

"Your mom and dad?" I wrap my arms around her. "They're one hundred miles away. They're far enough. I'm sure we'll hear from them as soon as the phone lines go back up."

She nods into my shoulder, and we stay huddled together until she stops shaking.

"You know I can't read that, right?" I nod to the paper city in her hand.

"Then it's a good thing I'm coming with. Where do we start?" She lifts her chin and blinks away the rest of her tears. I take a deep breath and blow it out, forcing away the fear rising up my spine.

"Coffee shop?"

"Sounds like a plan."

We shake off the cold and fog as best we can and make our

way toward the last place I saw Alfie. As we walk, I'm finally able to summon the memory of his brown curls, his warm smile. If all goes well, his perfect arms will be wrapped around me in the doorway soon, soothing my pounding heart.

But if it doesn't . . .

Cold sweat forms above my lip as my body shivers at the thought.

Please, Universe, let that not be the last time I see him.

Alfie

EVERY WINTER, I THANKED THE UNIVERSE FOR THE WALL THAT separated the neighborhood houses from the high school. Do you remember it, Mia? The one with all the pink camellias that only bloomed in the winter? That was my favorite thing about driving to school in the misty dark of late fall and winter. Well, until I realized I'd get to see you every day. Then the camellias came in a rough second.

After Josuè pulled that stunt with Coach's golf cart, I wasn't sure you'd ever talk to me again.

Not that we ever really talked, anyway, except a *Here you go* or *Thanks* in classes we had together. If a teacher liked to mess with alphabetical order, I might've been lucky to sit near you. But your last name is *C* and mine's a *T*. Mostly, I watched you from the other side of the room, deciphering the hidden meaning of your every expression.

In class, or in the cafeteria with the other cheerleaders, your smile functioned as a tool—a fast pitch turned curveball—purposeful, but ultimately off. I fell for the real smile, the one you saved for people like Simi. Your eyes sparked as your lips spread wide, a warm summer breeze.

When Josuè nearly hit you, neither smile was anywhere near your lips. I mean, the way you stared me down, I had to do something to get you to forgive me. After all this time, you'd finally noticed me, but not in the way I'd hoped. I had to take the chance that the whole mess was a sign to change that.

Except there was no way I could walk up and apologize in front of everyone. I'd have said something ridiculous, and that would've been it. I knew whatever I did had to be big.

I've always been better expressing myself writing words instead of saying them. That's why I stopped at the wall that day and picked all those camellias for you. I knew flowers and a couple of notes would definitely go over better than me stuttering all over myself.

My sister Anna threw a fit. Said I was killing flowers for a "stupid romantic gesture," but I reminded her pruning is what makes more blooms. Besides, I didn't care what she said. This was about to be epic or the worst disaster ever.

You should've seen your face when you saw the first one I put on your locker. My heart soared when the tiniest smile curled the corner of your mouth as you read the sticky note I left with the pink bloom: *Like this flower, your smile defies the winter gray.* When Simi ripped it out of your hand to read it for herself, you cleared your throat and rolled your eyes. But I saw how happy you were before you buried it under your typical nonchalance.

I just wish I'd gotten the nerve to tell you it was me who left them.

You've always been so guarded, Mia. Afraid that if you show the smallest amount of emotion, it'd swallow you whole. Like dipping your toes into the ocean will suck you into the tide and carry you away.

I loved that you carried that camellia all the way through lunch and set it on your desk in English. I'd gotten there early to see if you'd let yourself really smile when you saw the next one sitting in your seat. Luckily, I wasn't the only one in the room and my secret would stay safe.

"'Sup." Chuck skated in behind me and slapped my shoulder. I cocked my chin in his direction.

Right before the tardy bell, you and Simi slid into your own seats.

You were still holding the flower from your locker, but you stared at Simi, wide-eyed and biting your bottom lip. Her eyes darted between the newest bloom and you. She mouthed "Oh em gee" and glanced behind her, where Josuè should've been sitting.

"I know," you whispered.

Chuck knocked the back of my head with his pen, and I flipped around. He nodded at the two of you huddled over the note and raised his eyebrow. I pasted on a blank expression and shrugged. He flattened his mouth and narrowed his eyes, shaking his head.

Innocent face aside, my heart was about to pound right through my rib cage, and you didn't even know the flowers were from me.

"Who do you think they're from?" Simi asked you.

"I have zero clue. You don't think it's Josuè, do you? For being stupid yesterday? The golf cart thing?" You studied the note for clues. Chuck snorted behind me. Simi's face blanched and I held my breath. Then you tossed your brown curls dismissively. "There's no way. He's not the poetry type."

I almost told you right then. That it was me and not Josuè. Because he always got the girl. And normally that was fine. But you were you, Mia. And I couldn't stand the thought of you and him, even though I knew you'd never fall for any of his lines.

Simi chuckled and glanced at his empty desk, but there was something about her reaction that didn't seem too convincing. Like she thought Josuè was definitely the poetry type.

"You know who is, though." Simi subtly nodded at me, but I pretended to be engrossed in whatever worksheet Ms. Downing had us doing that day, with my EarPods firmly planted in my ears. "You don't think . . ."

"Stop! No way." You swiveled forward and buried your face in your hands. In muffled tones, you added, "I can't believe you said that."

The way you reacted so quickly, so pointedly against the idea that I might be the one leaving you winter camellias all day, turned my lungs into lead. And I had to inhale twice as deep just to get enough air.

And there was still the one I left on your car. The one I was going to wait with. To tell you it was me. That I'm the one who loves winter blooms—the way they remind me of you. I remember that day when you pretended to be annoyed that freshman was crying in front of your favorite mirror in art class. You always checked your hair in it before going to your next class. But that day, you were ten minutes late because you stayed to talk her through her first breakup.

If I could, I'd pluck every bloom and give them to you.

But the way your expression twisted into revulsion, like if it was me, you might be sick. I couldn't tell you. Not then. Not ever.

"Just a question." Simi's voice was light, but she stared pointedly at me like I was a piece of code she couldn't quite get right. I buried my head in the grammar lesson as Chuck patted my back. I shrugged him off, though, because if I reacted, Simi would've known. Then you would've too. And that couldn't happen. Not anymore.

When Ms. Downing asked us to pass up our papers, I looked at the first question—something about not using second person in writing—the *you*. And then I had an idea. I didn't turn in my paper that day. Instead, I drew tiny little sheep, tiny ewes holding fluffy pink camellias all around the border. In the blank space, I wrote: *I wish ewe could see ewerself the way I see ewe.*

I crumpled my page into a ball, asked to be excused, and threw it in the trash on my way out. You don't know this, but I'd planned on taking down every flower I'd left for you. The one at your gym locker I'd paid some freshman to place. The one at your usual spot in the library. And certainly the one on your car.

But when I made it outside, something about the way the sun peeked through the enormous clouds made me think that somehow, some way, some of your sunshine might find me sometime too.

And I'm so glad I left them right where they were.

Mia, I know it seems like the world opened up and swallowed us whole. And the thick fog swathing the city doesn't help. But when I find you, I will turn this broken city upside down to find you the biggest, pinkest camellia it has to offer, just to see your smile bloom one more time.

Mia

THE DUST IN THE AIR HANGS LIKE THICK FOG. I KEEP MY EYES
trained on the broken ground, careful not to twist an ankle in the
cracks between the broken chunks of cement that used to be sidewalks.

Across the street, water gushes into the road from a tilted fire
hydrant. I don't know what we'll do if a fire pops up.

The sun dips behind the horizon as the moist evening fog
winds its way through the bedlam of people in the streets. Some of
them pick up bits of plaster that used to belong on the buildings.
Others are hugging friends and crying while still others frantically
push buttons on their phones in a futile attempt to reach their
loved ones. A few gather in clumps, exchanging excited stories.

Simi whispers "Waheguru," the Sikh name for *God*, over and
over under her breath, something she does when she's nervous.
My heart slows to the rhythm of her chant—a bit of respite from
all the chaos.

Farther down, a group of guys—probably from a fraternity—
help direct traffic while others shout invitations to an end-of-the-
world party as cars slither by. As the weather's tendrils wrap around
my torso, I shiver and tug at my sleeves, wishing I'd had the fore-
sight to grab a jacket or hoodie or something. Simi bunches her
hoodie close around her neck. She looks me up and down, then
sighs, sliding her backpack over her arm.

"Put this on. At least it'll keep your back warm." She extends her arm, and I exhale some of the tension from my shoulders. I loop her bag over my shoulders, and the weight of what's inside collides with my bones. I puff out a breath.

"Geez, how much does your calculus book weigh? You could've warned me about potential broken spines." My stomach sinks at my biting tone. I start to offer an apology, but Simi interrupts.

"Yours or the book's?" Her eyes beg for a distraction from all the awful surrounding us.

"Very funny." I muster a watery smile in return.

"Besides, it's in the disclaimer you signed when we became best friends. 'Will carry heavy books and broken hearts for designated BFF.'" She air-quotes the last part, turning her attention to me. Despite her light tone, my breath catches in my throat.

No need for plural. There's only one broken heart.

My eyes fall to the ground just in time to see a large, jagged piece of a parapet from the nearby building right in front of her.

"Careful!" I grab her arm as she skips over it. "That was close."

I loop my arm with hers instead of letting go. Something about the rising darkness and the quiet of the fog makes me want her close—not to mention to protect us both from tripping on random rocks and broken cement. She burrows into my side, telling me she feels the same.

As we walk, my mind drifts to the day Alfie apologized for almost running into us with the golf cart. He didn't need to. He wasn't the one driving. But he never cared about that. He wanted us—me—to know how he felt. And he showed me the only way Alfie Thanasis could. Sweeping romantic gestures.

I saw the first pink bloom poking out from the slats of my locker before school even started. I thought for sure someone got the wrong metal door. I scanned the hallway, half-prepared for someone to claim the flower, saying, "Oops, wrong person!"

Alfie and Josuè were at the end of the hall, but they were laughing about something on one of their phones. No one else seemed to be paying attention.

I lifted the stem and settled the camellia under my nose. That's when I noticed the sticky note wrapped around the bottom. I unfolded it and read, thinking it'd be some cheesy *Do you like me, yes or no* thing.

My heart swelled when I saw the words. Who writes poetry these days? I must've turned eighty shades of red because I could feel heat rising from my back all the way up to my cheeks.

Then Simi was there, yanking the note from my hand, squealing with delight. Jumping up and down and listing possible suspects.

But then my stomach flipped. What if it really wasn't for me? Or what if someone was playing a joke? I rolled my eyes, trying to play it off, but Simi knew better.

When I got to English and saw the second camellia on my desk, all my muscles carrying the worry that this was a joke relaxed.

It *was* for me. They were for me.

Over lunch, Simi narrowed the culprits to Josuè and Alfie because of the golf cart thing. And when she saw the one in class, she almost gave it away.

How much I wanted it to be Alfie.

But I couldn't say anything out loud until I was sure.

He gave me five flowers that day. Then it seemed like a random number. Now it feels like one for every month we've been apart. One for every time my heart cracks just a little more.

After a while, Simi slows her pace over the broken sidewalks.

"I'm not entirely sure of the direction. Should we check the map?"

I realize I've been following her instead of thinking about which way to turn. I glance at the surroundings to hide the flush in my cheeks.

"Yeah, good idea." I release her arm and turn so my back is facing her.

She unzips the backpack and rummages inside until she pulls out her parents' laminated map of the city. I take out my phone for the light and am reminded of my low battery.

"Shit, I'm at ten percent. Can we use yours?" The flush of embarrassment in my face deepens into frustration.

She nods. After shoving my phone back into my pocket, I open the map and try finding the You Are Here spot in the fading light. Simi shines her phone's flashlight over the page, but the light is too strong and creates a glare. She tries a couple of angles, but none of them let us see all we need to.

We don't really know where we're going, and if those frat boys across the street have any say, they'll soon be drunk and out in droves. A wave of doubt washes over me.

Am I doing the right thing? Is it worth risking our safety to find Alfie? Will he even want to see me after the way I left things? The way he said my name before we were cut off . . . maybe? I close my eyes and tilt my face to the sky. If only we'd had five more seconds. I would know everything I needed to. Instead, I'm risking Simi's life to traipse through a broken city that might not be done breaking—just to hear him finish his sentence. He seemed happy to hear from me, but people do that when they hear from people they used to know. It's the polite thing to do. Right?

All I can think about is his arm around that girl earlier. But that wasn't even the worst of it. The way he looked when he was with her. Relaxed. Happy. Something I haven't seen in a long time.

What if they're not there? Or worse: What if the coffee shop looks the way Simi's dorm does? What if they're trapped?

A heaviness replaces the hope that burst in my heart only a few minutes ago.

Simi places a hand on my shoulder and squeezes. It helps.

A car slows to a stop next to us, and a group of teens hop out. My eyes pop open and my heart pounds. I instinctively stop and pull Simi even closer. The driver pops the trunk while the rest of them scavenge the sidewalk for broken bits of building and load them into the car. The car bounces low as they drop the larger pieces in.

"What are you going to do with those?" My voice snaps in the middle of my sentence. One of the girls shrugs before she dives into the back seat.

"Sell them for souvenirs!" the driver yells as he peels away.

"People will always be people." Simi shakes her head.

"Good or bad, that never changes." I keep my eyes on them until they're around the corner. When they're out of sight, I fish Alfie's letter out of my pocket and stare at his words. Simi's right. People don't change that much, even when they pretend they have.

Folding the paper into its familiar creases, I tuck it in between my phone and its case and place it all in my front pocket for extra security. We resume our trek until the last of twilight disappears behind the broken houses in front of us.

We walk in silence, careful not to disturb grieving neighbors as we navigate what's left of the sidewalks. As the sky deepens, people stand on their duplex stairs, calling to their neighbors.

Some wear bandannas over their mouths and noses. Others use masks left over from when the world felt like it was ending in another way. Some hug when they see each other. Others are sweeping broken glass and building detritus from their stoops. I find Simi's hand and squeeze and try not to let fresh tears roll down my cheeks.

Ahead, two large planters lie on their sides. I don't know why, but when we get close, I right them. I suck in a breath as a jolt shoots down my spine. One small camellia bloom dangles from one of the bushes, its neck broken.

I twist it the rest of the way off and bring it to my nose, even though I know they have no smell. Its tender petals against my skin are almost too much as the memories of Alfie's flowers come flooding back.

The wreckage around us reminds me of that last day I could call him my boyfriend. Haunts me as I make my way along the darkened backdrop of the emerging stars. The ruined sushi. Untouched ice cream in pools of sticky liquid. The text he sent after he walked away.

But then, there's this single camellia. Defying the ruins. A message.

Keep going.

The hope that my past mistakes could be fixed as soon as tonight pushes me toward the next block, and the one after.

Alfie

EVEN THOUGH I'D GIVE ALMOST ANYTHING TO GIVE YOU A CAMEL-lia now, by the end of class that day, I'd decided not to take credit for leaving you all those flowers around school. You seemed so happy that you had a secret admirer creating a mysterious game just for you. But when Simi asked if you thought I might be the one, your expression told me everything I needed to know—there was no way you wanted it to be me.

At least, that's what it looked like. And even though more flowers were waiting for you, I vowed right then and there at the end of English to leave it a forever mystery.

But Chuck wasn't going to let me off that easy. He never did, right?

"You only get one life, dude. Take your shot."

Honestly, I'm glad he talked me into waiting by your car that day after school, because senior year—my life—would've been a lot different if he hadn't.

When the last bell rang, I walked as quickly as I could to the parking lot without looking like some sort of fiend, so I wouldn't chicken out. But as the fates would have it, you and I parked in the same aisle that day, and I had to pass my truck to get to your car. And as soon as I saw my ride out of there, all the nerve drained from my body.

Chuck must've known that was going to happen, because he and Josuè were right behind me.

"Alfie, my dude, tell me you finally got the balls to tell Mia you like her. That the whole flower-palooza was you." Josuè tapped steeple-folded hands to his lips.

"I didn't tell her anything. Yet."

"But it was you." It was more of a statement than a question, and I nodded. He opened up for a bro hug and clapped me on the back when I accepted. "'Bout time, bruh."

"Let's not out him to the whole campus," Chuck said. "At least let the man be the one to tell her."

"Yeah right. Alfie's going to wimp out anyway." Josuè punched my shoulder and scanned the crowd. "Here she comes." He spun on his heels and propped himself against the back of my truck, his arms folded over his chest. Chuck rested an elbow on the tailgate and crossed one foot over the other, watchdogging Josuè like usual.

You and Simi walked straight to the car, making as little eye contact with people as possible. Like you knew the whole parking lot was watching. Waiting to see what was going to happen next. I had zero idea what to do with my six-foot frame. Suddenly it was too big, too conspicuous. I could've waved, said hi, anything. Instead, I stood there, backpack drooping at my side. You know, super hot.

Then Simi stopped in her tracks and pointed to your windshield. "Look."

Your gaze followed Simi's finger. Your eyes got so big when you saw it—the last flower. But instead of a smile, your neutral expression morphed into a grimace. Like the mysterious game you'd enjoyed this morning had become a torturous trial. Instead of a curious glance to find who might be leaving them, your eyes darted from person to person, accusing anyone who dared participate.

Your reaction was a knife plummeting into my gut.

Chuck rested his hand on my shoulder, and through the weight of his touch, compassion and strength bled from him to me. I blew out a breath and thanked God for extra-strength deodorant.

You approached your car like the last bloom of the day might explode any moment and slid it from under the wiper. And even though you had to know by now that camellias have no scent, you brought it to your nose and inhaled anyway. Like you weren't giving up on the hope that something so beautiful might smell good too.

God, Mia, I always loved that about you. Your determination to find beauty, even when it eluded you.

The whole time you were smelling the flower, Simi turned in circles, her eyes narrowing at potential suspects. When they landed on me, the corner of her mouth slid upward.

One girl huddled with the rest of your cheer pack yelled, "Go, Mia!" Others hooted and applauded.

Chuck squeezed my shoulder, then let go. Josuè waggled his eyebrows and jerked his head toward you. He never understood how hard it was for me to work up the courage to talk to any girl, especially you. It was always so easy for him.

"Shut it, Josuè."

"I said nothing." His hands rose in defense.

"You going over there?" Chuck's eyes landed on my throwing hand, which was opening and closing the way it does when I'm nervous. "You all right? Take a breath, bro."

I did, forcing my hand to relax. I wanted to walk over there to you, tell you all the flowers were from me. I wanted to believe you'd smile and hug me and everyone would cheer and Josuè would shout something stupid like *Get a room!* But as usual, you kept your true emotions hidden from the world, and I had no idea how you'd react. Only Simi's slight smile in my direction gave me hope.

Like he could read my mind, Chuck whispered, "There's only one way to find out."

I forced one foot in front of the other and walked toward you as casually as I could manage. Luckily, you were looking the other way, unlocking your car and throwing your bag on the back seat. Simi saw me and tapped you on the shoulder, nodding in my direction with an expectant smile on her face.

I knew that could be a good sign. They say you've got a better chance when the best friend likes you.

But then you turned around and, when our eyes met, your whole face went white. Like vanilla-sheet-cake white. Your dark eyes turned into saucers, and your normally soft shoulders resembled icebergs.

My whole world shifted, but we stayed where we were. Phones popped up from all sides as people awaited what they thought was coming next.

I couldn't tell you it was me. Not in front of all these people with eager fingers poised over their Instagram. Not with Simi's mouth scrunched together. Not with Josuè ready to remind me for the rest of forever what a loser I was with girls.

So I adjusted my backpack over my shoulders, swallowed the hope of telling you how I really felt, and bent my mouth into a *Hey there* smile.

"Uh, hi." I twisted my hand into a small wave. "Do you remember what pages we're supposed to read for English? I forgot to write it down."

You chewed your bottom lip for an eternity before you

answered. Some people lowered their phones and picked up whatever conversations they'd been having before I walked over. Others were still aiming cameras, hoping they wouldn't miss anything. I rocked back and forth on my heels, hands buried in my front pockets while I waited.

Part of me hoped you would ask about the flowers. If I was the one. But the rest of me knew that was never going to happen. Just as well, right?

"Yeah, she said the first thirty, I think?" Your voice was higher than normal, but I chalked it up to not wanting to talk to me. When Simi elbowed you, I knew you two would be joking about me later. I pretended not to notice, but hot humiliation crept up my neck all the same.

"Okay. The book looks kind of cool. Knights in shining armor and all that." You know I babble when I get nervous. That day was no different.

"I guess. If you're into that sort of thing," you said.

"Chivalry, romance. Who isn't into that sort of thing?" Simi raised an eyebrow in my direction, but you didn't react. "Honestly, I'm there for the sword fighting and not much else."

Mia, I can't believe I said that. Can. Not. I thought Simi's eyes were going to bug out of her head. You have no idea how much I begged for the earth to open up and swallow me whole right then. Still I managed to babble on. "Well, thanks for the reminder. Have a good afternoon."

Yep, I said *Have a good afternoon*, too. Who was I, the host at Denny's? No wonder you didn't reply. It was hot that day, right? I remember it being really hot.

I pivoted as fast as I could without looking like a lunatic and beelined it to my truck.

Josuè doubled over, laughing his ass off as I threw my backpack into the truck bed next to my gym bag. Chuck patted my shoulder but said nothing.

"Told you he wouldn't do it." Josuè wiped his face with his sleeve.

"Ease up, Guzman. Did you see her face when I walked up? You wouldn't have said anything either." I fumbled with my keys and unlocked the driver's door.

"If I'd walked up, her face wouldn't have looked like that." He flashed his famous smile and I rolled my eyes.

"You're a dick," I said, but dammit I smiled too.

"I'm aware . . ." He half walked, half danced to his car. "Peace."

After Chuck left, I positioned myself behind the wheel of my own truck and cranked the engine. You and me were probably never going to happen. I was destined to split the rest of senior year between Baba's restaurant and baseball training with Chuck and the team.

Mia, even though we ended the way we did, I've never been so glad to be so wrong about anything in my entire life. Because even a few months with you was worth what happened.

After that parking lot fiasco, I was pretty sure the chance I'd had to get you to notice me was over. That I was relegated to being the invisible guy sitting behind you for the rest of the year.

Then you and Simi walked into the restaurant.

Of course it was before the dinner rush, so the only people in there were the papous from church—the ones who'd lounge around, drink coffee, and play round after round of How Fast Is the World Going to Hell in a Handbasket. At home, Baba complained that all they did was sit for hours, drinking free refills and taking tables away from paying customers, but we all knew he secretly loved it. In fact, he'd been known to go a few rounds with them himself. Not that he'd ever admit it to Mama.

I'd cemented myself at the condiment station, filling ketchup and tzatziki bottles to avoid the eternal questions about baseball stats and girls and colleges, when the bell over the door chimed.

"Welcome to Zorba's. Sit anywhere." I waved my free hand without turning around. Shuffling feet and muffled whispers filled the room; then someone cleared their throat. I should've known then, because even the papous got quiet.

"Thanks."

I froze. I knew that voice. I heard it every day in English. Coming from the seat in front of mine.

Yours.

My eyes closed, like I was a stupid ostrich burying my head in the sand, but there was nowhere to go. My breath raced against my heartbeat, both trying to break some sort of record. My hands went a little numb, so I shook them in an attempt to get them to cooperate in filling the last bottle. I know it's lame, but I was glad for that last bottle since it meant I didn't have to face you and relive the earlier embarrassment in the parking lot.

Suddenly the condiment stand was my makeshift altar, and I prayed to the seasoning gods to let me spend the rest of the afternoon facing this way. I promised to be the keeper of ketchup, master of the mustard, and slayer of salt and pepper packets.

I couldn't think about why, of all the places in town to eat, you came to the one my family owns. I figured after what happened, the last place you'd ever want to be is around me. And since everyone in town knows we own Zorba's and I've worked there every day after school since eighth grade, you'd have a good idea that I would, in fact, be there.

I can't tell you how many stay-calm breaths I took in those minutes. Or how much I wished I'd applied a few rounds of that extra-strength deodorant because my shirt was beginning to stick to me like I'd run laps for Coach.

Muffled whispers and giggles filled the air as chairs scratched against the linoleum. "Don't lose it now, Thanasis," I whispered to myself. Fat lot of good that did.

Then Baba emerged from the kitchen and looked around. With a perturbed look in my direction, he switched on his Big Fat Greek persona.

"Ti kaneis. Come in. Sit. You want coffee? Cokes?" Baba was all smiles and welcoming gestures. "Alfie, what are you doing? Get over there and help that table. Go use those fancy words you're always writing in those books." He used hushed tones in Greek, like the place wasn't practically empty and his voice wasn't echoing off the faded blue walls. "Cute girls, come on." That last part he said in English.

Because of course he did.

I wanted to melt into the floor.

With a deep breath, I summoned the courage to turn around and face you.

Your flushed cheeks matched your pink hoodie, the same one you wore at school. Simi sat next to you, her eyes wide as she stared at the napkin-wrapped silverware in front of her. Thanks to Baba, there was no choice. I slid two menus off the counter and handed one to you and one to Simi.

"Hey."

"Hey," you returned.

"Can we get some waters?" Simi asked.

I nodded and practically flew to the kitchen, grateful to be free of the awkward, even for a moment. Two more old guys showed up, and Baba yelled for me to bring coffee. After placing the waters on your table, I asked if you wanted anything else. Which hello, of course you did. Because it was a restaurant. That served food. Pinching my lips into a tight grin, I waited for your answer.

"Alfie, bring the kafe." Baba's accent always got thicker when those guys were around, remember? Pretty sure he did it on purpose. Like he was trying to give the patrons a show.

I know it was just business to him, but I always hated it. Even though I was born in the hospital a mile down the road, his over-done accent and bigger-than-life gestures made me feel like the town saw us as outsiders. As you know too well. I know you don't like me to bring it up, so I won't. But just like the smile you like to keep hidden, that awful feeling of being unwelcome lies beneath my skin. A forever foreigner in your own town.

Anyway, what happened next was the worst. And the best.

After I got the coffee and dealt with the over-the-top, old-man head nods and overgrown eyebrows waggling in your direction, I turned toward your table, but the two of you were gone. You'd left a couple dollars poking out from a folded paper, even though you only ordered water. When I picked it up, I saw it was my paper, the one I'd thrown out. The one I drew all over. I unfolded it and saw what you wrote.

"Thanks for the flowers, Alfie. I knew it was you. Sorry I got nervous. Text me."

Quickly turning the opposite way, I tucked the paper and the dollars into my front pocket before anyone else noticed. A new tension pushed my heart to thump wildly against my chest, and I practically danced through the rest of my shift. Because you saw me, Mia.

I knew in my bones then that nothing would ever be the same. After talking to you earlier, I know it's still true. The fog is so thick through these streets, Mia, and I'm trying not to get turned around. I will find you again, and when I can hold you in my arms, I will show you how much I still mean everything I wrote to you.

Mia

IT'S HARD NOT TO GET TURNED AROUND. SURE, STREETLIGHTS and the electric glow of buildings are considered pollution, but it never occurred to me how dark a place could be without them. I'd seen the back roads of the wine country at night where I grew up, but something about seeing San Francisco fade to black as the sun disappears makes the shadows more foreboding. The dusty cement and ash mounting in the atmosphere makes it appear like the darkness is rising up from the deep, swallowing the city like Jonah's whale.

I clear my throat, and the sound falls flat, absorbed into the thick air. I breathe in extra deep to combat the caged-in feeling. Suddenly my collar is too close to my neck and the backpack feels a hundred pounds heavier.

Simi and I walk another block in the direction we think we're supposed to go, but it doesn't feel right. The darkness is so heavy, it's hard to focus. She unfolds her map at the next corner and attempts to find the You Are Here point one more time. With any luck, Alfie's date ran long and he's still at the coffee shop, helping to keep everyone safe and calm—even the girl he went with.

The thought of him on the phone with me while he was at the coffee shop with her tickles me more than I can admit. I add another stone to the guilt stack weighing on me.

"Do we go left here or should we have turned at the last corner?" Simi holds the map at an angle to catch whatever light she can find. "Or do we turn at the pedestrian bridge?"

I crinkle my forehead and bite my lip as I try summoning some sort of directional hint.

Under the ashy sky, the way the streets wind into each other looks more like a labyrinth than a city block. If any of the street signs are still standing, most of them are unreadable.

"I can't remember." I shift my weight from one foot to the other. I was so caught up in trying to not freak out about acting like a complete fool in front of Alfie, not to mention completely bailing on a job interview, that I barely noticed which direction I walked—okay, sprinted—back toward Simi's dorm. "Can you tell on the map?" My voice is tight.

She traces a path with her finger, shakes her head, and tries another way. "Don't worry, I'll figure it out."

I nod too fast and try to breathe normally. My lungs protest and won't fill all the way. Pressing my palm into my forehead, I take in a big breath and exhale.

As she tries to make sense of the map, my feet won't stay still. We made this decision awfully fast. We didn't really take the time to consider what would happen once we left campus. At least there, people could work together. Figure out how to get through all this.

But out here, it's just me and Simi. What if it all goes wrong?

My mom used to always say I'm too dramatic—that I want too much. My insides shrink. What if this is one of those times?

And what about Simi's safety? If anything happens to her because of one of my whims, as Mom would call it, I'd never forgive myself.

On the phone, Alfie said things were different now. The way he said my name was probably all in my head. What I wanted to hear.

I'd scream if I could, but it would probably be sucked into the darkness too.

This is ridiculous. One major catastrophe and I have some sort of huge epiphany? What is this, the end of a Ryan Reynolds movie?

"Let's forget it," I say. "I can't do this. I'm not someone who risks life and limb in the middle of a devastated city. I'm the person who packs what they can find and moves on. I'm not the hero."

That's Alfie.

Without waiting for her response, I turn and start back the way we came.

"Mia, stop." Simi's voice floats in the thick air behind me, but I ignore it.

I'm sure they won't let me stay on campus, but at least I can get her somewhere safe. My back rounds against the backpack as I fix my eyes on the ground in front of me. If I look back now, I think the darkness might suck me in too. Good. I'll wear my humiliation like a shroud and let the city swallow me

"That's the wrong way," she says, louder this time.

Except instead of wearing my humiliation like a cloak, I shove it down, force it into the dank space where the rest of it resides, deep in my belly. It feels like I'm swallowing fabric too silky and slippery to go down, so I swallow and swallow just to breathe. But the more air I take in, the bigger the cloak becomes. I gasp, but only the wet cement air enters my lungs. My vision goes black at the edges and my mouth stretches into a horror-movie yawn. It's probably better that this is where it ends. That I choke on my own failure and cowardice.

"Breathe, Mia." Simi appears beside me, and her arms steer me to what's left of the curb and guide me to the ground.

Alfie deserves so much more.

"Put your head on your knees." Simi rubs my back, and the pressure of her hand gets tangled in the satiny pitch clogging my lungs. I arch away from her, but she follows.

"Are you all right? Are you hurt?" a deep voice asks.

"She's just having trouble catching her breath. She'll be okay just as soon as she acknowledges her feelings."

I raise my head to her sharp eyes daring me to object. Instead, I turn to a man carrying a long, white cane. He stands in front of us, his free hand out like he wants to reach for me but isn't sure he should. I realize I'm sitting on the curb, my hair sweaty and matted, one hand on my knee and the other on my chest. The shock of a stranger approaching without me noticing does something to my fight-or-flight response, and my lungs open up, ready for whatever I decide to do.

"I think . . . I'm pretty sure I was having a panic attack." I take in a big, successful breath, which makes me yawn the regular way. "I think I'm okay now."

"See, doing fine," Simi says.

"No wonder," the man says. "Things are crazy out here. You lost?"

I stand and trade looks with Simi. Do we trust him enough to tell the truth? He's wearing a heavy coat and a baseball cap low over his eyes. Brown hair creeps down the sides of his face and bleeds into the raised collar. The soles of his shoes are thick but worn on the outside, so it looks like he's rolling his ankles. I used to stand that way to piss off Coach and the cheer captain, but I doubt he's doing it on purpose. His face points in my direction as he waits for my answer, but his eyes are glazed over and set into the distance. And then the cane makes sense.

"We got a little turned around is all." I force a smile so my words sound calmer than I feel. Of course, after what just happened, I'm sure he can tell I'm totally faking any sense of normalcy.

That I'm a complete fraud.

"Where you all trying to go? You should probably get home. Broken sidewalks, aftershocks, and the lunatics are dangerous." He smiles, probably to let us know he's not the danger. I'm still not so sure.

"We're coming from State, but . . ." I don't say that I was on my way to make sure a boy I once knew, who once loved me, is all right. To tell him I was wrong, that I love him and always will. How childish. What was I thinking? "It might be best to go back." I take in Simi's shocked expression from the corner of my vision but keep my eyes trained on the man.

"What?" she whispers through gritted teeth.

"Well, if you want to go back toward State, you'll have to walk that way." He gestures to his left. "You'll see it when you get close enough."

Instead of saying "thank you" and walking back the way we came, my head betrays me and looks over my shoulder, to my left. Toward USF. Toward Alfie. My feet are like lead.

"Miss? It is Miss, right?"

"Hmm?" My voice is still tangled with my thoughts and comes out raspy. I clear my throat and try again. "Yes, sorry."

"I hope you'll excuse my forwardness, but it seems like you don't want to go back. It feels like you want to go a different way. If you tell me where, I can point you in the right direction."

"But you're . . ." I close my eyes as the heat rises in my cheeks.

"Oh my god." Simi turns and steps away. Even she can't take my stupidity all the time.

Good job, Mia. Tell the man he's blind like he doesn't already know.

"Blind, yes." He chuckles and pats his chest with an open palm. "I'm a walking map. Got the whole city right in here."

"I'm sorry—that was so rude. I'm usually not such an idiot." Lies. I'm always an idiot.

"It's all right."

Simi clears her throat, and I jut my chin toward her, eyes wide with acknowledged guilt.

"I know better than that. Truly, I can be such a jerk." I make my words as round and warm as I can.

He makes a dismissive noise and swipes the air. We stand in an awkward silence for what feels like an eternity. I have to say something.

"Guess people show their true colors when tragedy strikes, right?" I scrunch my face and look at Simi. She rolls her eyes and covers her face.

"Well, now. Everyone has a little part of themselves they'd rather not let the world know exists. The messy part. These are extraordinary times, Miss, and I'm sure we're all going to see ugly parts of each other in the days to come. The best thing we can do is to be kind. Offer forgiveness. When the world goes to shit— pardon my French, ladies—kindness and forgiveness is all we have to offer." A breathy laugh escapes as he tosses his head back. "Now who's the idiot? Lecturing you when you'd rather go on."

"Go on," Simi echoes, and jerks her head the opposite way.

These *are* extraordinary times. An entire city—and probably more—was brought down by the earth itself. And I'm worried about looking stupid.

I straighten my spine and mentally set fire to the silky cloth of shame I choked on earlier and let the heat turn my fear into resolve. I can do this.

Alfie deserves to know the truth.

I will offer it up, and then he can decide what to do with it.

"Actually, there's a coffee shop near Stonestown we'd like to get to. Do you know the way?"

When I look at the man, he winks.

Alfie

GOD'S TRUTH, MIA, I ALMOST DIDN'T TEXT YOU THAT NIGHT at all. Not because I wasn't dying to talk to you, but because I didn't want to seem too eager, even though I was off work at six and home from the batting cages by eight. I know it's stupid, but the whole time at the cages, Josuè kept saying stuff that stuck in my head. That it would be better to let you wait. Build anticipation, whatever that means. He was only messing around, but you know me—gotta overthink everything.

I'd been lying in bed for an hour before I picked up my phone. And since it was nearly midnight, I didn't think you'd answer. Guess I have the chemistry gods to thank for the test you had that week. Because you were up. I didn't ask you then, but did you have as many butterflies in your stomach as me? I had so many, I was afraid if I yawned, one would fly up my throat and escape into the universe. I know it's ridiculous. Big, sporty guys like me aren't supposed to admit to butterflies and fear and all the rest. But I never had to worry about that with you. If anything, you seemed to like me in spite of all that. Or because of it, I'm not sure.

Anyway, remember that first text I sent you? There were about a million drafts before I settled on the one you saw.

1. Hey Mia, it's Alfie. From English? Thanks for the note. And the tip, lol.

2. Hi, it's Alfie. You stopped by Zorba's today and I got your note. Thanks for thinking of me.

Of course, there was this multiplatinum doozy suggested by Josuè:

3. S'up, girl? Alfie here. What's good?

I'm the one who's supposed to be good with words, right? Mr. Future Poet or whatever. But when it came to breaking the ice with you? Words became the enemy—something I'd never experienced before. And honestly haven't since. Things with you were always . . . bigger, more complicated. Before you go and get mad, I don't mean that in a bad way. It's just I cared so much about what you thought, how you'd react, what you felt. And I didn't want to mess anything up.

Maybe if I'd been less scared, tried less, let things happen the way they were supposed to, things would've turned out differently. But maybe not.

Do you remember the winning opener?

Me: It's Alfie, got your note. How'd you guess it was me? Also, hi :)

You answered almost immediately, which took off a thousand pounds of pressure. Thank God for those three dots.

You: Hi back. It was kind of obvious. Also, thanks. They're pretty.

Me: I'm glad you like them. Sorry for almost killing you with Coach's pimp-mobile. Josuè has a lead foot.

You: Not your fault. Did you get in trouble?

Me: Not much. Coach yelled at us for like 20 minutes, but it wasn't bad.

You didn't answer right away, and the weight of your silence crept back onto my shoulders. I didn't want to go down the conversational path we were headed. Talking about Coach and Josuè and all that. What I wanted was to see if you might like to explore the idea of an Us, but I couldn't get past the whole reason we were texting in the first place. I will never understand why dating is so hard, no matter how much time I have to figure it out. Right?

I had to think of something.

Me: So you liked the flowers?

Even if it wasn't very good.

Me: I mean, was it fun to find them or should I have manned up and given you a bouquet like a normal person?

You: If that's normal, please never be that.

I wish you could've seen the smile on my face. I must've looked like that meme—the one of the dog with squinty eyes and stretched-out, grinning lips in pure bliss.

Me: Haha that's something I can be good at. Normal is . . . not me.

Me: Did I just tell a cute girl I'm not normal?

You: Idk but you definitely just told me.

And there it was. The time to take this conversation from flirty to fruitful. With the courage only found behind a screen and a closed bedroom door in the middle of the night, I took a breath and hit send.

Me: Do you think you'd want to hang out sometime? Me and you? In a not-normal kind of way?

Me: I mean, normal-ish. Definitely on this side of normal and not at all doing anything that might be construed as overly weird or creepy.

It was at that point in the conversation where I considered that maybe Baba was right and I shouldn't go to college. I should just stay home and work to take over the restaurant someday. You don't need fancy words to serve gyros and baklava, and I'd almost certainly used up my share. I almost put down my phone, but then I saw those three dots pop up.

You: I'd like that. Maybe this coming weekend?

Me: That'd be very cool. Dare I even say rad?

You: Rad is good lol

Me: I'll text you tomorrow then :)

You: Or you could just talk to me at school.

Me: Rad.

You replied with a pink heart emoji and there was no going back. Even after that . . . not-normal first date we had. Maybe because of it.

Honestly, that's probably true. If we did anything right, it was definitely because we kept things . . . not normal.

If our phones worked right now, I would send you the most not-normal but completely rad text I could think of.

I can't wait to see you.

Mia

ONCE WE'RE ON THE RIGHT SIDE OF NINETEENTH AVENUE, WE
practically run the rest of the way.

My heart pounds in rhythm with my feet hitting the pavement. When I decided to tell my truth, I could hardly wait. That
man was right. People go through their day trying to survive. We
keep quiet because we're told what we think doesn't matter.

But in times like these, when the world feels like it really is
ending, we have to tell the truth. We have to tell the people we
love how we feel. Because if not now, when?

We're so close. Finally.

Simi hardly ever leaves campus, under penalty of death by
parental execution, and I got turned around in all the chaos after
the dorm evacuation. To be fair, most of my way back from the
coffee shop was on the light rail, and I was sort of distracted by
the humiliation of dropping an entire iced coffee all over myself in
front of my ex and the girl he had his arm wrapped around.

I'm not calling her the girlfriend until all evidence indicates
I must.

Also, I kind of figured one side of campus was like the other
and I'd find a cross street soon enough. Everything in the valley
where I grew up is squared blocks the way Benjamin Franklin
intended. I hadn't counted on so many hills and lakes and curvy
streets.

But after a quick navigation lesson by the nicest stranger ever and an additional twenty-five-minute walk, we finally stumble across the right street. There I stand, my best friend by my side, at the corner of anticipation and fear, hoping against hope that Alfie will be here and, above all, okay.

Clumps of people litter the street. Some try their phones while others point at the stores, animatedly recounting what'll eventually turn into their *Where were you when . . .* stories.

The air turns crisper but still feels heavy against my bare skin. I pull the backpack tighter and wrap my arms around my waist.

The buildings don't look how I thought they would after such a huge earthquake.

"Look at that." I point to some across the street. Most look normal, except some stores don't quite line up with each other. Like puzzle pieces forced into the wrong place. The one right in the middle looks like a ruined soufflé, its center an open vortex sucking it inside out. In the street, a huge gap—maybe three feet wide—divides the asphalt.

Simi nods, her brows knitted closely together. Sirens from the main road echo off the large building on the other side of the street. She tugs at her sleeves and wraps them around her clenched fists.

"You okay?" I nod at them and take in the grimace painted on her face.

"Me? Oh yeah." She softens her scowl. "Just taking in the damage. Weird how things we take for granted can be taken away so easily."

"Yeah." What she says punches me in the gut, but I force myself to breathe normally.

We're literally across the road from where I last saw Alfie. A million scenarios go through my mind all at once, and only a few of them end with him and me together. I blow out a shaky breath.

So much for normal breathing.

She must sense my rising panic, because she grabs my hand and pulls me through the crowds toward the coffee shop, all the while avoiding the fissures in the street.

Some guy keeps telling people he's an off-duty cop as he looks over cuts and bruises. He groups them together by seriousness of injury. Simi leads me around a group of four or five with bleeding faces or hands.

A brown beanie in another group catches my eye, and I freeze. Simi jerks to a stop and points.

"There. Is that him?"

Alfie

OUR FIRST OFFICIAL DATE WAS THE SATURDAY AFTER THANKS-
giving, and it almost didn't happen. As I approached you and Simi
in the hall the day after we texted, you jerked to a stop. I brought
you one more camellia, just for fun. Just to see your smile up close
instead of from a seat behind.

Even though you suggested it first, I asked if you wanted to
hang out that next weekend even though it was a holiday and even
though you probably had family stuff. It was my way of giving you
an out in case you'd woken up and realized you didn't want anything to do with someone who'd nearly hit you with a golf cart and
then admitted he was a total weirdo. Who could blame you? This
way, you could politely say you had family obligations or whatever
and neither of us would have to feel bad.

But you didn't. You said you'd love to hang out. You wanted
to do it even sooner, but with midterms and cheer practice and
student journalism deadlines messing everything up, you couldn't.

"But definitely next Saturday," you said. It was all I could do
not to mark the day as a national holiday in my phone. Well, at
least an Alfie-and-Mia holiday. November 21st: the day we celebrate a not-normal but mostly-kinda-normal first date and hopefully many more to come.

"Sounds great." I know I smiled like a lunatic and probably
stared too long, but I couldn't help it. Your cheeks turned pink,
and you buried yourself in your locker to hide it. I know you did,

no matter how many times you've denied it. It was never like you to show too much emotion until you fully trusted a person. Believe me, I know that now.

"Text me later?" you asked.

"Consider yourself texted."

The Friday before our date, you messaged me. I didn't see it until after my shift at the restaurant and nearly choked when I did.

You: Alfie, I'm so sorry. I might have to cancel tomorrow. I did something . . . stupid.

Hundreds of scenarios went through my head. You changed your mind. You thought about dating a baseball player just as spring training was starting and you didn't want any part of it. Or worse. You decided another baseball player was a better, more normal choice. Or even worse than that, a football player. After all, you came from a two-parent, church-on-Sundays family with a dog you walked every night around your normal block. I was a Greek kid who went to a strange church, had lots of relatives that spoke too loud and hugged too much, and roasted an entire lamb on a spit in their backyard every Easter.

Of course you'd changed your mind.

Me: That's okay. I get it. Maybe some other time.

I knew in my gut there wouldn't be another time. And the way my insides ached told me exactly why they were called crushes. But then three dots appeared.

You: No, you don't understand. My parents and I do this thing every year the Saturday after Thanksgiving. It's stupid. I thought I could finally get out of going because . . . I don't know. I just thought I could. But they're making me go and I'm stuck.

Something flickered underneath the rubble of what was left

of my heart. It wasn't that you didn't want to. You just couldn't.

Me: That's all right, I totally get it. My parents are always making me do things I don't want to. 😵

You: I was kind of hoping you might want to come with us? It's stupid, but at least we'll get to hang out.

Turned out that flicker in my heart was a phoenix rising from its ashes, and now it soared over everything. Of course I'd go. Of course I wanted to. You were going to be there, and that's all I cared about.

Me: Sure, I can go. I already got the day off, so why not?

You: You don't even know what it is lol

Me: Will you be there?

You: Duh.

Me: Then I'm in.

That Saturday morning, when you and your parents picked me up from my house, I realized I probably should've asked more questions. I know we were all about not normal, but I never thought that for our first date we'd be doubling with your mom and dad. At a cow palace. One hundred miles away.

Mia

THAT CAN'T BE ALFIE. HIS BUILD IS WRONG. DISAPPOINTMENT wells in my chest. For all I know, he could be a hundred miles away.

"No. False alarm." I press my palm to my forehead and let out a sigh.

With a sympathetic smile, Simi pulls me into the coffee shop. Blotchy patches of light splatter the walls under emergency flood lights. I search every face as fast as my eyes can take them in. My shrinking heart racing faster with every stranger.

Porcelain shards and broken glass litter the floor in front of the shelf-lined walls. A jagged crack splits the food display case next to the registers, distorting the muffins and breads inside. Coffee beans from broken bags riddle the floor and mix into the sea of spilled drinks that'd dripped from the tables.

Alfie isn't anywhere. My stomach turns as I inhale the pungent, sticky smell.

A couple of employees mindlessly sweep at the scattered messes. Only a few people remain inside, and neither Alfie nor the girl he was with are among them. The manager who interviewed me writes furiously on a clipboard as he takes down a customer's information.

"That's the manager," I whisper to Simi. She nods.

We sidestep some of the bigger messes and wait for him to finish. When he sees me, he inhales sharply.

"I thought you left." He smiles at the exiting customer and attempts to put his clipboard on the counter, but it's too full of debris. Instead, he clings the board to his chest and looks me up and down. "That position you applied for probably isn't a thing anymore."

I blink at his harsh tone, and even though I'm sure it's because his entire store is ruined and not because I ruined my interview, my cheeks burn anyway. I force a smile and try to stay calm. Alfie could've just left. He could be right around the corner.

"Yeah, I mean, I kind of figured. Sorry I spilled my coffee everywhere." It's all I can think to say.

"Doesn't matter much now." He gestures at the floor and laughs bitterly. I feel the heat in my cheeks spreading. "Did you two need something? We're not really serving right now."

"Oh, no," Simi says. "That's not why we're here."

"You didn't happen to notice a guy in a beanie at the door when I left, did you?" I ask, my voice as liquid as I can make it. Butterflies flurry in my stomach as he draws his face into a frown. "He was with a girl."

The thought of Alfie's hand resting on her shoulder tangles with the pungent aroma in the room, and a wave of nausea washes over me. I breathe through my mouth to clear my head.

"Let's see. A guy in a beanie with a girl. At an indie café in the city. You just described eighty percent of my customer base."

Simi arches an eyebrow and tilts her head. "She did ask about a specific time."

"Nope," the manager says, shrugging. "Can't think of anyone specific."

I squeeze my eyes shut. Who knows when he left? I was right the first time. He could be anywhere.

"Now, if you don't mind, I've got to figure out what I'm going to do with this mess." He shoos us with a single wave and starts barking orders at the poor employee sweeping behind the counter.

"Thanks anyway," Simi says loudly, then mutters under her breath, "Thanks for nothing."

When he walks away, I add, "He was nicer during my interview."

"Still, he didn't have to be so curt. It's a good thing you didn't get the job, or I'd be down here side-eyeing him every time you had a shift."

My stomach reels. "Let's give him the benefit of the doubt that he's acting like such a jerk because of the massive destruction he's dealing with and get out of here."

I shuffle to the exit, and through the window I see a dad comforting his small, crying daughter. She can't be more than five. He wipes at her tears and smooths her pigtails in between embraces. I swallow my own tears and cringe as they swirl, stormlike, in my gut.

A woman walks by and smiles at the man the way women do when they see a dad doing his job. Like he deserves some kind of medal for doing things moms do every day. Women used to look at my dad like that when he and I would go for ice cream, just the two of us. Or when he pushed me on the swings at the park. I loved spending time with my dad. It never felt like he was being forced to babysit. My heart balks at the memory. We used to be the family on the cover of our church directory. Now we're the one everyone whispers about in dark corners and private messages.

"You're green," Simi says. "Let's get some air." She opens the door, but my feet are glued to the glossy cement floor.

I've felt about a thousand different emotions since we left Simi's campus. And right now, they're a cyclone, the debris of what my entire life has become in the last five months churning in my stomach. I keep my back and neck flagpole-rigid. Because I know what's going to happen when I take a step. Simi tugs my hand, and it takes me a moment to stumble forward.

Once I come unstuck, I race to the trash can by the door and vomit out everything inside me—the fear, the longing, the hope, the dread. Lightning bolts jolt my spine as I wretch.

The next thing I know, I'm sitting in a chair just outside the café as Simi places a cold towel around my neck. The manager hands me a small cup of water and leers over me while the off-duty cop holds his finger in front of my face, telling me to follow it with my eyes. I wave it away.

"I'm fine. Just ate something that didn't agree with me." It's a lie, but they don't need to know that.

"Certainly wasn't the iced coffee I made you, since you wore more than you drank." The manager snorts at his joke. If only I could have the confidence of this neck-bearded barista, I wouldn't be sitting in front of a ruined coffee shop three thousand miles away from the future I'd planned.

But we all make choices.

I ignore him and focus on the father as he situates his daughter in her wagon and covers her with a blanket. When she's tucked in, he pulls her along, checking every few seconds that she's okay. The protective expression he has all over his face makes me ache for a time when someone looked at me like that. A time when, with a simple expression, my own dad could make me feel like everything would be all right.

What Simi said earlier about taking these shops for granted

haunts me. I did the same thing with Alfie. With everything, really.

I trace the choices that led to me sitting in front of a decon-structed coffee shop, wiping vomit from my lips. Leaving home in the middle of the night. Begging Simi to let me sleep in her dorm until I could figure out what to do next. The choices weren't all mine, though. I didn't choose to throw away my chance at going to Sarah Lawrence. I didn't choose for my family to implode.

But I did force Alfie out of my life. What if we don't fit together anymore? What if we're like these buildings, disjointed and out of place? Or worse. What if we're the one in the middle that folded in on itself? *Things are different now.* I'm clinging to our phone call like some magic shoehorn that can slip us back into our rightful places. I could've imagined that catch in his voice, the familiar way he said my name.

Even if I did, I have to tell him the truth, no matter if he's moved on or not. He deserves the truth. I only hope that if I do finally find him, he'll let me explain.

Alfie

TO TELL YOU THE TRUTH, I DIDN'T TOTALLY MIND YOUR DAD'S cow jokes on the way to the Cow Palace.

"You see, Alfie," he said, "during an earthquake, cows are called milkshakes. And the reason they have hooves is because they lactose."

"Dad, stop. No one thinks you're funny." You rolled your eyes so many times, I lost count.

That's the first time I saw the warning flash in your mom's eyes. *Don't rock the boat, Mia. Mind your manners so everyone sees our perfect family. Don't show the cracks because that's how the devil works his way in.* But outwardly, her perfectly painted lips stretched wide across her teeth as she playfully pushed your dad's arm. She'd *Oh honey* and *Stop your teasing, Jeff* him as he continued his jokes. I chuckled to be polite, but it wasn't really funny.

The comedy was too on key, the timing too perfect. It was a well-rehearsed, heartless show.

Of course I didn't know any of that then. It was more an instinct, so different than the chaotic energy and belly laughs of my own family. And even if you had an inkling, you'd never have admitted it, because the faux patina that glossed over everything was better than uncovering what rotted underneath.

Despite the disdainful looks you kept tossing toward the front seat, I think on some level you liked his joking around—or at least you liked the idea that the two of you had a relationship where you shared something. A dad-joke relationship.

You could've told me there weren't actually any cows at the palace. You could've told me it wasn't actually a palace. You could've told me we were headed for the reincarnation of Victorian England at Christmas. Or that we were going to the Dickens Fair. But you chose to be complicit in your dad's silliness. And even though it was rare, I loved it when you two played off each other. I miss that a lot.

I'm sure you do too.

When we finally parked and made our way to the entrance, you should've seen your face. Eyes bright and cheeks flushed. On the phone, you told me how over this whole outing you were, that you didn't want to go. But the way your voice clamored higher with every detail, I knew you were right where you were supposed to be.

"Mom, oh my god, get off your phone," you said. "You're going to miss the entrance."

"Don't take the Lord's name in vain, Mia. And I'm not missing anything." Your mom—Maryanne, as she insisted I call her—tucked her phone into her purse and looped her arm through yours. You offered your other one to me while your dad found his spot next to her. And that's how we went in—linked arm in arm. It felt good to stand next to you, to connect. It was the first time we touched, and I'll never forget it. Well, honestly, I do try to forget that we were also linked to your parents because, weird. But if that's what it took to be close to you, I'd do it any day of the week.

I'm just sorry that we couldn't stay that way.

I know you watched me as we glided through the entrance, observing my reaction to our trip back in time. And you're right, I'd never seen anything like it.

As soon as we rounded the corner, carolers harmonized their welcome, dressed up in Victorian finery. To the right, women in large skirts and men in high collars and long-tail jackets pulled willing visitors into a waltz as music wafted from the band onstage.

Roasting chestnuts, grilled meats, and sugary goods wafted through the air, my stomach rumbling in response. And thank you for not saying anything. I know you heard it, but I couldn't help it. It was a long car ride, after all.

The aisles-turned-streets were decorated with storefronts selling jewelry, photos, and other souvenirs. Christmas ribbons and pine wrapped their way around signposts and streetlamps alight with golden flames. It was like we stepped out of our own time and straight into a Dickens novel, which I guess was the point.

"What do you think?" Your eyes met mine, then looked away. "Dorky, right?"

"It's kind of cool." I didn't want to tell you how amazing I thought it was—how fantastic it was that someone could transform the regular world into something so beautiful—because I didn't want you to think I was the dorky one. But walking through the lobby into the grand concourse with its fake snow and roaming carolers and roasting chestnuts and sellers crying their wares? I loved it. Every inch. And even more because you were the one who showed it to me. And you loved it too. The look on your face said it all.

That's what relationships should be, don't you think? Opening worlds for each other. Experiencing them together.

I'm so glad we had that together, even if it was just for a little while.

"What do you guys want to do first?" Jeff clapped, then rubbed his hands together as he waited. "Food or shopping?"

My stomach rumbled again at the mere possibility of something to eat, but I didn't want to be the one to suggest it since I was only along for the ride.

"I don't know." Your eyes grazed my midsection. "What do you want to do, Alfie?"

"I could eat." I shrugged as nonchalantly as I could manage. "But whatever you all want to do."

"There's a really good Greek place," Maryanne said. "We could go there if you want."

"We don't have to. Whatever you guys want is fine with me." The truth was, the last thing I wanted was Greek food. I mean, I eat it all the time and I really wanted to try something new.

"Mom, I'm pretty sure Alfie wants anything but. He works at his dad's restaurant, remember?" You leaned into our still-linked arms, which your dad watched with a less-than-enthused expression.

"Really, anything's fine." I stepped away from you, but only enough so that the scowl on your dad's face lessened into more of a blank stare. "What do you normally get?"

"Mom's favorite is bangers and mash." You grinned in her direction but she was lost in some conversation on her phone. A shadow darkened your eyes. "Earth to Mom, hello?"

"I'm sorry, dear, what did you say?" She finished her text and smiled expectantly.

"I said your favorite food here is bangers and mash."

Her back straightened as her eyebrows knit together. "Oh hush. Don't say words like that. It's not polite." Her eyes darted everywhere, like people were suddenly going to appear with pitchforks and torches or something, and that made you crack up.

"Why don't you like bangers? Or mash?" Your voice was more

teasing than a question, but it was obvious your mom was not having it. "And I thought today was a no-phone day. Who do you keep texting?"

"Come on, Mia, leave your mother alone. She has important church business to figure out before the Christmas pageant. Isn't that right?" He kissed the top of her well-sprayed hair and winked at you. "And no more talk of banging and mashing."

"Jeff, honestly!"

"Let's head to the food court and we can decide then." Your dad rounded his arm over your mom's shoulders and led her away from us. I took the opportunity to lean closer to you.

"What exactly is bangers and mash and why is it rude?" I whispered.

"*Bangers* is British slang for sausages, and *mash* is potatoes. Obviously we use the words differently here." You smile proudly. "I just like messing with her uptight ass sometimes."

"You think she's uptight?" I laughed, despite the fact that I was highly aware I was making fun of your mother. Couldn't help it. My family was so different from yours, not that I need to remind you. They're all fart jokes and recipe sharing and bear hugs and corner takedowns by the cousins. Yours was just you and your parents—well-mannered, polite, and almost formal. Like the Dickens Fair, sometimes walking into your house was like walking into a different world. "I don't see it."

"Right." You tilted your head toward them. "Let's catch up so we can take care of that rumble in your tummy, Pooh Bear."

With an embarrassed sigh, I followed your lead past the haberdashery-and-wig shop to the food court—and your parents.

"You get enough meat pie, there, Alfie?" The way your dad eyed my plate, I couldn't tell if he was annoyed or impressed by my ability to eat. And to be fair, I did offer to pay for my second pie. He just wouldn't let me.

"Yes, sir," I said as I swallowed the last bite. "Couldn't eat another bite." Even as I said it, I knew it wasn't true. I was definitely trying the bangers thing later. How could I miss it after all the hype? I just had to figure out how to sneak off and get a tray.

"Good deal." He nodded to your mom. "You ready to make the rounds?"

"I want to take Alfie to see the puppets." Your long curls brushed my arm, sending butterfly kisses through my veins. "Don't worry, it's not as lame as it sounds. They're actually pretty violent." Your eyebrows rose and your face brightened.

"Should I be worried that violence makes your face that happy?"

"Maybe." You shrugged, all nonchalant.

"Mia, play nice." Your mom peered at you over her glasses in a rigid teacher way, and you rolled your eyes. It didn't take me long to figure out that was basically how you two communicated. You'd say something, she'd judge, you'd roll your eyes, and she'd retreat. Seemed harmless at the time.

"Let's all go," your dad said. "I like a little violence myself." He made a point of frowning at me, then winking at you. I knew he was kidding, but damn. It was bad enough our first date was a parental double, but lunchtime threats too? Awesome.

"Dad."

"I can't help if I like Punch more than Judy. It's a thing."

I must've looked as confused as I felt because you said, "I'll explain as we walk. It's a whole thing."

"Hmm, bangers, mash, two out of three violence-seeking companions obsessed with puppets. What have I gotten myself into?"

You laced your fingers with mine and lifted your chin to my ear. "Oh Alfie, if you only knew."

Do you remember that chimney sweep guy that followed us around at the Dickens Fair? He had that ball of mistletoe and ribbons hanging off the end of his broom. He'd dance around, pushing it into crowds of people, holding it over couples' heads, cheering for them to kiss.

Your dad pointed him out to your mom when we were finishing the second meal of the day. Not that I minded, but a lot of eating happens in the Dickens world. If I'd known, I probably wouldn't have had that second meat pie the first time we ate. Total rookie move.

"Look, hon." Jeff nodded toward the chimney sweep prancing around a nervous couple, then winked at your mom. "He's trying to get them to kiss. Think he'll come over here?"

"Jeff, stop." The slight smile that crept up the side of her mouth hinted that she might not mind.

I swear, it was like the sweep heard your dad all the way across the room. He swiveled in his unstrapped boots and pranced right toward us.

I tried not to freak when he started for you and me, especially with your mom and dad right there. Plus, we'd barely gotten to know each other. And yeah, this is stupid, but your dad put so much vinegar on the fish and chips he wanted me to try. I thought for sure I'd taste like lemony acid forever. If Victorian England at Christmas sold Juicy Fruit, I would've paid just about anything for one measly stick.

"Um, Dad, I think he heard you." Your voice was about as shaky as my hands. The man with soot all over his face and fingerless gloves wouldn't wave his mistletoed broom over our heads and try to make us kiss with your dad there, right?

Luckily for us, he switched direction at the last moment and traipsed toward your mom and dad. Remember how she half-heartedly swatted it away?

"People will stare," she said.

"It's all right, milady, you're allowed a snog or two from the love'a your life, idn't that right?" The chimney sweep smiled, revealing two blacked-out front teeth. His accent was so over-done, I had to bite my cheek to keep from cringing. Of course, making you laugh by mimicking his terrible cockney all the way home was an added bonus.

The sweep swung his broom back and forth over your mom and then your dad, waggling his eyebrows like some sort of luna-tic the entire time. But your mom wasn't fazed in the least. She poked her cheek toward your dad and he kissed it even though her eyes were on her phone. The sweep withdrew his broom and frowned.

"That's it, loves?" He elbowed your dad like he was a cross between a comedian and a bad mime. Then, to my extreme cha-grin, he turned his attention to you and me. "What about you love-lies? Fancy a round under the mistletoe?"

Since all the air had just disappeared from my lungs, I did the next best thing and gulped the vinegary vapors in the back of my throat. Supercool, as always. Was this guy for real? Your dad was right there. When I glanced at you, your expression wasn't much different than how I felt, so at least we had that going for us.

"Oh, for heaven's sake, they're just kids." Your mom waved him off and nodded toward the next section. "Let's go to those shops. I saw a little purse I want to have a closer look at. It'd be so cute for church!"

"Jesus, Mom, you act like church is some sort of runway competition. God doesn't care what you look like."

"You stop that talk right now." Her eyes raked over me like you were a puppet and I'd just stuck my hand in your back and made you say that. Not the impression I was going for. But then she sighed one of those mom breaths where they're trying to control themselves. "Don't take the Lord's name in vain. You're embarrassing yourself—and us—in front of your friend." Her eyes grazed over me in a way that I didn't love.

I wasn't sure what to do or say, so I stayed silent.

"Everyone ready?" Your dad clapped his hands as the chimney sweep slinked away. Then he herded us, your mom first, toward the row of shops on the other side of the building. But you let them walk a few paces ahead of us before you followed. The way you glared at the back of her head, I could tell you didn't even want to be in the same breathing space as her. I remember shooting you a confused look as you rolled your eyes and made a face behind your mom's back. Like we were five and she'd just told you not to eat any more cookies.

"What was that about?" I half whispered so she wouldn't hear me. "Like, it wasn't that big of a deal, right? What you said."

"She's so touchy about church, I swear. She dresses up like it's goddamn fashion week and expects me to do the same. I don't even like going."

I opened my mouth to sympathize, because my family not only went to church every week, but my brother and I were expected to help out in the altar every time. No sick days. No exceptions. But you were on a roll. And in a family with lots of strong women, I've learned to let them finish when they're ranting because, otherwise, they start ranting at me, so I properly shut it and continued listening.

"And isn't 'God'"—you put His name in air quotes—"supposed to love you as you are? Unconditional love and all that shit? Why would He care if I wore ripped jeans and a hoodie?" You stopped walking and crossed your arms over your chest. "I'm sorry, I don't know why I'm getting so emotional over this. I'm just tired of her America's Top Christian drama. It's not even that big of a deal."

"I hear you, I do." I faced you, and the fact that we were inches apart set my heart thumping. We were definitely breathing the same air. "Can I tell you what my yia-yia told me?"

"Yia-yia?"

"My grandma. That's how we say it in Greek."

"Yia-yia. I like that. Okay, what did your yia-yia say?" Your arms relaxed, but only a little.

"Well, I used to complain because my mom makes me wear a whole-ass suit to church. And what's worse is I have to take half of it off to put on altar robes. It's a pain." I sighed at the thought of all that effort. "Anyway, she told me that going to church is like going to see your king. And wouldn't we want to wear our finest clothes and be as inviting as possible so the king would show his grace to us?" I shrugged. "I don't know, but that kind of put it into perspective for me."

Your expression changed from expectant eyes and a relaxed mouth to crinkled forehead and set jaw. Not a good indicator I was making our "first date" memorable for the right reasons. Naturally, I panicked.

"Not that ripped jeans and a hoodie are bad. I mean, for a lot of people, that is the best they have. And do you know how much some pairs of ripped jeans are these days?" A nervous laugh escaped, and I sort of wished the sweeper guy would come back just so I'd have something else to do with my mouth.

"No, you're right. Dang, your yia-yia just puts it out there, doesn't she?" You sort of slumped as you took an exaggerated breath. "Meeting your king. Okay, I get that. Just not the way she does it, like it's a beauty pageant instead of a place of worship. She's all about how she looks to everyone else. I highly doubt she's thinking about God when she's sending her secret little waves to all her other overly-made-up friends in between songs and the preaching. Nothing about her rules have anything to do with faith, just about what people think."

"This is a bit of a trigger for you, huh?"

"I guess." You ran your hand through your hair and sighed. "I'm sorry. I'm ruining this . . . date? Can we call it a date? With them here?" Your eyes cut toward your parents in the leather shop across the way.

"I vote yes, especially if we're still abiding by the not-normal mandate we established early on."

"Cool." You laced your fingers with mine and blushed. You actually turned pink. It was the cutest thing I'd ever seen. And my stomach flipped, which was probably a good thing since the recently dormant butterflies exploded into action when you touched me.

But then, a shadow of a ball caught my eye. My heart pounded so hard because I knew what it was. When I looked over, the chimney sweep was waving his mistletoe over our heads while he winked and nodded.

"Not takin' no for an answer this time, loves."

Trying to read your face, I crinkled my forehead. Your blush went from pink to full-on red, and your lips were completely folded into your mouth as you chewed on them.

"What do you think?" I asked.

"We should do it. I mean, if only to get rid of him." Your eyes sparkled the way the sun hits the tiny ripples on a lake at sunset.

"Not exactly the answer I was hoping for, but okay."

"Also, I've kind of wanted to kiss you since last year, so this could be the time to check that off my bucket list." You licked your lips, and I couldn't concentrate on anything else.

"Seems fair. I mean, I've kind of wanted to kiss you since the homecoming dance in tenth grade when you wore that white dress. So I get it."

"You have? And you remember what I wore? Okay, creeper." Your shoulders shook from silent laughter, but all I could concentrate on were your lips, fuller from your earnest chewing a moment ago.

"Thirty-five percent creepy, I'll give you that. But me remembering how you looked on the night I started crushing on you is definitely sixty-five percent adorable."

"Are you going to shut up and kiss me, or what?"

"Definitely the former. This is me shutting up."

I'd kissed other girls. Once after youth group behind the swings of the church's preschool. And once at one of Josuè's parties because of a dare. But never had I felt anything close to the way your lips pressed against mine made me feel.

When you let go and I opened my eyes, I'd almost forgotten we were in the middle of a crowded fair with an eccentric actor practically forcing us to kiss. But his cheering brought it flooding back. You seemed to have the same reentry because you cleared your throat and smoothed your hair.

"We should go find my parents before they send a search party. Don't want them thinking we snuck off to do the devil's work or anything." Your hand found its spot in mine and, with a wave to the creepy sweep, we headed toward the leather shop.

Your dad was at the register, paying for the purse your mom had picked out, and she was outside, texting frantically. Seriously, I've never seen anyone over thirty move their fingers over a phone that fast. There was no way either of them saw us kiss. We could keep it for ourselves.

And Mia, I know what happened later broke your world. And I know that deep down, you blamed us for not seeing it earlier. Looking back, it's easy to see now. How she was on her phone the whole time while your dad got swept away by the dancers and the performers, one after another in each row we explored. She'd barely noticed the mistletoe hanging over her own head, let alone ours.

But we were caught up in our own dance, and I guess no one can blame us for that.

Mia

WE HIKE UP NINETEENTH, DANCING AROUND THE GLASS AND
plaster from more broken stores. What used to be a House of
Pancakes is leaning sideways on a pile of sticks, a car buried
beneath. A few people dig through piles of brick and debris from
the restaurant while others find more beams to help support the
crooked structure. Simi huddles close to me, and I wonder if she's
wishing she stayed on campus.

Cars inch their way up and down the avenue. Some impatient
ass lays on his horn every few minutes, like that's going to make
the street magically clear up. I jump every time, and Simi looks
like she might rip the horn right off his steering wheel.

"I'm sorry I dragged you out here." Guilt winds its tendrils
around my spine. I loop my arm with Simi's and lean my head
against hers.

"You didn't. There's no way I would let you come out here
alone. At least this way, if something happens, we have each other
to get help." She tightens her arm against her side and quickens
our pace as if we could outrun any danger. "And I get to watch the
greatest reunion of all time."

"Maybe." I press my tongue to the roof of my mouth so I don't
scoff. Or sob.

"No maybe." She offers her trademarked assuring smile.
"We're doing this. We're finding him."

I purse my lips together and nod, but only so she stops trying to be my cheerleader. Where do we even start? The only lead I had was the coffee shop, and that turned out to be a bust.

My hand slides over my phone in my pocket. I could try calling again. Just stay on long enough to find out where he is, then hang up before my battery dies completely.

I suck in a breath.

Simi has a phone. *Why didn't I think of this sooner?*

Before I can register the thought, I'm making grabby hand gestures to her.

"Give me your phone. I'm going to try to call him."

Immediately she pulls it from her pocket. Her face falls. "No service." She holds it up for me to see the missing icon in the corner, but I don't look.

I feel like my bars shrank to zero too.

Honestly, who knows what we'll be walking into. The last thing I need is to disappoint my best friend again.

On the next block, a hobbled billboard across the street advertises this year's Dickens Fair—Christmas fun for the whole family. My parents and I used to go every year on Thanksgiving weekend. Kick off the holiday season right, Dad used to say.

I absolutely loved going when I was little. I'd always beg to play croquet with the stuffed flamingos like Alice did in Wonderland. And I was always the best at the pickpocket game from *Oliver Twist*—always won the big peppermint stick. But as I got older, the whole day became more of a chore than a holiday. Mom's disapproval of the pickpocket game and telling me to "be good" and only have a taste of dessert nearly ruined it all. Except the last time we went. A warm ribbon winds its way through me as I remember the year before, my first date with Alfie. Well, if you can call it that.

Who goes on a first date with their parents?

The ribbon wraps itself around my insides and tugs. Showing the fair to him reminded me of everything I loved about being immersed in Victorian England. But what I loved most was watching Alfie figure it all out.

The entire car ride home from the Cow Palace, Mom driveled on about how good the food was this year and how the dancers were especially agile and wasn't the purse she got the cutest thing we'd ever seen. Dad nodded his head and laughed in all the right places.

Neither Alfie nor I paid much attention, though. The fact that my hand lay nestled in his underneath the coats on the seat between us took up my entire brain. The way our fingers laced together, the way our energies intertwined to create something stronger than what we could be alone, transported me out of the car and right back to that moment his lips touched mine. Not that my parents would get weird about us holding hands—at least I don't think—but like this, it was still just ours, like the kiss we shared under the mistletoe.

The entire day was magical. That is, until we dropped him off.

As soon as Alfie waved from his porch and went into his house, the entire mood in the car shifted. Dad's plastic smile withered to his serious driving face—squinty eyes and puckered lips. Mom shifted out of her *Queens don't cross their legs* posture and crossed her legs away from my dad. She even changed the radio from some generic oldies station to a Christian one, turned up the volume, and engrossed herself in her phone. Dad's frequent glances at me through the rearview mirror the rest of the way home only confirmed what was already obvious. Mom wasn't happy.

In normal families, a mom would simply say what was bothering her—at least that's how Simi's mom is. Sometimes Simi doesn't like what her mom says, but at least she knows where she stands. But with my mom, we're all supposed to guess why she isn't happy. Like if we really loved her, we would know. And if we can't, we're stuck with this intrinsic guilt of not being good enough—for what, I'm not sure. Love? Respect? To matter? The ironic thing is, she drives us to church three times a week so we can feel all that Divine love from worshipping some whitewashed guy in robes. It's an endless cycle—mess up at home, feel bad, go to church to be forgiven. Rinse and repeat.

It's like a goddamn drug addiction.

But I can't say all that. In this family, we don't talk about what we really think. We move on, doing what we're supposed to do, and behave like the good Christians God intended us to be, feelings be damned.

At home, we usually settled into our own little universes once the dinner dishes were cleaned and put away. Mom would change into her pj's and start on her nightly skin care ritual. Dad would fall onto the couch and flip open some book from his memoir-obsessed collection while I typically tucked in my earbuds to watch videos. But that night was different.

Mom practically jumped out of the car before it was even in park and was in her room with the door closed when Dad and I came through the back door. With a heavy sigh, Dad set his keys in the dish by the door and lumbered toward their bedroom. After he closed the door behind him, I tiptoed through the hall, making sure to avoid the squeaky part, and beelined to my room. He might not have gotten his peaceful reading respite, but I wasn't about to stick around to play her what's wrong now game.

The last thing I needed is to hear another one of my parents' passive-aggressive "discussions."

I couldn't be sure, of course, but I had a pretty good idea what they were talking about anyway. I'd never brought a boy to a family event before, let alone one my parents didn't know or know of through their Bible study or Bunco circles. Mom tried to balk when I told her I'd invited Alfie, but I knew she'd never risk the public shame of reversing an invitation.

Sometimes it's better to apologize than ask for permission.

This was all-new territory. Sure, I'd been on a date or two, but they were usually with someone from church. Our parents would've known each other and had certain expectations about how the night would go. Don't stay out too late. Stay with the crowd. Don't ruin the family's reputation and risk our place in the pews. All of this went unspoken, of course. Just like everything else. But the pressure was there. The underlying anxiety that people might find out we weren't perfect and heaven would be forever closed to us by the jury of our peers.

They didn't know Alfie, not really. They knew his family owned the Greek place in town and he played baseball. But they didn't know much else except that he wanted to date their daughter.

Later that night, I came down to the kitchen for a snack to find Mom and Dad sitting at the kitchen table. Soft music played under the dimmed overhead light. Mom faced the opposite direction, her stiff posture keeping her back to me. As soon as Dad noticed me standing by the fridge, he jumped up and offered me his hand.

"There's my little girl," he said. "Dance with me." His face was twisted with pride and something else I couldn't quite figure out. Looking back, there was a quiet desperation mixed with the green-and-gold flecks in his eyes, the one facial feature we have in common.

"Dance with you? Like when I was five?" I tried frowning, but he stuck out his lower lip and made such a ridiculous face, I had to laugh. I glanced across the room to see if Mom was laughing too, but she stayed facing the opposite wall, her head bent like she was studying her nail beds or something.

"Come on." He dragged the *n* as he reached for my hand. "Can't I dance with my little girl before I'm totally replaced by some guy with a nerdy name and a killer batting average?" He draped himself over my shoulder and fake sobbed while he scooped me up and rocked us both back and forth in tiny circles.

"Ew, Dad, gross. Stop stalking my . . ." I stopped before I labeled Alfie as anything, especially *boyfriend*. My eyes darted to Mom out of reflex.

"Little girls have to grow up too." Mom spun around on the chair and surveyed our dancing. After a cool glance looking us up and down, she smiled her *I know best* smile. "You know, Mia. You should really think about dating this Alfie. I'm sure he's nice enough, but I just don't see how dating a non-Christian is a good thing. That's not who you are."

I pulled away from Dad and crossed my arms.

"Now let's not—" Dad said, but I interrupted.

"Mom, Alfie *is* Christian. He's Orthodox. They're like the OG Christians. Just because he doesn't go to our church doesn't make him some heathen who worships Satan." I rolled my eyes, thinking I'd made my point. But instead of apologizing or asking an actual question, Mom raised her eyebrows as she pursed her lips and stared at the floor for what felt like an eternity.

"You know what I mean."

"No, Mom, what do you mean?"

"No one's saying that Alfie is a bad guy," Dad said. "Right, hon?" He looked at Mom, who only turned her face away from the conversation.

"All I'm saying is to think about your choices. So you don't get hurt."

"You mean so you don't look like you can't control your daughter to your friends. Jesus, Mom."

"Language!" She slapped her freshly lotioned hand against the table.

Before she could say anything else, I grabbed a bag of chips from the pantry and scuttled to my room. Shutting the door behind me, I set the bag down and pulled out my phone.

Me: Thanks for coming today. I had a really good time.

Alfie: Omg I'm so glad you texted me. I was trying to be cool and not seem like the minute I left the car I wanted to talk to you again. I was failing pretty hard, tho haha

M: You can text me any time.

A: Is any time really two words?

M: Not the time to discuss the finer points of grammar.

A: I've really been spelling it wrong this whole time.

M: Aren't you supposed to be flirting with me or something?

A: The next time I see you, I'm going to write ANY TIME on the inside of your wrist. That way, when you look at it, you'll know exactly what time I will want to talk to you.

M: That'll do, pig. That'll do.

I closed my eyes and bit my lip to remember how his lips felt on mine. Warmth spread from my chest through my arms and down my legs, and I drew my shoulders to my ears, like I could still feel his arm around them.

Closing out the text, I switched to Netflix and opened the chips. I wasn't going to let Mom ruin this feeling. Not for anything. As I picked through the bigger chips in the bag, I forced myself not to focus on her disapproval. What I didn't realize, though, was that I should've been focusing on those last minutes with Dad. Because that was the last time he would ever see me the way he did that night. The last time he would ever behave like my dad again.

"What are you thinking about?" Simi asks, jerking me back to the shambled streets.

"Nothing really." I shake the faded colors of the past from my vision. There are too many things to trip over, too many people out to let myself get lost in memories, as sweet as they could be.

"Your face went through fifty-seven different expressions. I doubt it was nothing."

"Just thinking about that Cow Palace date." I nod toward the billboard. Simi coos.

"Where you had your first kiss?" She drags out the *s*.

"Yessss . . ." I do the same. "And the part after." My voice is quieter.

"It's kind of ironic. Your mom was so picky about who you could date, and I'm the one who's supposed to have the 'oppressive' arranged marriage." She air-quotes *oppressive* and rolls her eyes.

"Simi." I squeeze her arm. "I can't imagine anyone ever using the word *oppressed* next to your name."

"Damn straight."

Simi's been an unstoppable force since she refused to let the first-grade class bully steal my crayons out of my cubby. We stayed friends after. Then in fifth grade, when I walked her home every day for three weeks after she hurt her shoulder in a rough game of dodgeball, we became pretty much inseparable. There wasn't anything she didn't know about me, and I could swear I knew everything about her. By senior year, we rarely needed words to communicate—that is, until I screwed everything up.

"One day, when I grow up, I want to be just like you," I say. She scoffs and lifts a brow but says nothing.

In the distance, candles glow in the palms of people standing together. As we get closer, we stop and listen. Their soft singing settles into my chest and spreads through my limbs. Something about their mournful harmonies and the way they huddle together makes the pain of missing Alfie that much sharper.

"Prabh Kai Simaran Pooran Aasaa," Simi whispers.

"What's that mean?" I whisper back.

"In the remembrance of God, hopes are fulfilled."

I take a deep breath and let it out in a slow exhale. I push myself to keep going as their musical prayers soak into my soul.

I will find Alfie.

Alfie

ONCE THIS FOG CLEARS, MIA, I WILL FIND YOU. THE FOG WAS never this bad back home, even on those early December days. Like the morning of the Parade of Lights.

What was it you said about pep, Mia? That it's "a socially acceptable way to pretend you're better than someone exactly like you." I think you even said it was the only way a white boy could ever feel good about himself, pretending like he's better than his competition. Some philosophy for the number two cheerleader on the varsity team.

That's why I fell so hard. You call people on their shit, no matter who they are. Even me. But I think you were always hardest on yourself.

You called yourself an ironic cheerleader because the only reason you did it was for your college applications. I thought I knew exactly what you meant because even though I loved baseball, it was a means to an end for me, too. But then I saw you that night before the parade, and it all made sense.

I knew you weren't looking forward to riding on a float all through downtown, pretend smile and fake laughter on your lips and trying not to freeze in your uniform. And maybe because the flowers at school worked so well, I came up with the ridiculous idea that landed us on the cover of the newspaper the next day.

That night, Baba made sure I was all but handcuffed to the koulourakia-and-kafe cart in front of the restaurant for the whole evening. "It's my way of letting you be part of the fun," he said. Even Mama rolled her eyes at that one. He didn't care if we got to see Santa waving to the crowd or the Shriners Club guys in funny lit-up hats throwing candy to the kids' hungry hands. Baba wanted people to buy the coffee. Business first, community second.

Even though I was stuck working, I paid my sister Eleni to get some art supplies at the dollar store down the street. In hindsight, I should've given her a list instead of telling her the general idea of what I wanted. Twelve-year-olds tend to like shiny things too much. Together we made that huge sign for you—complete with the eighteen tons of glitter she bought. I'd tucked it behind the cart so that when your float rolled by, I could hold it up. Then you'd know there was at least one person in the crowd that was cheering for you, the way you cheered for everyone else.

But, as is par for the course, you surprised me.

"What's a girl gotta do to get a cup of coffee around here?" You looped your pinkie with mine as you slid shoulder to shoulder with me. The goose bumps on your bare arm visible as it brushed against my sweater.

"Hey, what are you doing on this side of the route? Aren't you supposed to be warming up your super smile or cheer muscles or something?" I kissed your frozen cheek while I pushed the poster farther behind the cart with my shoe. "Not that I'm not happy to see you."

"I really don't want to go." You picked up one of the readied cups of coffee from the cart and wrapped your hands around it. "I don't even like cheering. Too much drama and way too much pressure to be perfect all the time. And I actually can't with these ridiculous tube tops they call skirts." You gestured to your bottom half. "Anything you have to wear shorts under so you're not flashing the entire school shouldn't qualify as a skirt."

"I don't know. I kind of like them." I ducked as you punched my arm. "Kidding! Take it easy, Ronda Rousey."

"That's exactly what I'm talking about, though. Objectification." A knowing grin emerged from behind your cup as you swallowed a sip. "Of course, I don't mind if you're doing the objectifying." A deeper red appeared under the frost on your cheeks, and you buried your attention into your next sip.

An older lady with short gray hair and a wool overcoat ambled up to the cart and asked for two cookies and a coffee.

"I would never," I said to you.

"Uh-huh. Then why do you keep staring at my bow?" You pointed to the two enormous loops pinned to the top of your extremely high ponytail. "My eyes are down here, mister."

"Hey, if you don't want me to stare, you shouldn't be so adorable. Them's the rules, sister."

As the lady handed me her money, she gave me the most indignant look and walked away in a huff. You burst out laughing.

"Nice job, Alfie. Now you're going to have a reputation as a rake among all the old biddies in town."

"Nah." I tried my best Chris Hemsworth impersonation and ran the back of my hand across your cheek and winked. "I only have eyes for you and your bow."

You rolled your eyes, but I could tell by the way you tried to hide your smile that you liked our stupid little game.

"Alfie, you need anything? Kafe? Baklava?" Baba half scowled, half smiled as he leaned out the restaurant entrance—a look every Greek man masters sometime between getting married and having a child. I'm sure of it. You lurched away and turned your focus on finding a trash can. I groaned.

"No, Baba. Everything is okay for now." I silently pointed to the city's can in front of the shop two doors down and shrugged an apology to you. Baba was never one for privacy or boundaries, and I knew that was different than what you were used to. I'm not going to lie—I was more than a little embarrassed. I mean, not of my family, but about the way I could see them through your eyes. Big and loud and in your face. I just hoped they wouldn't scare you away.

"You tell me when you need, all right?"

"Yes, Baba."

After he went back inside, I sold another cup or two while you waited. When I was done, I slid my hand into yours and almost got lost in the marbling of hot and cold—ice and fire. If I closed my eyes, I was sure we'd melt together in a puddle and I wouldn't have even cared. But I knew you had places to be, so instead, I checked my phone for the time.

"When do you have to be on the float?"

"I'm probably supposed to be there now." You took a deep breath and let it out slowly, leaning on our intertwined arms. "Cheerleading is so not the business. I can't wait to go to a school where I can focus on my studies and not on who's dating who and what we're all wearing so we're twinning at the Saturday car wash."

"Then why do you do it? Why are you on the squad?"

"Because it looks good on college applications." You studied me for a time, then sighed. "Also, my mom was on the squad and she likes to 'help' out the team every now and then. It's, like, the one thing we can talk about without us ending in a screaming match."

It struck me then how many differences our families had. My parents yelled all the time, but that was just how they communicated. None of their heated discussions and flailing arms ever made any of our faces look the way yours did right then—haunted by the thought of being truly alone.

I hate that you felt that, even for a second.

"Besides, my dad's only willing to pay for some Christian brainwashing center that masquerades as higher education where all the girls major in literal husbandry, and the boys pretend they're righteous and play golf while cheating through their accounting classes. If I have half a chance at a real journalism degree, I need to go somewhere else far away from here."

"Oh wow. A journalist, huh?" It's all I could think to say because all I could hear were two words over and over: *far away*. I didn't want you to go far away. We were just getting close.

"Yeah, women journalists are really making a difference in the world. Like that team of female reporters who investigated backroom deals of powerful groups and discovered that they spent hundreds of millions in dark money to promote anti-abortion misinformation all over the world. Almost every major news source picked up their story. I want to do that too."

"You want to find dark money?" I raised a brow. You rolled your eyes and laughed.

"Not specifically, goof. But yeah, kind of."

"You're amazing, you know that?"

"No, just tired of being fed lies and propaganda. The world deserves better. So here I am whoring myself out for scholarships."

"You're going to be a kickass journalist."

I meant what I said, but despite how good your hand felt in mine, a shiver tiptoed down my spine. Looking back, I think a tiny fissure appeared on my heart when I realized we could be far apart in a few months.

"Sarah Lawrence has a great reputation, and so many smart and successful women graduated from there. That's what I want for myself." You stood taller as you spoke, almost instinctively, and a heaviness burdened my heart. Selfish, I know, but feelings are what they are. Your eyes flicked to mine and back to the ground like you were nervous to say the next thing. "I don't think I could ever live my mother's life—wife to a small-town orthodontist and judge and jury of all that's righteous in this world. No, thank you."

"My mom stays at home." I squeezed your hand so you'd know I was trying to be more of a comfort and less of an argument.

"Your mom is raising four kids and maintaining a home while helping your dad with the restaurant. That's work. My mom does nothing, yet she wears the stay-at-home-mom label as a fricking badge of honor or something. Like driving a big-ass Suburban and carrying a Coach purse bought on your husband's credit card means you win at life."

"Hmm, I'm sensing some strong feelings here." I lifted my free hand to my chin and attempted my best Sherlock Holmes.

"I just want something more is all." Your voice seemed smaller, like it always got when you tried fitting yourself into your mom's world. Like even the idea was too small, too tight. An out-grown shoe you were forced to wear way beyond its time. I wanted your real voice back. The full-throated sandpaper that resonated through me all the way to the base of my skull.

"All that to say you don't want to cheer in the parade tonight?"

"I'll cheer like I always do—ironically." You bit your lip as a smug twinkle flickered in your eyes.

"How do you cheer ironically?"

"They think I'm cheering for them, but what I'm really doing is thinking of the day I can put my last suitcase into the car and wave goodbye to this one-horse town."

"Oh now, I think this town has at least two." I lifted your hand and brushed it with my lips. "Maybe even three."

"Maybe."

"I'll be here when you're done, if you want to hang out after."

With a nod—half-sad, half something else, you let go of my hand and headed toward your spot in the parade. The air iced the spaces between my fingers and in my palm, where the heat of your touch left me aching for more.

I need to rest a minute, Mia, but I'm still looking for you. I'll only rest until this fog lifts. When it does, it'll be easier to navigate these windy streets.

I will find you.

Mia

UP NINETEENTH AVENUE, PAST THE SPONTANEOUS CHOIR VIGIL, silence overtakes the usual electric humming of the city, despite the wind whipping through the streets. Even though I can't see it, I can tell San Francisco's famous fog began its descent into the hills, because the chill in the air doubles almost instantly.

Simi tucks her hair into her hood, and my whole body tenses from the colder air. I try to imagine somewhere warm, but that only makes it worse.

"How many times do you think your parents have tried to call you?" I ask.

"I wouldn't be surprised if they're halfway here already, demanding they be allowed across the bridge, whether it's still there or not." Her attempt at humor lands with a thud on the broken sidewalk. Rumors of the Bay Bridge collapsing travel through the city in whispers, but no one can say for sure. It collapsed in the last big quake, so I guess it's possible. Simi takes out her phone and tries it. Still nothing. "I'm sure things will be restored soon." She offers a tight smile. I nod in return, but neither of us believe it.

I wonder if my own mother is worried, or if she even knows what happened. Home—her home—is over a hundred miles away, probably far enough to be safe from the quake, and I doubt she's watching TV.

On the block ahead, groups of people line up at different tables. We cross the street, and a small older woman meets us with a heartfelt smile. She's wearing a Giants baseball cap over her short salt-and-pepper hair and a too-large brown utility coat with the sleeves rolled up mid-arm.

"You need water?" Her warm brown eyes invite us. "Come here, we have water." She gestures for us to follow.

My suddenly dry mouth tells me to go with her. She scoops a small bottle out of a blue tub and hands one to me and one to Simi.

"Drink." She nods and smiles. We do.

The water is cold from the city's natural refrigeration, and I shiver as it slides down my throat. A renewed clarity perks me up as I drain the last bit. After all that walking and breathing in the dusty air, I guess I needed it.

"Thank you." I twist the cap on the bottle. Simi does the same. The woman takes them, throwing the empty plastics into another tub. I wonder if Alfie's sister Anna would think using plastic in a crisis like this is okay. She's our hometown's version of Greta Thunberg.

All around, volunteers hand out granola bars and water in front of what looks like a church. A darkened sign over the door reads KOREAN 1ST BAPTIST CHURCH, confirming where we are. Simi nods to a small group of church members standing on the lawn in a circle, tule fog winding around their feet. Their arms are raised and eyes closed. One person leads the prayer and the rest chant or respond, so they're all talking at once. I can't understand what they're saying, but I'm sure they believe God does. It's how my parents pray too.

The woman is by our side again, handing us granola bars. We take them gratefully. As I unwrap mine, I take in its sweet scent. A few months ago, such creature comforts weren't even a thought worth registering. Even if my parents were awful, at least I never

THE QUIET PART OUT LOUD • 107

had to worry about an empty snack cupboard or not having a warm bed at night. Now granola bars count as a meal.

But if this night works out the way it's supposed to, I'd do it all over again.

"This makes me miss making food at the Gurdwara, handing it out to people who need it," Simi says. "I never thought I'd miss that." She bites a huge chunk off her bar and chews.

"I was thinking something similar," I say.

"What's your name?" the woman asks. I clear my throat.

"Mia. This is Simi."

"I'm Chin-Sun." She smiles and her whole face is sunshine, and for some reason, I want to shade my eyes from her warmth. "Why are you two out here, honey? You should be inside, where it's safe."

My spine automatically stiffens, a defense mechanism I adopted at home to prepare for judgment, but she's waiting for an answer with no preconceived notion in her eyes. I glance at Simi, hoping she has an answer that sounds less ridiculous than the truth. Instead of answering, though, she takes another large bite of her granola bar.

"We're fine. I'm just trying to find someone. Make sure he's okay." My words come out curt.

Simi's face blanches. I wish I could be different, sound nicer, invite conversation. But it's almost second nature to cut people off now, keep them at arm's length, even when I don't need to. I'd take it back if I could, but as usual, it's too late.

"She means we're worried about our friend and really want to find him." Simi side-eyes me, then smiles at Chin-Sun. I widen my eyes at Simi just long enough for her to get my apology, but she's already moved on.

"You can't wait until morning when it'll be safer?" Chin-Sun takes my hand and nods. I let myself feel a little of her warmth.

Of course, that's a more logical idea, something past me would've been swayed by. Risk was always Alfie's thing, not mine. But the earthquake shook something loose inside me. When it became evident I could lose him for real and forever, I realized that I have to tell him the truth. That I've always loved him. The image of him with his arm around that girl pops into my head.

Hopefully it's not too late.

"No, I—we—need to see him now." I pull back my hand and cross my arms over my middle. Simi stares at me, jaw jutted forward. "What?" I mouth. Instead of answering, she turns away.

She doesn't really need to. I know I'm coming across as ungrateful, but I can't help it. As great as Chin-Sun is, I want to keep going. It's only going to get darker and colder. Just the thought makes me shiver.

Chin-Sun pinches her lips together and looks around. "We're out of coats, I think, but I can at least give you a blanket. Keep you warm." She digs through a box under the granola table. She wraps a thin red blanket around my shoulders and holds another one out to Simi, who says something about saving it for someone more in need. Immediately, warmth bleeds into my shoulders and arms. I wrap the blanker tighter around my body and smile. She hands us two more water bottles, which we tuck away for later.

"Thank you." I exhale and look at the ground. "I didn't realize how cold I was."

She takes my hand again. "Can I pray for you?"

My eyes jerk upward and I meet her gaze. Nothing about that ever felt real to me. In my house, public prayer was always for show. Let the neighbors see how faithful we are. My whole body pulls me away from her and toward the sidewalk.

"That's okay." My smile becomes tight, automatic, like I'm back at my mom's house. Simi's *Let her* look and something in Chin-Sun's expression—honesty, vulnerability, I'm not sure— makes me want to back away, keep going, forget we were ever here.

It's too much like home. But she takes my "That's okay" as permission.

Before I can resist, Chin-Sun takes my and Simi's hands, then bows her head. Simi reaches for my other one, and the three of us form a lopsided circle of our own. Chin-Sun speaks softly in a language I don't know. Even though there is hope and love in her words, all I can hear are my mom and her Bible study circle.

In my family, prayer was a weapon. We prayed for people to stop doing the things we thought they should. We asked God to save people from themselves, even when they were just living their lives. We prayed our wishes out loud so other people would hear them. Never once did I hear a prayer like Chin-Sun's. Her prayer is warm and kind and vulnerable.

I've spent the last five months—maybe my entire life, if I'm truly being honest—shoving my emotions somewhere deep inside. But the earthquake didn't just break down the dorms and neighbor- hoods. Alfie's letter was its own sort of quake that brought every- thing to the surface. And Chin-Sun's soft pleas shatter my heart in a thousand pieces. Tears form, and I try to blink them back.

If I break now, I'll never go any farther. And I need to find him. I need to find Alfie.

"I'm sorry, I can't . . ." I jerk my hands away from both of them and fold them into my new blanket.

The tears come anyway, and I can't stop them. I don't know where to begin to explain myself, so I turn away before they slide down my cheek and onto my new red blanket.

"Thank you, Chin-Sun," Simi says.

"Be safe. I hope you find your boy," Chin-Sun shouts behind me. I croak out a goodbye, but I doubt she heard. I can barely breathe, let alone talk.

We walk in silence until the ruined gas stations and restaurants become rows of dark houses. People sit on their porches, watching others clean up overturned garbage cans and reset car alarms. Cigarette flares and flashlights are the only illumination. Some people wave or nod to us. Others continue the work of cleaning up the mess the earthquake left behind. A lot just hold each other. Even though they don't speak, there's an air of community, a togetherness that unites the neighborhoods in a common goal.

"She was nice." Simi catches up to me.

"She was."

"You, not so much."

I don't look at her. I can't. Because if I do, I won't be able to hold everything inside, and that's exactly what I have to do in order to keep going.

"Everything okay? You didn't even let her finish her prayer."

"Yep, all good." I quicken my pace.

"Are you sure?"

"Just really want to get across the city."

"You're walking too fast." Simi's voice is heavy with something unfamiliar. I ignore it and keep going. "Want to talk about why you're running down the street?"

I stop at the end of the block. She almost slams into me.

"I am not running down the street." My voice is even and subdued.

"Yes, you are. You're running away . . . again."

I flinch, her words are arrows hitting me straight in the chest. My thoughts fly everywhere at once.

"I'm not running away, I'm running *toward* something. Toward Alfie."

"Are you?"

I scoff even though my blood is spiraling through my veins. How dare she? My dad is the one who wrecked my relationship with him, not me. And after my mom humiliated us in front of the entire town, how could I stay? That wasn't running—that was survival. This is ridiculous. I turn and face her. But when I see her face twisted in exasperation, I can't deal.

"Fine, I'm running." I throw my hands up and step off what's left of the curb. She jerks the strap of her backpack I'm wearing. It scrapes my shoulders as it thuds to the ground. My mouth drops. I stare at her bag while cold seeps in between my thin blanket and skin where it used to be.

"Mia, look at me."

I turn around but can't bring myself to meet her eye. I tap my foot and sigh.

"You can lie to yourself, but I'm right here, seeing what I always see." She evens out her stance and puts a hand on her hip. I jerk back like she slapped me.

"Do you have something you want to say to me?"

"Pretty sure I'm saying it." She exhales frustration. "You always do this."

"Do what?" Anger rises in me, slithering up my spine, binding my tongue.

"Run. Chin-Sun made you feel something you didn't like, so you took off. It's the same with Alfie . . ."

"Stop." I close my eyes like that could stop sound.

"And your dad." She reaches for my hand, but I step away from her grasp. "Now you're doing it with me. You always do this . . . and leave me to pick up the pieces you leave in your wake."

I open my mouth, then close it again. She doesn't get that I'm doing this to try to fix all that. Just because I don't want to listen to someone pray doesn't mean I'm running.

The group from the church has spread out to help others for the next few blocks. Among the broken glass and chunks of plaster on the streets, people come together, directing traffic and assessing injuries.

On regular days, these strangers would probably pass each other without acknowledging that others exist. Everyone's too wrapped up in their own drama to notice anyone else. Disaster changes all that. When it really counts, people come together and forget about what normally separates them. Everyone is equal.

Except right here, on this corner. Because Simi doesn't get it, and I can't find the words to explain. The air feels heavier, like it's struggling under the weight of the dust and fog it's forced to carry.

"I'm not running," I say again. She doesn't reply. I take a few steps into the street. She doesn't follow.

"I didn't run from . . . what I did to you."

"You knew I'd forgive you." She blows a burst of air through her nose. "Don't I always?"

"What does that mean?" I'm shrieking now. My feet can't decide where they want to be, so I end up pacing between the curb and the gutter.

"Mia, I love you. And you've been my best friend since before

I even knew what that meant. But sometimes you make things hard for no reason. You're so hell-bent on exposing the messed-up things in the world, but you can't take two seconds to look at yourself."

She's wrong. At least about this. I fold my arms across my middle. Tonight isn't about the past. Tonight is about finding the truth. Saying the truth. For the future. For Alfie.

We cross another street, and the path ahead is darker than the last few blocks. Rows of houses become rows of trees that block the sky. The air feels warmer against my face, but I wrap the blanket Chin-Sun gave me tighter around my shoulders anyway.

"Why are you here? If I make everything so difficult, why'd you come with me?"

"Aside from the fact that I couldn't let you traipse through all this by yourself?" Her face twists into her classic *Duh*, but then I realize maybe that's not what that expression means. Maybe I've been reading her all wrong this whole time. "I thought because you reacted the way you did to his letter that maybe this time was different, but . . ."

"But what?" I exhale hard and hold it so I feel it in my chest, a heavy pressure just over my heart.

"We never really talked about what happened—we just brushed everything aside. I'll take the blame for that, but I can't do it anymore. If you want to push everyone away, do everything alone, then fine. You win." She steps off the curb and walks past me the way we were headed, the backpack looped over her shoulders now.

I realize that I'm still holding my breath, and a part of me wants to remain like that, the weight pressed on my chest, but I have to keep going. I take in the icy air, and it's like daggers, shooting straight though the shield over my heart. I follow a few steps behind, clutching my thin, red blanket, hot tears rolling down my face.

I wish she'd stayed at the dorm. I sniff, sucking snot back into my nose. Right now, I wish I'd never asked to stay with her at all.

How awkward will it be when we do find Alfie? What's she going to do—say hello, then try to catch a ride back to campus?

It occurs to me we never really talked about after. Just another Mia special—act now, think never. I blow out a breath and my entire torso deflates.

Out of nowhere, a small girl appears. She grabs Simi's hand, pulling her in my direction. I shoot a confused look to Simi, but her attention is on the little girl. She's probably about seven with a pink-and-purple coat buttoned all the way up. Her dark hair is pulled into a tight ponytail.

When they reach me, the girl grabs my hand too, and practically drags us to where two men are circling each other, throwing punches. My insides shrink as my eyes go wide. Simi and I trade looks, our fight forgotten for the moment.

"Papa, stop." The girl whimpers and sniffs, and my heart sinks.

Immediately Simi is kneeling and asking if she's okay.

Something twists inside me. She's so young. Her mom probably loves her and misses her. She needs her mom to hug her and tell her everything's going to be okay.

I'm going to make sure she gets to her mother safely, even if it means I have to stop for a while. Alfie would do the same.

Alfie

I KNOW YOU THINK IT'S CORNY AND DON'T UNDERSTAND WHY everyone in town started setting out chairs along the parade route at six a.m. And you thought it was "the awful rot of capitalism" that made businesses stay open late to let people window-shop downtown while sipping hot chocolate and spiced cider. But I loved it.

My favorite part is how all the wineries, schools, and organizations around town create floats to celebrate who they are. I know you hated having to ride on one, but the view is always so good. There are so many lights—you'd think they could see our tiny town from space. Oh, and how Budweiser brings their Clydesdales, and the Coca-Cola Company has Santa giving out free Cokes to the crowd at the end of the night. With all the winter cheer and everyone being so nice to each other, it's the perfect time of year.

When I was younger, Mama let me watch the parade on her lap. Now most of us had outgrown that, and even though Coach wanted me on the school's float with the rest of the team, Baba expected the whole family to pull our weight with the business—although I suspect he'd rather do without Anna's constant nagging to switch to environmentally friendly take-out cups and bags. Even Eleni had to make sure the sidewalks stayed litter free around the storefront.

When the coffee-and-cookie crowd thinned and the piped-in Christmas street music faded from the speakers hidden in planter boxes and streetlights, I knew the parade was about to begin.

"Was that her, Alfie?" Eleni's bright eyes shone over her cherry nose. She shivered in the cold.

"What do you think? I hold hands with strangers?" I winked and made a big deal about shaking my head in disgust.

"Why are you so weird?" Before I could answer, she rolled her eyes and went inside the store, probably to apply the fiftieth layer of lip gloss—the only makeup Baba allowed in middle school, although my money was on her sneaking a full case of blush and mascara buried in the bottom of her backpack. Mama and Baba got off easy with me, Elias, and Anna, but they're going to have their hands full with her.

I wiped the cart down as I cleaned up leftover cups and crumbs, but I couldn't keep my eyes from the parade route. I refused to miss you passing by, Mia. Not when I had my glitter-ific sign to cheer you on.

Mama surprised me by coming out from behind the register and gently taking my rag.

"You go." She nodded toward the street where the parade would soon be coming, her tired eyes crinkling at the edges. "Go with your friend."

"But Baba wanted . . ."

"Never mind Baba. You go and have fun. I'll take care of him."

Before she could change her mind, I whipped off my blue-and-white-striped apron and grabbed the poster. I might not be able to be on the float with everyone, but at least I could be part of the crowd.

"Thanks, Mama." I kissed her cheek and she waved me off with her typical *Get out of here* face, even though I knew she loved it.

As I walked, a new idea formed—the one that got us in the paper. I raced around the back alley and found an open spot on the first corner of the route. If you were going to cheer ironically, or whatever, I was going to cheer for real. For you. Because you deserved it. And, I'll admit, I wanted to see your real smile. Not the one you pasted on for the crowd—I wanted to see the one meant just for me.

Floats appeared and passed by, one by one, their lights shining like stars for our little universe.

Then yours turned the corner.

My eyes searched the sea of gigantic bows until they finally found yours, nestled in between two others, almost hidden from this side of the street. But I knew it was you. There was no mistaking your squared shoulders and brown ponytail cascading down your back in an explosion of waves.

It was time.

I held up the sign, glitter raining down onto my hair and face and arms, but I didn't care. And I shouted as loud as I could so my voice would rise above the crowd.

"Mia! Woo-hoo, go Mia! Yeah!"

Your head whipped around so fast, I thought for a moment your flying hair might blind the girl next to you. When your surprised eyes found mine, they filled with panic. As they darted between the others around you, your smile went from plastic to cement. It hardened on your face as you drew your arms around your middle. For a moment, I doubted my not-so-well-thought-out plan.

But then Josuè shouted back at me from the float, his football jersey covered by his well-decorated varsity jacket. "Alfie, my dude! What's that say?" He nodded his team baseball cap toward my sign.

"You're the sugar to my Christmas cookie!"

Josuè flicked his chin at me, the universal sign of fellow-dude approval.

Your shoulders relaxed a little as the rest of the float started cheering too. This only made me jump up and down and yell louder. "Get it, Mia!"

The poster jiggled above my head, making more glitter rain over my face and shoulders, making me your own personal ornament. Then Chuck was at my side, jostling my shoulder and pumping his fist.

"Come on." Chuck jerked his head to the next corner. "Let's beat them there."

Without thinking, I took off behind him, weaving my way through the cheering crowd. As I bobbed through the chairs and blankets, my foot caught on a trash can, and I stumbled, scaring the older couple directly in my path. Luckily, I was able to right myself at the last minute and pivot toward the street.

"Watch it, young man!" a crusty voice boomed.

"Sorry!" I waved behind me like I'd cut him off in the fast lane, but kept going.

When I got to the corner, not only was Chuck waiting, but a few other guys from the team were standing by as well. I stood in front of them, poster high over my head, smile toothy and wide.

Your float approached and we started yelling. I screamed your name as you buried your face in your hands. The girls around you swooned, and Josuè shot me a thumbs-up with his ultimate-approval head nod. And when you slid your hands from your face and looked at me, I saw it. The smile that's meant just for me. Eyes glinting, one side of your mouth higher than the other, creating a tiny dimple right in the middle of your cheek.

The whole float erupted into cheers and waves and fist pumps while you shook your head. But that dimple was still there, your definitive happy tell.

Our group raced your float, adding people every time and growing larger block after block so that by the time we were near the end of the route, there were about as many of us as there were people on the back of the flatbed. Standing between the two groups, I couldn't tell which was louder. As the tires of the float rolled to a slow stop, Chuck took my sign and nodded toward you. As I neared, you made your way to the edge. Josuè jumped down, and he and Chuck flanked my sides, holding their hands out.

Cameras flashed and phones recorded me putting my arms into the air.

You grasping the hands of my two best friends.

Me wrapping my arms around your middle.

You sliding against my chest so your face met mine.

Your arms around my neck.

Our lips colliding.

The morning headline read LOCAL TEEN SCORES A HOME RUN AT THE LIGHT PARADE, and even though rain was sparse that year and farmers feared for their next year's harvest, they at least predicted a romantic winter. Love conquers all, even in the darkest of times.

How naive we all were.

Mia

I CROUCH DOWN WITH SIMI AND THE LITTLE GIRL. *SHE TURNS* her tearstained face to me and points to the men, her breath coming out in between broken sobs. I may have been a little naive to think we could fix this on our own, but we have to at least try.

"Are you hurt?" Simi asks, looking her over. The girl shakes her head. Simi asks her something in Punjabi I don't understand. She nods.

"Help him." More tears. More sobs.

"One of them is her dad," Simi says.

"Okay, I'm going to see if I can help, or get some," I say, my voice too fast, too shaky.

"Hey, get away from my daughter," one of the men says. The surprise of his voice brings me to my feet, and I snap my attention back to him. Every bone in my body tells me to run. But I can't leave the little girl alone. As he's looking at me, the other guy sucker punches him and knocks him to the ground. I flinch like he was aiming for me.

"Daddy!" the little girl screams.

Adrenaline floods my body as my feet beg me to run. What can I do against two men so determined to hurt each other? My only physical training is some cheers and gymnastics. What am I going to do, backflip them until they stop hitting each other? I slide my hand over my hair.

Think, Mia.

The little girl says something to Simi.

"They live down there," Simi tells me. She asks her something else.

"Risha," the little girl says.

"Hey, Risha. Let's see if we can find your mom." Simi takes her hand and nods for me to take the other. Unsure what else to do, I take her hand and squeeze it the way Chin-Sun squeezed mine, feeling very much like the world's biggest hypocrite. "Do you know which house is yours?"

Risha points at a building down the street.

"Let's go," I say.

Simi yells something to Risha's dad.

"I told him we're taking her to her mom."

As we hurry over the sidewalk, I yell for help. I put all the force of my cheerleading lungs behind my cries for intervention, but no one responds.

"Please, a man needs your help!" I cry. Simi tries in Punjabi.

No one comes.

I look back and Risha's dad is on the ground, the larger man looming over him. Risha whimpers. My teeth click against each other as I try to figure out what to do. Then I remember something from a self-defense class we had to take for PE sophomore year. I don't know why it picked now to show up in my head, but I'm glad it did.

"Fire! Fire!" I screamed it over and over in all directions, hoping someone would hear me and want to help.

"Aga! Aga!" Simi yells too.

Shades of light pass over windows as they open and people peer out. Too many flashlights shine in my eyes to see where they're coming from, so I point with my free hand to the men duking it out in the middle of the street.

"Over there!"

"Risha!" a woman cries from her window. "Stay there!"

"Mama!" Risha tugs on my hand for me to let go, but I hold her tighter.

"Let's stay here so she can find you," I say.

She stops pulling as two men speed past us toward the fight. Risha's mom flees out the main door of her building. As she gets close, she kneels down, swoops up her little girl, and spins her in a hug all at once. Then she sets Risha down and gives her a proper mom inspection. Her worried eyes tug at my heart.

"Are you hurt? Where is your dad?" She opens Risha's jacket and checks for injury. Risha shakes her head and points toward the fight. Her mom gasps and yells her husband's name. When he looks, the other man kicks him hard and he cocoons into a ball. The man kicks him one more time and flees into the trees.

One of the men who ran past us stops to check on Risha's dad while a few others chase the kicker into the dark trees. Without thinking, I race to the man on the ground. As I'm running, I whip the blanket from my shoulders and bunch it into a ball. Once I'm with him, I carefully prop it under his head. The other man makes eye contact with me and stands, dialing something on his phone. He puts it to his ear, curses, and shoves it back in his pocket.

"Circuits are overloaded."

"At least you have service." I stand.

Simi, Risha, and her mom rush to her dad's side.

"Are you okay? What happened?" her mom asks.

"They were fighting, but I don't know why," I say.

The dad's eyes are closed, but he rouses when he hears his wife's voice. Her eyes graze mine, then shift when he moans.

"The car," he says. "He was trying to take the car."

The mom looks toward the sky and mutters something.

"You're trying to get yourself killed for the car?" she says. "That can be replaced. You cannot." Her eyes shift back to me. "Thank you for helping, both of you." She smiles at Simi. "Risha is lucky you were there."

Simi and I exchange uncomfortable looks. I nod to the mom, unsure anything I could say would be right for this moment. We're outsiders infringing on this family's moment. At least Simi can speak the language.

"Yes, thank you for your help." The man sits up and moves his jaw in circles. "Sorry I yelled at you. I thought you might've been with him."

"Of course." Simi smiles and bows her head. I remember Chin-Sun's water in the backpack. I take it out and offer it to him.

"I have this. You should drink it."

Risha's mom hands me my bunched-up blanket, which I take with my free hand. He refuses the water and stands.

"You two have done enough. I can get fixed up at home."

His words sting a little, reminding me that I no longer have a home of my own. But I'm glad at least some of us have the option. I tuck the water back in its pouch and fold the blanket over my arm.

The guys who ran after the thief come back, out of breath and frustrated.

"He got away."

"Probably for the best," Risha's dad says. "The cops aren't coming out for things like that tonight anyway."

The men trade glances. I shudder and pull the blanket over my shoulders. Risha's dad holds out a bruised hand.

"I'm Avi. This is my wife, Safa, and my brother, Raj. Thanks again."

"I'm Mia, and this is Simi," I say.

"Sat Sri Akaal," Simi says. A Punjabi greeting, one of the few phrases she's taught me. I don't say it, though. I'm worried I'll screw it up, and I don't want to embarrass myself or Simi.

"Sat Sri Akaal," Safa and Avi say together.

"Do you two live around here?" Avi asks.

"No." I motion toward the park. "We're headed that way."

"I go to State," Simi adds like she'd rather be back there than here with me. Safa asks her something I don't understand, and the two of them step away to talk.

"She's helping me get to USF," I say.

Avi's face blanches. "You can't go in there with that maniac car thief on the loose." He nods to Raj and tosses keys to him. "My brother can drive you."

"Happy to," Raj says.

The back of my neck tingles, but there's no new breeze. I look at Raj with new eyes. Getting into a car with a stranger—both big and male—isn't something I'd normally do. His own eyes are kind, though, and I could really use a break from walking in the cold.

Simi looks at Risha's mom, then after a deep breath, hugs her. Risha's mom holds Simi's hands in her own and says something, and they hug again.

When they separate, Simi glances at me. I raise my eyebrows, but Simi doesn't respond, and it's clear that she's still furious with me. Another icy dagger hits the shield over my heart.

"Safa says they're going to the Gurdwara to hand out food once they clean up." Simi's tone is distant and she avoids my eyes.

"You should go with them," I say, my tone equally icy. Inside, I'm frantic for us to stay together. She's the one who keeps me calm, helps me find my direction. A blade of fear slices through me, but I need to stay focused on finding Alfie, to be strong. She'll be better-off with people who can help her instead of constantly causing her so much pain. She deserves to feel safe too.

I offer Simi a neutral smile, but she doesn't reciprocate. Instead, she busies herself rummaging through her backpack. My jaw ticks. Even calculus is better than having to talk to me, I guess.

"Can I go too, Daddy?" Risha asks. Avi looks at his wife, who nods. If she's okay with her daughter going with him, I guess I should be okay going with him too. I blow out a breath.

"Ready?" Raj tosses the keys into the air and catches them. "You coming, Risha?"

"It's the least we can do. Not many people would have done what you did." Avi puts his arm around his wife. "I was trying to defend my property and got a little more than I bargained for." He laughs, but not in a happy way.

"You held your own, bro," Raj says.

"I appreciate the ride." Just thinking of sitting in a warm car makes my legs ache. "We've been walking awhile."

"Done." Raj lifts Risha over his head and flips her onto his shoulder. She squeals and motions for me to follow.

I turn to wave goodbye, and nearly run into Simi. Without saying anything, she holds out the map. I swallow and lift my chin, then take it silently and slide it into my back pocket. This time, there's no psychic communication between us.

Just my best friend going one way and me, the other. Again.

As I climb into the passenger seat, she runs to the door. My heart skips as the *I'm sorries* float on my tongue.

"Take this, too." It's her SFSU embroidered sweatshirt. Because even when she hates me, she doesn't want me to suffer.

It takes every ounce of strength I have to not dissolve onto the worn floormat beneath my feet.

"No way. You'll freeze," I say.

"You're going to need it more."

Reluctantly I take her sweatshirt and close the car door. As she walks away, I try for one more telepathic message: *Thank you. I love you, too.*

I don't think she gets it.

A sliver of the new moon peers over the trees. I take a deep breath and try focusing on what's in front of me. I'll see Alfie soon. As I settle into the warm seat, relief washes over me for the second time tonight. But it doesn't last long.

Based on the mess I witnessed as I walked along the newer parts of the Avenues, I can't bring myself to imagine what Alfie's ancient dorm might look like. At least with a ride, I can get there faster.

I just hope it's soon enough.

Alfie

Alfie: Is it too soon to tell you how much fun I had with you last night? You can jump into my arms and kiss me anytime. *inserts Greek eyebrow emoji*

Mia: You know there's no such emoji, right?

Alfie: There should be. Where are you?

Mia: Ugh, my mom's in a mood. I'll probably be late to homeroom.

Alfie: Don't forget they're making the winter court announcements today. You don't want to miss that.

Mia: It's whatever.

Alfie: It is indeed not whatever. It is totally a what. I saw your face when you filled out your ballot. You want to be on the court.

Mia: Only if I get to be with you. 😍

Alfie: Um, excuse me. I'm the flirty one. You take those heart eyes back.

Mia: I will not. It'd be kind of fun to be up there with you.

Alfie: Just get here as fast as you can. I'd like to reenact that kiss asap. Gotta go. Ms. Newton is giving me the stink eye.

Alfie: They just announced.

Mia: I heard. Congrats. 😊

Alfie: I won't do it without you.

Mia: Don't be stupid. You're going to be great.

Alfie: *sends pic of a cartoon sheep with a crown and sash* Ewe'd make the best queen.

Mia: ♥♥♥

Alfie

MIA, I WANT YOU TO KNOW THAT UNTIL THAT DAY IN HOME-
room when my name was announced and yours wasn't, I'd never
even considered going into one of those trinket stores where
they sell stuffed heart emojis and every nine-year-old girl goes
to get their ears pierced. But I couldn't handle watching your
beautiful smile twist into forced happiness for all the others
who were on the court. Girls from your squad jumping up and
down, hugging you and squealing *This is so great!* even when
you clearly didn't agree.

So that day, after school and before my dinner shift, I dragged
Chuck to the mall in the next town and bought you the best thing
I could find that would let you know, court or no court, you were
my queen and that's all that truly mattered. I didn't even mind
that he teased me the entire way back, because I couldn't wait
to see your face as you opened your gift. I had to force myself to
drive the speed limit the whole way.

After dropping him off, I parked in front of your house
instead of the driveway. I don't know why, but I could never bring
myself to park there, even though your dad practically insisted on
it. Something about parking in the driveway is too personal. And
your parents, as nice as they could be on the outside, seemed to
harbor some internal yardstick they kept between me and them.
Like they said come in, get comfortable, but then made sure I was
only allowed on the company couch. Yet it was my fault for not

relaxing on the stiff cushions. Anyway, driveways are for parking without yardsticks in the way.

I made my way to your front door and knocked. You answered, a shocked look on your face.

"Hey! You didn't text me, did you? I didn't know you were coming over." You glanced over your shoulder and stepped onto the porch, barefoot and in cutoff sweats.

"I wanted to surprise you," I said. You closed the door and motioned to the chairs on the porch.

"What's that?" You pointed to the bag as you sat down and folded your legs underneath you.

"A present."

"For me?" A slight grin tugged at the corners of your mouth.

"Mm-hmm."

I handed the bag to you. You untied the ribbon so carefully, like the bag might explode if you pulled too hard. Then you pulled the tissue paper out one by one, folding each piece into a square and placing it on the table between us. You always unwrapped things that way. Like the wrapping itself was part of the gift. My dad always gave my mom her gifts in the bag he got at the store— no paper or ribbons or anything. I loved that you paid so much attention to those little details.

You lifted the rhinestone crown out of the bag. A cloud passed over your expression for just a moment. Then you blinked and there was water pooling at the corners of your eyes.

"You got me a crown?"

"There's something else, too." I nodded toward the bag, my heart swelling with each breath.

You dug through the bag and unraveled the pink satin sash as you lifted it out.

"Oh my god. You didn't. You didn't!" You stood up so fast that the bag fell from your lap, forgotten on the porch. I stood too.

"Here, let me help you." I straightened the sash around your torso while you secured the crown in your hair. When you were satisfied it would stay, you pulled the sash tight as you read.

"Prom Queen."

"Couldn't get one that said anything seasonally appropriate at such short notice."

You should have seen your face when I got down on one knee. If I could paint your expression and hang it in a museum, I would call it "Panic with a Side of Romance."

"You are my queen, and you deserve to be on every court of every dance at every school." I pulled a camellia bloom from the inside of my jacket and held it up to you with both hands. A tear rolled down your cheek and off your chin. You took the flower and held it close to your heart. Could you hear mine beating? I thought it was going to come out of my chest.

I stood and you wrapped your arms around me so tight.

"Thank you, Alfie," you whispered. "This is so sweet. It's everything."

Then the door creaked open and you jumped back so fast. I didn't have time to register how your entire body language changed in the one second it took your mom to walk onto the porch. Now it's so obvious how simply being in the same room with her made you feel.

"What's all this?" Your mom wore a pasted smile that didn't come close to her eyes. She looked more like she was asking what the special of the day was than what your boyfriend was doing at your house.

"Alfie brought me a crown." You raised your hands to either

side of your head and turned right and left to show it off. "I was kind of sad I didn't get nominated today, so he wanted me to know he thinks I should've been."

"You're darn right you should have been nominated." Your mom took your hand and twirled you around. "Who wouldn't want someone this pretty on their stage, ruling over the night? Oh Alfie, you did good. Well done." Her tone was more condescending than impressed.

Then she did the thing she inevitably always does. And I still hate that I couldn't change that for you, Mia. More than anything, I wanted to save you from all that pain. I know, it's not my job to save you and you can do it yourself. But when you love someone, you just don't want them to hurt. And I hated to see you carry all that pain.

Her hands were in your hair and wrapped around your crown before you could react.

"This is right out of a storybook." She placed the crown on her own head and twirled in a circle. "I could wear this for our anniversary party!" She pushed her lips together and posed her chin on her raised shoulder. She posed in a few different positions and then handed it back to you.

After she went inside, you just stood there, eyes wide and fixed on some ghostly scene playing in your head. I stepped in front of you and gently took the crown from your hands and put it back in your hair, smoothing the parts where your mom ruffled it out of place.

I wish I could've smoothed away all the hurt she left with you.

"She ruins everything," you said in a whisper. I wrapped you in my arms and held you until you stopped shaking.

"She won't ruin us," I whispered back. "I won't let her."

In that moment, I believed it. The way your body pressed against mine, you believed it too.

Mia

IT TAKES FOREVER FOR RAJ TO GET RISHA BUCKLED INTO HER seat. When he does, I press myself against the fur-lined passenger seat and do the same. She wants me to sit in the back with her, so I sit as sideways as I can in the front to see both her and Raj. This family has been super nice, but I can't help thinking about child safety locks on the back doors. As nice as Raj is for driving me, he's still the guy who took off after a violent thief.

"You going to school here too?" Raj closes the driver's door and starts the car. He buckles his own seat belt as the car warms up.

"Um, not yet. Hopefully next semester." It's not exactly a lie. I've been thinking of applying because Simi's heard good things about the journalism department.

Simi.

I look out the window, hoping to wave or pass on an *I'm sorry and I'll be back* or something, but she's already halfway inside.

"Oh, okay." He pulls away from the curb and makes a left toward the park.

A part of me reaches out for Simi, hoping she'll feel it and turn around. But the door closes behind her instead. I almost ask Raj to stop, but in classic Mia form, I don't.

"You can come play with me!" Risha perks up.

"Thank you. That'd be fun." I reach over the seat and offer a fist bump.

"You know the reason Avi wanted me to drive you, right?

Besides your safety, I mean." He jerks his head subtly toward the back seat. "Give them time to clean him up without eyes."

For some reason, this relaxes me a little, and I lean into the seat.

"You live here with your family?" Raj asks.

Maybe it's the warmth from the heater or the adrenaline leaving my body, but suddenly I'm too tired to think of a lie.

"No, I don't really get along with my parents."

"That's too bad. Family is always good to have around. If you can depend on them."

We pass a sign that reads STRAWBERRY HILL, and I glance at Risha. Her eyes are closed and her head is limp, but I don't want to tell parental horror stories in front of someone who just almost lost their dad.

"That's true." I don't add more.

I turn in my seat to look out the window and breathe in the warm air blowing from the heater. If only I could've depended on my family.

The morning of the winter formal, I woke up to the aroma of Saturday pancakes à la Dad, a rare weekend treat. But the last time he'd made them, they'd sent me to Bible camp for two weeks instead of the cheer camp they'd promised I could go to if I got all As my junior year. Yeah, it was cheer and not an internship at a newspaper, but a couple weeks away from home would've been a nice break. Ruined my chances to be head cheerleader, too. Sure, I was still the second, but being in charge would've looked better.

Instead of warm and delicious things, now pancakes smelled like broken promises and empty dreams.

Downstairs, Mom had just come in from her morning run. Her hair was windblown and her cheeks were pink from the cold, a look we rarely saw.

"Ooh, pancakes!" She took off her windbreaker and hung it over her chair at the kitchen table. "What's the occasion?"

"Committing me to a nunnery this time?" I grab a pancake off the pile next to the stove and bite into it. No cinnamon. No vanilla. Just the sweet tang of boxed batter.

"Mia, that's ridiculous." Mom pulled her phone from her fanny pack and checked it. A smile heated her face as she read.

"Besides, we're not Catholic." Dad kissed my cheek, took the partially eaten pancake out of my hand, and put it on the plate he held. He handed it to me and nodded to the table. "Now go eat like a person, please."

I was about to ask what a person eats like, but I decided not to chance anything, especially since the dance was that night. Instead, I carried my plate to the table and sat down.

"Are you excited for tonight?" Mom asked.

"Of course."

Mom tilted her head and studied me. I swallowed the bite I'd been working on.

"What."

"Oh, nothing." She sipped her coffee. "Was Alfie able to find a matching bow tie and cummerbund?"

"No one does that anymore. He's wearing black tie."

"But he can afford an actual tux, right?"

"Yes, Mom, he can afford a tux."

"Don't get defensive." She held up her hand. "I just want my little girl to have a perfect evening is all."

I forced myself to look at the plate in front of me and not roll my eyes. The last thing I needed was to be grounded the night Alfie was crowned king.

"Your mom's right." Dad joined us at the table with his own

plate and a huge stack of extras he set in the middle of the table. "She wants it to be perfect for you." He patted her knee. She returned a tight smile.

"Are you sure you wouldn't rather go with Chuck? He plays baseball too, right?"

Dad nodded. I stood so fast, my chair squeaked against the tile.

"Are you serious right now? Alfie is my boyfriend." I struggled to contain my volume.

"Oh, no need for labels in high school." She scrunched her face and waved me off. "You're babies."

"Besides, you're going to meet a lot of people when you go off to school in the fall." Dad motioned at the pancakes with a questioning look toward Mom.

"No thank you, dear, I'm going to be good." She patted her thigh and looked at my plate. "What about you? You don't want to be bloated in that gorgeous dress, do you?"

For that, I ripped a pancake in half, dunked it in syrup, shoved the entire thing in my mouth, and shrugged. She didn't say anything, just pursed her lips and looked away.

I hope it grossed her out.

"You know, you're probably going to get a sweet offer from Liberty, and I'm happy to make up the difference," Dad said. "And there will be plenty of good, Christian boys to choose from."

"Are *you* serious right now?" I poured myself orange juice from the pitcher and gulped it down.

"You'll meet someone more like us." Mom drank the last of her coffee and took her cup to the sink.

More like us? Did she mean uptight and fake? Caring more about what people saw on our outside than what they thought of us inside? Even I didn't want to be like us.

"I'm not going to college to shop for a husband. I'm going to . . . you know what? Never mind." I clenched my hands into fists, arms straight by my sides.

"What were you going to say, Mia?" Dad's voice was like the pancakes, plastic and bland. His warning voice.

I wanted to tell them that excluding Alfie because they didn't take the time to understand his culture was prejudiced bullshit, not to mention un-Christian. That the reason I'd all but begged to go to Sarah Lawrence was so I could become the kind of badass journalist who exposes small-mindedness like that. That even if I ever decided to get married, I would bend over backward to make sure that I didn't end up like them.

But the dance was that night, and I wanted to see Alfie.

"Nothing." I sat back down.

"Maybe that's the only school I will pay for. It certainly is the best one." Dad's voice wasn't so neutral anymore.

"Oh Jeff, we don't know which school will be the best until we visit." Mom stood behind him and rubbed his shoulders. "You made this beautiful breakfast for us, so let's not spoil it. Let's just have this time together and be thankful."

The pancakes cemented themselves to my insides, but I stayed silent. Something was really wrong. They usually hardly talked to each other, and she barely let him kiss her on the cheek. But here she was rubbing his shoulders, making a big deal about a breakfast she would never eat.

The scariest part was that she didn't say no to my choice of school—one that clearly went against everything she thought was good for me. A tiny glimmer of hope sparked in my chest, but I quickly clamped it down. It was probably just some reverse-psychology crap she'd heard about on one of the podcasts she was always listening to. But hey, if her shoulder-rubbing and sweet-talking were going to get me closer to my dreams, fine with me.

If I could just get out of there, I knew everything would be okay.

"Besides, this Sarah Lawrence might give her more money," Mom added. "Our girl is smart and beautiful and kind. Who wouldn't want her representing their school?"

That sort of thing was so typical. Insulting my weight one moment, then telling me I was beautiful the next. Riding that emotional-manipulation train day in and day out my entire life was exhausting. So much so that I'd rather be riding through a darkened park with a stranger in a city miles away from them.

I glance at Raj, his bushy brows forming a V over his eyes as he slows the car to a stop. Lights flash in front of us.

"Looks like there's a roadblock," he says. "I don't think I can go any farther."

The yellow lights flash over an electronic sign that reads ROAD CLOSED AHEAD. Risha wakes up in the back and stretches.

"Are we there?" she asks.

"Looks like it, kiddo." I gather my things and open the car door. "I can walk from here. Thank you so much. This was so helpful."

"What if you can't get through? Want me to wait?" Raj shakes off the cold snaking in from the open door. "You going to be warm enough?"

"I'll be fine." I hold up the red blanket that Chin-Sun gave me, what seems like days ago. He nods.

"You should be able to get to the school if you go through the Presidio. It's just up ahead." He nods toward the intersection where people are waving flashlights to direct oncoming cars. "Oh, don't forget this." He hands me Simi's sweatshirt. I pull it over my head. My heart splinters as her vanilla spice scent envelops me.

"Thanks again." I wave to Risha, whose eyes are already closed. "Tell her goodbye for me," I whisper. Then I shut the door and head toward the crowd.

Alfie

I SHUT THE DOOR ON THE FRESHLY WASHED AND VACUUMED church-mobile—the 2005 minivan that could pack in the entire Thanasis family and a few friends, too—and wished Baba drove something just a tad cooler. At least it was clean inside and out.

"Go ahead, agapi mou, you work hard," he said. "You deserve it."

I know I should've been grateful. And I was. It's just a tiny bit embarrassing pulling up in a tux, rented shoes, and a royal blue tanker that seats eight.

He just had to get the bright blue. Not to mention the matching Greek flag and cross on the back bumper. Like we weren't different enough.

Josuè did what he always does to make it better. He found the old-school aux cord and blasted music from his phone on the way to pick up you and Simi.

"Dude, your dad needs to stop messing with the sound experience." He pressed buttons and switched audio settings, making my seat vibrate with bass.

"You're messing with the sound experience."

"Yeah, but I'm making it better." He lifted his hands and moved around like he was dancing in a TikTok challenge.

When we parked, your dad was sitting on the porch, sipping from a mug and doing the casual dad thing that's actually pretty terrifying.

"Dad alert," Josuè said. "Is he the kind of guy who squeezes your hand while he shakes it, or does he make the *Hurt my daughter and you die* threat more overtly?"

"Somewhere in the middle." I handed him the corsage I'd picked up for him when I got yours. "Here, give this to Simi. I made sure it matches her dress."

"You're such a good boyfriend." He pinched my cheek and I smacked him in the gut. "Getting flowers for the best friend will definitely get you laid. You get a room?"

This time, I punched his arm and climbed out of the van.

"You know, you could be a little more grateful I agreed to go with Simi." He pretended the corsage was a basketball and mimed going for three points. "Not really my type." He popped the *p*.

"Any breathing female is your type. And you're lucky *she* agreed to go with *you*."

"Bruh, that is objectively not true. I respect and admire all the ladies, but only a select few get the Josuè experience."

"Really. So what's Simi getting tonight if not 'the experience'?" I air-quote my last two words.

"Simi gets her best friend's boyfriend's best friend to show her a wholesome fun time at the winter formal."

I stop walking. "Why are you the way that you are?"

"Just sayin'."

"So you'd date her if she wasn't Mia's friend?" I teased.

"Doesn't matter. You don't mess with group dynamics. Watch a few nineties sitcoms and you'll figure that out real fast." Before I could respond, he tugged at his lapels and strolled up the walkway.

"Good evening, boys," your dad said. "You're looking handsome."

Josuè spun in a circle on his heels and shot him finger guns.

"Thank you, Mr. C." I frowned at Josuè, and he winked in return. I made a mental note to murder him as soon as we drove away.

"The girls will be down in a minute. You have enough money for dinner? Gas?" He reached into his back pocket, but I put up my hand.

"Yes, sir. We're okay. Thank you."

"Nothing is too good for my little girl."

"Boom, there it is," Josuè mumbled under his breath.

Maybe murder was too quick.

Inside, your mom zoomed around the living room, testing lighting and adjusting pillows and yelling for you to hurry up.

"But don't come down without announcing yourself first!" she shouted up the stairs. "I want to get pictures!"

"Speaking of, this is an interesting one," I said. "Is that Mia next to . . . a hippopotamus?" Josuè snickered and did a double take. Even now, I still can't get over that picture hanging in the hall.

"That was taken while we were volunteering in Africa." Your mom adjusted an ornament on the tree and checked it through the camera lens. "Mia was only about thirteen, I think."

I know you hated that trip. Not because of where you went or the things you got to see. What was it you called it? Voluntourism?

"I just love that we were able to offer hope to so many children in that village," your mom said. "And we had an experience of a lifetime! Isn't that right, Jeff?"

Just then, you cleared your throat at the top of the stairs. I about lost my mind when I saw you—I'm sure it was all over my face. Your long hair all done up in loose curls. Some strands floating down your back and around your shoulders. Your dress looked like it was sewn just for you. A royal blue, fitted tank and matching long, fitted skirt slit almost the entire way up your left leg. Frosty-white sandals, a shimmery wrap, and your tiara completed your look.

Suddenly I liked the Greek flag a lot more.

You floated down the stairs, and I think I forgot how to breathe. The look on Josuè's face as Simi descended behind you said that '90s sitcoms didn't teach him everything he thought they did.

After the trading of the corsages and the fifty million pictures your mom made us take, we escaped.

The rented hall was covered in balloon arches, glittering lights, and fake snow sprayed in all corners and around the dance floor. Tiny tables with white tablecloths and bowls of flowers in the middle huddled in the far corner. The DJ bounced with the music against the opposite wall.

With you by my side, everything was perfect.

Josuè high-fived guys from the team as we walked toward the tables. Simi stayed next to you, and you both did a great job of looking like you were ignoring him, but I saw you watch him out of the corners of your eyes. With all the analyzing you two were going to do later, I almost felt sorry for him.

Almost.

We'd barely sat at our table when Madi appeared and pulled me away for court pictures. I know you grew up with her. Same schools. Same church. Practically the same life. On paper, you two should've been best friends, but no one could have picked two more opposite people if they tried. She was on every social committee the school had and made sure that if someone knew something about anything, she was their BFF until she knew it too.

"I want them done before everyone gets sweaty from dancing and the girls end up with raccoon eyes." She tilted her head and aimed a tight smile at you. "Don't worry, Mia—I'll have him back in no time. You won't be alone for long."

"Don't worry, Alfie. I'll keep her company." Josuè bobbed his eyebrows and finger-gunned me. "I'll take care of both these ladies."

I shook my head.

By the way, the punch you landed on his arm was impressive. I think it might've actually hurt. And Simi's ice-cold stare could've given real snow some competition.

"I love your crown, Mia." Madi's eyes grazed over your tiara, and they weren't saying anything about loving it.

"Thanks." You smiled, but not at her. And I could tell you were thinking about me and you on the porch the day I gave it to you.

I hope you still smile like that. I can't wait to see it again.

Madi carted me off to the foyer and posed me and the rest of the kids on the court more ways than your mom could've imagined. At least I had Chuck to talk to since he was nominated too.

When we finished, Chuck found his date and joined me at our table, but you were on the dance floor with Simi and Josuè, taking selfies and laughing. You looked so happy.

I think we got to dance twice before Madi was back with another task. I swear, if I'd known I had to be away from you as much as I was, I never would've agreed to be on the court. All I wanted was to stand next to you. Dance with you. Hold you in my arms.

After the big sash-and-crown ceremony, I found you in the hall by the bathroom, remember? Tears in your eyes, your arms crossed and mouth pulled tight. You looked pissed.

Those girls should never have said those things to you. Saying you had no right to wear a tiara because you weren't chosen. Madi probably orchestrated the whole thing. Probably followed you into the bathroom. Waited all night for the chance to make you feel bad.

And her dad was the pastor of your church. You'd think she'd be nicer.

I told you then, and I'll say it now. You *were* chosen, Mia. I chose you, every day.

I tried to make it better, but you did what you always did. Shut it down. Pushed the pain somewhere deep and locked it away beneath your armored smile. You only ever let me in so far.

I've never met anyone else who could draw me in and push me away at the same time like that.

The rest of the night, you were School Mia. Laughing at the right times, dancing to the right songs. That curveball smile misleading everyone but me.

Madi pulled me away one last time, and I saw the thunder pass through your eyes. As she pushed me and Chuck into the foyer for "one more group picture," Josuè pulled you and Simi onto the dance floor.

I'm glad they were there with you, keeping you company.

When the court was finally released from duty, a slow song was playing. I hurried back to the table so I could scoop you up and hold you for at least a little while. But you weren't there.

I found you on the dance floor, arms resting on Josuè's shoulders. His arms around your waist. Simi nowhere to be found.

His fingertips curved perfectly into the small of your back, and your head hit his shoulder at just the right spot.

I felt like I'd just taken a pill that didn't go down right.

And his smile wasn't the typical one he wore when he was with a girl. I would've felt better about that, but he looked peaceful. And that set my teeth on edge.

"Dude, Josuè is just being Josuè." Chuck put his hand on my shoulder, the other one in his pocket. He nodded toward the bathroom hallway on the opposite side of the room, where Simi was watching them too. All her attention was on Josuè. "See that dreamy look on her face? He's definitely got plans for later."

"Dude, that's my girlfriend's best friend. He better not." I shook off whatever eeriness had crept over me as Chuck laughed.

"Did he mention the 'Josuè experience'?" he asked.

"No, he was more focused on nineties sitcoms and group dynamics. I have no idea."

"I don't know," he said. "She looks kind of into him."

Maybe the auditorium's warm, stale air was getting to me, but I hoped Chuck was right. I hoped Josuè would go for Simi. Then maybe tonight would be the last time your face would be that close to his.

Mia

MISSING THE WARM AIR AND SOFT SEAT FROM THE CAR, I bundle the blanket around my shoulders and shiver. My throat is still thick with goodbyes, and my eyes sting from the rapid change of climate. I blink a few times and look around. Raj said to go through the Presidio, but I don't see any signs telling me which way that is. With a determined sigh, I continue on the road around a curve and find a footpath that leads to a wide street.

Yellow safety lights flash atop portable barriers blocking further entrance into the neighborhoods. One or two police cars have their lights on in their rear windows as the officers direct cars safely out. Down the road, more fraternity brothers in their pledge sweatshirts are directing intersection crossings. The heaviness in my chest lightens. When I get to one of the guys directing traffic, I ask a tall Kappa brother if I can borrow a flashlight to check my map. My phone is almost dead, and I need to keep it in case I can use it later. Who knows when I'll get to charge it again?

"I'm kind of depending on it so I don't die." He gestures to the road and the cars taking turns as he waves them through.

"Oh. Just thought you might have an extra." An idea pops into my mind. "Or maybe you can help me figure out which direction I need to go?"

He doesn't respond. Exhaling through my nose, I mouth "Okay" and look around for someone else. So much for help. Maybe he missed the day the frat trained the brothers in emergency traffic policies and has to concentrate. Must be a national fraternity mandate that they direct traffic in a crisis or something. These guys are all over the city.

It's getting colder, and the light from the new moon isn't really helping with all the muck in the air. I feel like I've been walking forever and I'm not any closer. I press my hands over my face, letting my trapped breath warm my nose and cheeks.

Get it together, Mia. You can do this.

Tension rises in my body and grips my heart, making it beat faster. I run my hands down my sides and tap my fingers against my legs. My eyes land on a pile of belongings on the opposite street corner. A couple of guys are hunched over it, pouring something from a brown bottle into their Hydro Flasks. A tiny ray of hope blooms in my chest. I make my way across the street in between cars. "Do you have one I can borrow?"

"One what?" The Gamma with shaggy brown hair sips from his bottle and offers it to me.

"Flashlight."

He flicks his chin to the pile at his feet where a large silver flashlight rests. Back home, I was taught to smile, be polite. Don't make waves. But I'm not there, and there's already enough waves that any I make probably won't get noticed.

"Can I use it?" My tone brims with impatience.

"I don't care." He nudges his buddy. "Not mine." They both laugh.

"Charming." I shine the light on my map, but the glare on the laminate makes it hard to read. With an irritated sigh, I eye the two guys watching me try to figure out which direction I should be heading. "Is it possible you know how to get to USF from here, or have you had too many of whatever's in your water bottles?"

"Shit, bro, that's where you're trying to go?" The other guy stands behind me and grasps my shoulders, turning my whole body east, and points to an endless sea of houses and trees. "Head straight down that way and you'll run right into it."

"Are you sure?" In my excitement, I face him too quickly, then have to step back to avoid his alcohol-laced breath. My cheeks flush, and I try not to breathe in. "The guy who dropped me off said to go through the Presidio."

"Nah, dude." He contorts his face into a frown and shakes his head. "That's way up there." He gestures behind him.

"Your friend probably meant the road," the other Kappa says as he points east. If you go down that way, you'll see a street called Park Presidio. But don't turn on it. Keep going straight like Kev says."

I nod a thank-you as I fold the map as best I can and tuck it into my back pocket. My whole chest expands, and I take in a full breath. Heading east, I wave a grateful goodbye to Kev and his friend and follow the flashlight train block by block until I see Park Presidio. Motivated by this discovery, I quicken my pace and jog across the street.

A car hugs the curb as it makes a right turn, forcing me to jump the last couple of steps to avoid getting hit. I land with a thud against a tall, skinny bearded man wearing a wooden sign. He smells like spray paint.

"Watch it." His voice is higher than suits him, almost off-key. He frowns as he straightens his huge sign, which reads THE END IS HERE. REPENT NOW!

"I'm so sorry." I pick up the water that fell out of my pocket when we collided and take a sip. "That car almost hit me."

"Repent now, child, before it's too late! The end is here!" He barks his words like a junkyard dog, and I know better than to say anything more. I give a small wave and turn to go. "Only whores walk the streets at night. Jesus is coming!"

I know I shouldn't, but I do. Maybe it's the cold or the trauma of the night. Hell, maybe it's the trauma of the last five months. He's clearly not well. But right now, I'm not all that great either, and this person does not get to talk to me that way.

I turn around and smile at him as widely as I can, channeling every bit of my mother I have left inside me.

"I'll pray for you."

"Whore." He spits in my direction.

The blood running through my veins is hot, and my entire body pulses with rage. This is exactly what's wrong with religion. How did a Black Jewish man living in the Middle East thousands of years ago questioning authority and practicing kindness devolve into this?

I know better. This man needs compassion and maybe a bed in a mental hospital. But I'm exhausted and I'm only one person. I can't fix any of it.

"Go fuck yourself." I keep walking, and he turns his attention back to the passing traffic.

Another neighborly exchange on the streets of San Francisco. How proud Jesus would be.

Growing up, I thought Christianity was more of a popularity contest than a religion. Then Alfie took me to his church, and I saw something bigger, something meaningful in a way that is larger than one group of people. I mean, sure, there were the families in the front rows that wore fancy coats and expensive jewelry, but most people were just happy to see you.

Even though I didn't understand much of the language in the

actual service, I didn't need to because the metaphors spoke to me. The presentation of the Bible; the incense carrying prayers to God above; the responses chanting in perfect rhythm with the priest. The humility and respect of those worshipping while children were side by side with their parents, the whole place alive with humanity, but an elevated version.

I still have a tough time believing the stories I grew up on, no matter which church tells them, but I can see why people go back to that service week after week. If only for the company.

I walk several blocks, passing more flashlights directing when to go and when to stop. Finally, as my feet remind me sitting is also fun, houses turn into businesses and then churches and finally USF. I push them faster until I reach the campus proper.

And my eyes don't know where to look first.

Alfie

THE NIGHT I PICKED YOU UP FOR OUR LAKE DATE, MY EYES didn't know where to look. You were so beautiful with your long curls setting off the porcelain of your skin. I could barely keep my hands from shaking as I gripped the steering wheel. Sure, we'd been alone together before, but never *alone* alone, and never with blankets and pillows in the back of my truck, overlooking an evening winter lake.

After the flurry of winter formal, we both decided it would be nice to have some quiet time away from everyone. For whatever reason, I couldn't get the image of Josuè's arms around you out of my head, and all his jokes later that night about getting a room fixated in the back of my mind. If anything, it only made me more nervous.

We drove to the far side of the lake, and I backed in as close as I could to the shore. Once we parked, I spread out the blankets and pillows in the bed of the truck while you carted the snacks from the cab. The inky water echoed the new moon, and the crisp winter air invited the stars to come out and play. I'd never seen so many at once in our little valley. It was like the gods themselves were watching over us.

Starlight shimmered against your skin, and the way your lips curled into a shy smile when I smoothed your hair made the blankets more of an accessory than a necessity, winter frost be damned.

"Um, Alfie?" You stacked the pillows behind you in a pile, pulling out one from the bottom and holding it up. The one I'd hoped you wouldn't see. "I'm not judging or anything, but why do you have a Jonas Brothers pillowcase?" A playful smile dusted your lips.

"That was on the bottom for a reason." I wiped my hands down my face. You raised an eyebrow. "You know that's not mine. Don't tell her I told you, but that's Anna's from her Disney-obsessed days. She loved Joe, and we all suffered for it, believe me."

"If you say so."

"Come on now. You know I'm more of a Nick guy," I teased.

"Oh yeah?"

"Nice strong Greek name. What's not to love?" I winked and settled into the stack of pillows, lifting my arm. You nestled in next to me as I curled it around your torso.

"What should we watch?" You clicked on your Netflix app and scrolled to your watch list.

"Can I watch you?" I kissed your cheek.

"Don't be weird." You pushed me away and laughed.

"I'm not weird, just not normal."

"Mm-hmm, not normal is right." You kissed my cheek. "But I like it."

I leaned in to kiss you, but before I could, that stupid duck started quacking and wouldn't stop.

"Ohmigod!" You shot up and crawled to the edge of the bed. "Hi there, little guy!"

I scooted next to you and peered over the edge. A mallard stood tall, flapping his wings and quacking.

"Do you think we're in his spot?" you asked.

"He has this entire lake." I gestured in front of us.

"Well, he's mad about something."

I shrugged and leaned back into our pile of pillows. You followed.

And so did the duck.

He flapped his way to the back of the truck bed and stared us down, quacking under his breath.

"Um, should we be worried?" I brought my knees up and mom-armed you. "Are we about to be eaten by an angry duck?"

"You were the one who said you liked not-normal. And this qualifies." You made smooching sounds. "What's wrong, little duck? You hungry?"

"Don't encourage him!"

"I'm going to give him some of our snacks. Are you seriously scared of a duck?" You dug around in the bag and found popcorn. Then you scooped a handful and tossed a piece to the duck. He lunged for it and gobbled it, beak high in the air.

"I'm not scared of a duck. I'm scared of rabid ducks."

"Can ducks be rabid? I don't think ducks can be rabid." You tossed another piece, which was gone just as quickly. "Aw, he likes it."

"As long as he's not eating flesh, I'm good."

"I think he needs a name. What should we name him?"

"Hmm." I made a big deal stroking my chin in thought. "What about Cannibal Duck?"

"He's not a rabid, flesh-eating duck, ohmigod." You threw a piece of popcorn at me, which I grabbed faster than I thought I could and tossed it to the duck.

"Hey now, don't bait him!"

Your grin blossomed into a full smile, and your rich, throaty laughter followed. You laughed until you cried. It was like watching the dawn break. When you could breathe again, you tossed the rest of the popcorn to the edge of the bed and our new friend went to town.

"How about Ruchard?" I asked.

"Ruchard? You mean Richard?"

"No, Ruchard." I gave you a sly grin and your eyes went wide.

"Because Dick is short for Richard . . ."

"And Duck is short for Ruchard."

You clamped your hands over your face, then buried them in your lap and squealed.

"It's perfect!" You raised your arms in victory and shouted to the sky. At the sound, our new friend Ruchard flapped his way off the truck bed and into the water, quacking the entire way to the other side of the shore. "Oops, I think I scared him."

"Nah. He just ate all the popcorn." I pulled you into me and wrapped you with a blanket. You snuggled into my side and pulled the blanket over me. We must've looked like one big burrito. "Look at you, making friends wherever you go."

"Yeah right. Hungry ducks are easy to please. It's the humans I have a hard time with."

"I don't believe it. Besides, you have me hooked." I kissed the top of your head and you snuggled deeper into my chest. Ruchard and his friends quacked in the distance.

"I feel like my whole life is a lie." You jerked your head up, leaving a cold spot where your cheek had been, and looked at me. "Everything but you, that is. You're the only one who lets me feel like I can be myself."

"What about your family?" For me, family was always my safe space. Sure, they could be a little much when everyone was together, but never once did I consider they wouldn't have my back. I'd never thought about it any other way until I met you.

"Please." You tucked your head back into its spot, and the warmth flooded back. "They're the worst offenders. You've seen how they are."

The truth was, I had seen, and you were different around them. But nothing I could say would make you feel any better, so I chose to hold you, build an imaginary fortress around us both. One that would keep us together in that moment forever.

"Can I tell you something?" you asked.

"Of course." Your body pressed into mine. I squeezed as you exhaled, letting you know I was right there.

"I think . . . I don't think I believe in God."

"Oh." I stared at the trees around the lake, shadows blacking out the stars' edges, creating patches of abyss in the sky. You sat up.

"It's just that everything my mom and dad do and say is exactly the opposite of what the Bible tells them, you know?" You shook your head and looked at the sky, your own shadows haunting you. It was difficult to see the details of your face now that the sun had disappeared, but I could feel your frustration radiating off your skin. "How can something so backward and contrived be real?"

"The actions of the people don't make God fiction, though. Right? I mean, people aren't perfect. They sin, despite God's grace." I sat up next to you and reached for your hands. I wanted you to know I was there with you, not against you. I just wanted to understand.

"That's my point. They say God is love and He forgives us and we're made in His image and all that. We go to church and pray and give money and bask in His grace. But before we're even out of the driveway, it's all *Did you see what so-and-so was wearing and can you believe she had the nerve to sit in the front after how much wine she drank at Bunco?* It's *Pay your tithing so your pastor can drive a nicer car.* It's *Love your neighbor unless they look different than you.* It's *Protect a fetus until it needs something from you besides thoughts and prayers."*

Waves of thunder radiated from you as you spoke. Your voice shook with it too. I imagined myself absorbing all that energy and releasing calm and peace back to you.

"How can any of it be real if it's all so fake?" You pulled your hands from mine and crossed your arms over your middle. I leaned over and brushed your lips with mine.

The truth is, I didn't know how to answer. Until I'd met you, I never thought to ask any of those questions. I never considered what I'd been taught wasn't true. I didn't know what to say, so I did the only thing I could think of.

"I'm real." Another kiss. "You're real." This time you kissed back. "Tonight is real."

Then your hands were around my neck, and your fingers wound their way through my hair. Our mouths pressed together and my tongue found yours. We fell against the pillows, locked together. We kissed until we were all that existed. And in that moment, it was enough.

Neither of us was ready to go all the way. Not yet. Despite what Josuè said, we were going at our own pace. Honestly, I'm glad we waited. I don't think I could've handled the guilt of what came next. Especially since neither of us had done anything like that before.

Nestled in the pillows and blankets, we watched the stars. Ruchard and his friends were tucked in for the night, the lapping of the water and your soft breaths the only sounds as we counted airplanes and settled into the quiet.

"I can't wait until I can be up there," you said, pointing to airplane number three.

"Am I that bad of a kisser?"

"I meant for school." You smacked my chest with your fingers, too relaxed to move your whole hand. "Sarah Lawrence."

"Oh."

My stomach sank into the bed of the truck. I'd Googled the school as soon as I got home from the parade. You wanted to spend the next four years—maybe longer—in New York. I'd been hustling to get my game good enough for University of San Francisco, and now that Coach was saying they were coming to scout this year—it could really happen—I met you. And you wanted to move across the country.

When you told me about your plans, we'd just started dating and the end of high school still seemed far away. But now that our last semester was right in front of us, the idea of moving to opposite coasts was terrifying.

"So many amazing women went there and went on to do great things," you said. Then you whispered, "I want to be like that too."

I've always loved your energy. The way you aim all your force at something, even if you're not sure where you'll land. You pick a direction and know that's where you need to go. I wish I had half your bravery. Maybe if I did, things would've been different.

"You will do great things. I know it." My lips found yours, and I lost myself all over again. You pulled away so fast, I thought something was wrong. "What? Did I hurt you?"

"What? No. It's just, I didn't ask you where you wanted to go."

"That's why you stopped kissing me? For a status report on college applications?"

"It sounds dumb when you put it like that, but yeah, I guess. I realized I have no idea what your plans are."

In that moment, I was so glad the new moon gave off almost no light. How could I tell you we were most likely going to be on opposite ends of the country? Would you still let yourself fall in love with me if you knew we were going to be ripped apart so soon?

I know, I should've given you all of the information, then let you choose. I took that away from you, and I'll regret it until I die. Maybe even after. But I couldn't take the chance.

I loved you so much already, and I was selfish.

"I'm kind of waiting to see if I get any baseball scholarships."

It wasn't a lie, but it wasn't anywhere close to the truth. I knew that if I went to college at all, it would be close to home. Close to family. It's the only way they would've let me go since Baba wasn't happy about me leaving the restaurant. I knew it was his dream for me to take over. If I wanted to chase my own dreams, I'd have to do it in a way that still kept them happy. And the only way to keep my parents happy was to keep the family close.

I know it was hard for you to understand why they were like that, but it's all I'd ever known. The only kind of love I'd known. But now there was this new love. Ours. And I couldn't risk it.

You didn't question my answer. Didn't doubt the validity of my choice. That made kissing you even more intense. Like I could say sorry every time our lips touched. Every caress a confession.

On the way home, you smiled with swollen lips and laughed with husky breaths. I wondered how a person like you with so much love inside them could feel the way you did. Could lock yourself away when it was so obvious how much you wanted to be free. The way you were when you were with me.

I guess I'd locked away a part of myself that night too.

Watching you transform from my Mia to the one your parents knew as we parked in front of your house shattered my heart into a thousand pieces. Everything back then was so heightened. Every first felt like it could be the last, and we were desperate to hold on to it all. If I could see the stars right now, I'd wish on every one that I had been braver.

Mia

MY HEART SHATTERS INTO A THOUSAND TINY PIECES. THE dome of the large church next to the campus has melted into the sidewalk, glass exploding into constellations in the street. Its two towers stand tall, although with another aftershock, they could collapse at any time.

The other side of the street isn't much better. The law school's columns are piled up like Lincoln Logs dumped in the street. The overhang of the building droops onto the stairs leading inside, its once-hungry jaws clamped forever.

My windpipes shrink, and I gasp for air. If the newer buildings look like this, what about the older ones? Panic climbs up my spine and lands in my throat.

On the other side of the church, half of a large grassy area is roped off. The other part is littered with students. There are two kinds of people. Some sit on the lawn, wrapped in blankets, crying. Others clump together behind them on the bits of walkways and ramps that aren't broken, joking and pushing each other playfully.

I look everywhere at once, taking in every brown-haired boy and beanie I see. My shoulders get tighter each time there's a wrong nose or a boy not quite tall enough. The tension bleeds from my neck into my shoulders. Did I really expect it'd be that easy? Get to campus and he'd be up front with a big welcome sign?

I want to throw up.

"Hey, State!" some random, half-drunk guy yells. "You're on the wrong campus." He and his friends crack up as they high-five each other.

I run my hand over the letters across my middle. The reminder of Simi and everything I left with her tugs at my chest. I wish I'd said something different, been honest about how all this feels. But I can't afford to be soft now, especially around rowdy guys on a strange campus.

Helping Risha find her mom and telling that end-of-times guy what to do with his judgy ass must've made my spine straighter, my mouth more brazen. Small-town Mia never would've said or done those things. And she would've ignored this guy too. But I'm San Francisco Mia now. I've been baptized not in water this time but by the earth.

"I left my USF one at your mom's."

The guys roar with laughter. One of them even pours a little of whatever he's drinking onto the ground and crosses his fist over his heart. I roll my eyes and turn my back to them, allowing myself half a grin. Adrenaline pulses in my veins, and I'm not as cold as I was, but cross my arms over the SFSU logo on my sweatshirt in case anyone else decides to be a smart-ass.

Walking through the groups of people on the lawn, I resume my search. My eyes invade every possible face as I look closer for signs of Alfie and the girl he was with. At the end of the grass, a girl with the same blond hair works herself through a crowd. My heart beats two thumps at once. I chase her to what looks like a soccer field. There's more order here. RAs and emergency services have set up a check-in spot under a makeshift tent. Hundreds more people huddle in groups all over the field.

Hundreds more possibilities.

People check their phones and huff when they don't have service. Some stare habitually at their screens anyway.

The girl stops at the tent, and I'm right behind her, pounding heart and all. While she's speaking, she turns in my direction and I get a better look at her face.

Not her.

My stomach drops, but I'm also a little bit relieved. I'm not exactly sure how to approach a complete stranger and say, *Hey, do you know where your boyfriend is because I came to tell him I love him thanks k bye.*

I approach one of the RAs.

"Can you tell me if a student has checked in here?" I ask.

"Name?" She tosses her long brown bangs out of her eyes and opens a roster.

"Alfie Thanasis?" I hate myself for saying his name like a question. "Thanasis."

"Don't see that name on here. You can ask around, though." She gestures behind her to the people on the grass. His name is a stone sinking into a lake. I close my eyes and see our lake with the different sky. One that has stars that shine for years even after they're gone.

I go farther into the field.

"Do you know Alfie Thanasis?"

"Have you seen a tall guy with longer brown hair? He's on the baseball team."

"Anyone here know an Alfie?"

I work in a big spiral around the field. Starting wide, I slowly wind my way to the middle. Not one person knows or has seen him. If I knew more about the girl, I'd probably do it again and ask about her. But my body is heavy with the empty answers I've collected.

"Don't know him."

"Haven't seen him."

"Sorry."

I'm sorry too.

I cross my feet and lower myself onto the grass. Both my arches and my back immediately thank me by cramping. I unfold my legs and stretch over them.

After checking behind me for room, I lie back and stare at the sky. Instead of stars, though, a gray cloud hovers just above—part building, part ash. If Alfie were here, he'd call it manifested memories lost forever in a haze of grief, or something poetic like that. It feels like, if I reach out my hand, I could touch it.

I don't. I can't even bring myself to try. Eventually, it will settle. We will breathe in parts that will live in our lungs. The rest will sink to the ground and stick to the bottom of our shoes. We'll build something else in the empty spaces, and people will create new dreams. Make new memories. Build new things in the empty spaces inside them.

All of it seems so far away.

The silky black cloth threatens to choke me again. I made a mistake coming here. There are too many people. Too much time has gone by. He could be anywhere. I'm too late. Again. I tilt back my head and inhale as deep as I can. Over and over until the air reaches all the way to the bottom of my lungs.

A tremor roars through the ground, and that sickening, dizzy feeling returns. My head feels like when you swim too long and get water in your ears. I drop my hands to my sides and grasp the very thing threatening my life. Screams sound off around the field. One rises from somewhere deep inside me, too, but I swallow it down. As fast as it started, the shaking stops. I sit up. Someone on a megaphone tells everyone to remain where they are because this is the safest place, but I stop listening.

Some girl is standing right in front of me, pointing at my sweatshirt.

"Are you the person looking for Alfie?" she asks. My heart in my throat, I bolt to my feet, much to their chagrin.

"Yes! Do you know him? Do you know where he is?"

"Not exactly, but he lives in Hayes-Healy. He might be back there." She points toward the back of the campus. I could kiss her.

I immediately start walking, then turn back. "Sorry, where is Hayes-Healy?"

She relaxes her expression into a smile.

"I can get you on your way, but it might not be possible to get over there. Most everything is blocked off. I'm Jenna, by the way. She/her."

"Oh, I'm Mia. Same." I offer a patient smile, but the blood pumping through my veins at rapid speed is screaming for me to run.

"I heard they all evacuated to the baseball field over there. You might be able to get there."

"Baseball field?" I'm not usually a big believer in fate, but my ears perk up anyway. I think about the man who gave me directions way back when, who told me things will unfold the way they're supposed to. At the time, I went along with it to be polite, but maybe he's right. Maybe this is a sign. Maybe I'll finally see Alfie on the baseball field, where he belongs.

I shiver.

Jenna takes me to a road she says will lead me to the field if I follow it far enough, and I have to force my legs to not sprint ahead of her. After her directions, I actually hug her. I practically skip until I come full stop in front of caution tape and markers with DO NOT ENTER printed between bright orange cones. The parking lot is completely blocked off. There's a huge patch of darkness a few hundred feet ahead on the right—that has to be the field.

My whole body sings.

I follow along the tape and duck under where it's tied to a tree, my jaw set and eyes alert for any holes in the path. I am getting to that field. I don't want to waste the battery, but I turn on my phone to light the way. The last thing I need is a broken ankle or twisted knee.

I work my way over cracked asphalt and broken sidewalks to the entrance of the field. Another tent is set up here, this one with camping lanterns hanging from the metal frame. On the backside of the tent, a triage table is set up where med students clean up cuts and scrapes and assess the more seriously injured. Students with clipboards hand out cups of water from one of those giant yellow drums they use to hydrate teams during a game. The idea that Alfie's name could be on one of those clipboards drives me toward them.

One of the girls filling the cups sees me. She flicks her eyes over my hoodie, then twists her mouth into something like resolve. She leans over the table and hands me a cup, which I gladly take. In one gulp, I swallow the water. It stings the back of my parched throat. Before I can say thank you, she turns back to the Igloo and resumes her cup-filling duties.

I guess competitiveness never really dies, even when people are being nice to each other. Maybe that's why we always go back to our corners when the tragedy ends.

The light from the lanterns makes it hard to see into the deep parts of the darkened field. I wind through the groups huddled together and try to make out Alfie-shaped postures or blond-girl curls.

A lyrical but tinny laugh wafts into the crowd from the corner of the field, its sound setting my spine rod-straight. That's the laugh I heard earlier at the coffee shop. When Alfie whispered something in the blond girl's ear that made her head tilt.

I follow it like a bat, tracing its echoes in a curvy path through uneven mounds of blankets and people scattered on the ground. This time, the aftershocks work their way into my heart and lungs and vibrate all the way down my legs and out my toes.

And then she's there, right in front of me. With an Alfie-shaped shadow on her right.

Alfie

I FEEL LIKE YOU'RE RIGHT IN FRONT OF ME. IF I COULD ONLY reach you. I don't remember it ever being this foggy in the city before. At least it isn't raining.

It rained the first day of baseball practice, but Coach made us play anyway, shouting at us every time someone stopped to wipe their face or wring out their shirt.

Winners train. Losers complain.

I don't know how many times he said it, but I'm pretty sure I'll be hearing that in my head for the rest of my life.

I gained a couple miles per hour on my pitch, which was pretty amazing considering the ball and I were soaking wet. That fall workshop we did really paid off. I only hoped my arm would hold up when the scout from San Francisco showed. Overall, it was a pretty good practice.

But the best part was you waiting for me when it was over.

You were so cute with your yellow polka-dot umbrella and matching boots. You must've gone home and come back because your hair was tucked into a bun on the top of your head and you were wearing leggings instead of the jeans you had on at school.

When Coach finally excused us to the locker room, I detoured toward the fence where you were waiting to say hello.

"Isn't there a song about yellow polka dots?" I took the umbrella from you and held it over both of us, kissing your cheek.

"I think that's a bikini, not an umbrella."

"Fine with me."

Did I ever tell you how my heart skipped a beat every time your cheeks turned pink like they did that day? I think it's my favorite color in the entire world.

"I doubt it'd go as well with the boots." You circled your foot in the air. Water dripped from my hair onto my face, and you wiped it away with your hand. I took a step closer to you so our lips almost touched.

"Want to bet?"

"Thanasis!" Coach bellowed from across the field. "Get in that locker room and ice that shoulder. You have scouts coming!"

A lump formed in my throat and I closed my eyes, too afraid to find yours. We were so good, so happy finding who we were together. The last thing I wanted to do was think about the future, especially one where you might not be in it. But then your lips grazed mine and you smiled into my mouth, sending me straight into the sun breaking through the clouds.

"Busted," you said. I opened my eyes to find a playful smile in your own. But like the storm swirling in the sky above, something else hid behind your amusement.

"Guess I better go." I offered the umbrella back to you. "Thanks for coming to visit."

"Anything for the starting pitcher. I'll talk to you later?" You took a step back, and the cold inched its way in between us.

"I'll text you when I'm off." I wiped at the water sliding into my eyes and watched you walk toward the parking lot. At the curb, you turned back, your umbrella resting on your shoulder so it looked like you were in the center of the sun.

"Alfie?"

"Yeah?"

"Do you think you might tell me which schools the scouts are coming from someday?"

Thunder rolled across the sky. The lump in my throat was back.

"Of course." I gave you my best smile and waved. "Text you tonight."

Before I could see how you wore my words on your face, I turned and jogged to the locker room, looking forward to the numbing feeling of the ice bath.

Alfie

Alfie: I'm finally home. I need another ice bath. Baba made me clean the condiment station. Side note, people are gross.

Mia: Ew, I'm afraid to ask.

Alfie: Let's just say I won't be eating tzatziki anytime soon.

Mia: Gross.

Alfie: So can we talk about this boot-matching bikini some more?

Mia: Ha.

Actually, I was wondering if we could talk about something else. Hello?

Alfie: Sorry, Anna needed help on her math. We can talk about anything you want.

Mia: What if we end up far away from each other next year?

Alfie: That's a long way off. We don't need to worry about it now.

Mia: It's not that far. Only 8 months. I don't want to think about it, but I can't help it.

Do you think you'll stay in California?

Alfie: Depends on the offers I get. But if it helps, thinking about being far away from you is too much. I can't even let my mind go there.

Mia: Do you think you'll get offers from East Coast schools?

Alfie: I guess it's possible. I don't think Coach talked to any schools out that way.

Mia: Could he?

Alfie: I mean, yeah, I guess he could.

Mia: Then we wouldn't have to worry about being apart next year. Do you think your parents would go for it?

Alfie: If the offer was good enough, they couldn't say no, right?

Mia: It makes sense.

Alfie: This isn't fair, you know.

Mia: What's not fair?

Alfie: That you're hot AND a genius.

Mia: Omg stop

Alfie: I'm serious. Genius. I'm loving this idea *googles New York colleges*

Hey Mia?

Mia: Yessss

Alfie: I've never felt like this before.

Mia: Me either.

Alfie: I think I'd follow you to the end of the world ♥

Mia: What are you saying?

Alfie: I'm saying . . . it's my birthday in a month and I better get a really big present.

Mia: Wow.

Alfie: Wow indeed.

Mia

I don't leave things to chance. I plan everything. But now everything is out of my control.

The blond girl's leaning against the fence, one foot crossed over the other, mug in hand. She's wearing the same clothes as before except she's added a long, dark trench coat over the ensemble. She sets her hand on the arm of the person next to her, and my heart flips upside down.

Now or never, Mia.

I take a deep breath and force my feet to cover the area between us. I feel her eyes on me, but mine are focused on the guy she's standing next to. When he notices her looking at me, he turns and my heart plummets to my feet.

A fully bearded man leers at me from behind thick-rimmed glasses. He's wearing a hoodie similar to the one Alfie had on, a tie-dyed tee poking out the well-worn neck.

My breath hitches and a weird sound escapes my throat.

Not Alfie.

I force my eyes back to the girl, now my only lead.

"Hey, uh, hi." Nice, Mia. Super smooth. She waits with a pleasant *What do you want?* pasted on her lips. "This is weird, but I'm an old friend of your boyfriend, and I'm wondering if you know where he is."

She and the bearded guy exchange confused looks.

"My boyfriend?"

"Alfie. I saw you with him earlier today."

She thinks for a few seconds and nods.

"Ohhh, no. Alfie's just a friend." She glances at the bearded guy. "Not really my type."

I crinkle my forehead and she leans in for a dramatic whisper.

"I usually prefer the guys I date to be girls." She and her friend share a laugh.

My mind reels with this new information, but I don't have time to consider it too long. She's still talking and I don't want to miss where Alfie is.

"I met Alfie in Psych 1. Professor sat us alphabetically and we have the same initials. I'm Alice Taylor, she/her. He's Alfie Thanasis, he/him. Whenever he sees me, he loves to high-five and say 'That's where it's AT.' He's a nerd, but it's cute."

My heart fills with images of him high-fiving random people and making everyone smile. Yes, he's both of those things. He's everything. He's my everything.

Before I can stop them, tears well in my eyes and throat. They fall down my face toward the green-black grass below. I bow my head as my shoulders start to shake and my stomach muscles clutch in the sobs. I let them come. Because that's my Alfie. The one who makes silly jokes and has never met a stranger.

I can't find him. And I need him. I really need him.

"Oh honey, you okay?" The girl's hand rests on my arm and, despite hating Alice Taylor down to her last molecule until a few minutes ago, and ignoring that I'm still a little jealous of her because she's in his life and I'm not, I lean into her touch. She takes me into her arms and rubs my back with her free hand until the sobs become short breaths and finally regular ones.

"I'm sorry," I say when I catch up to my breaths. "I'm not usually a crier."

"No worries. Tonight has been a night." She sits on a blanket beneath her that I hadn't noticed before, and I realize the guy with the beard isn't there anymore. She must see the question forming because she waves a dismissive hand. "He left mid-cry. No worries, though. Just shootin' the shit until we figure out what we're going to do."

I sit next to her after she pats the empty spot to her right.

"So how do you know Alfie?" She sips the last contents of her mug and sets it down. I remember my own water and practically empty the small bottle in one gulp.

"We were . . . We knew each other in high school." I pick at the dewy grass. How do I say we were going to start a new life in New York together, but then all our plans imploded overnight? "We dated for most of senior year."

"Are you Mia?" She claps her hands together and rolls backward. "Holy shit! You're *Mia*! He never shuts up about you."

Strange threads of pride and embarrassment string themselves through my insides and wind around both my heart and brain. He still thinks about me. He still talks about me. That means he still loves me.

A small breeze shimmers through my hair and over my face. The icy air contrasts with the heat in my cheeks. I breathe in its crisp bite, hoping it'll slow the thread's work inside me too.

"Do you know where he is?" My voice is small, like it's too scared for her answer. She tilts her head and looks up to her right. Her mouth twists in the way people shape them when they try to remember something.

"I think he said he was working tonight." She sucks in a breath through gritted teeth. "He works at a vintage vinyl shop in the Haight. Do you know how to get there?"

I shake my head and she tells me the way.

"Might not be easy to get to," she says.

After all I've done to get this far, now that I know where he is, I have to try. I have to give it everything I have, because that's what he deserves.

Alice asks if I want to get another water for the trip, and I say yes. As we make our way through the crowds of people, I pause a moment and look around. So many huddled together. Helping, comforting, listening. This place is a real community. A sick feeling turns over my insides.

"Alice, can I ask you something?"

"Of course." Her eyebrows lift and her whole face brightens. I see why Alfie likes her.

"Is Alfie—is he happy here?" Suddenly I wish I could suck the question back into my mouth and swallow it. Because if the answer is yes, that means he's okay. He's moved on. But if it's no, then we've wasted so much time. Dread blankets my chest and limbs.

Alice contemplates the question, and the longer she thinks, the more I want to sink into the ground. She tilts her head and pinches her lips together, looking me right in the eyes. I stop breathing.

"Sure, he's happy," she says. My stomach falls straight to my feet. I suck in air and nod. "But, like, happiness is a relative thing, you know?" Her hands weigh something invisible between us. I'm pretty sure it's my heart.

"Relative?" I barely squeak out the word.

"Yeah." She hands me two waters. "Alfie's the kind of guy that'll make the best of anything."

I'm nodding and crying again because she's right. He is. And I know what she's going to say next.

"But he'll be his happiest self when he sees you." She lowers her head and winks. I throw my arms around her, knocking her back with my forgotten water bottles I'm holding. She grunts.

"I'm so sorry!" I step back and shove the bottles into my pockets. She laughs, breathy and free.

Someday I want to laugh just like that.

"Thank you, Alice. For everything." I face my new direction, and she does too. We stand a minute, looking into the hidden horizon beyond the shadows of the field. I have to have faith that I'm going to find it. Find him. I take a deep breath and turn to her. Taking her hand, I offer my best smile, even if it's a bit tattered and worn at this point. She returns her own bright one. "I'm glad you two met. Maybe when this is all done, we can all get coffee together."

She nods and offers a last hug.

"Good luck, Mia. I hope you find him."

"Well, I've come this far. What's a few thousand more steps?"

Alfie

WE'D COME SO FAR SINCE THAT DAY IN THE CAFETERIA. IT'S hard to believe the first time you'd ever been to my house was my birthday. You became a part of the family; it's difficult to remember a time you weren't rolling cheese puffs with my mom or at the kitchen table helping my sister with her math.

I met you at the door before you could knock. Remember I told you to text me when you parked? I had to warn you.

"Okay, you're about to meet three hundred closest members of my family," I said.

"Three hundred?" Your voice was incredulous.

"And they're all going to want to hug you." I nodded as seriously as I could.

"I highly doubt three hundred people are on the other side of that door who want to hug me."

"And possibly spit on you." I rolled my lips between my teeth.

"Why are you the way you are?"

"Okay, maybe not three hundred, but after all the hugging and spitting, it's going to feel like it." I kissed your cheek. "Hi."

"They're really going to spit on me?" A mild panic floated behind your eyes.

"It means they like you." I grabbed your hand and led you inside before you could flee in fear. "Just keep your head down and follow me. I'll try to sneak us somewhere with less spitting."

We glided straight through the living and dining rooms, eyes on the floor and not the cousins and theas and theos huddled in groups along the way. But then Baba yelled from the family room down the open hall.

"Ela edo, Mia!" He threw his arms into the air, calling you to him.

Busted.

I pulled you into the couch-lined family room that stood opposite the kitchen, separated only by a long counter. He turned to the crowd grazing around the kitchen table in the corner and then to the papous on the couches.

"Everybody, this is Mia, Alfie's . . . friend." He drew out the last word so that everyone, including the people who didn't speak English very well, knew exactly what he meant. "Mia, this is everybody!"

A wave of people washed over you, and for a moment, I lost sight of where you landed in the throng of hugs and bodily inspections.

"Let me see your face, agapi." Thea Irene held your chin and turned your face side to side. "Pthu pthu." Her spitting sounds make your wide eyes shoot to me. I could only shrug.

My koumbaro, Nick, shot me a wink and a thumbs-up from the recliner.

"Your hair is so long," said Yia-Yia. "Do you have to tie it up all the time or do you let it get in the way?"

"Okay, everyone," I said. "Let's not scare her away before the baklava comes out." I slipped into the crowd and wrapped your hand in mine, leading you to safety.

"Alfie, what you mean put out sweets. We haven't put out the spanakopita yet—what's wrong with you?" Mama gave me the stink eye from the kitchen. I led you to the back door and hopefully outside.

"It's a saying, Mama." I winked at you. "We'll be in the back."

"Check on your sister." She waved us away and dove back into her cooking.

"Yes, Mama."

Outside, you collapsed into a lounge chair, obviously exhausted.

"You weren't kidding. That was only three hundred?" You brushed your fingers through your hair to settle its waves and exhaled. I shrugged and cozied in next to you.

Eleni, my youngest sister, and some of the littler cousins were running around on the grass. She'd been tasked with keeping the kids busy while their parents took turns shooting Metaxa and visiting with the over-thirty crowd. The rest of the cousins our age were upstairs in my brother's room, taking turns playing some video game I didn't care about. But I was sure we'd make our way up there eventually. At that moment, I was happy to have you to myself.

"Hey, Mia." Anna came out of the house and sat on the lounge next to ours. "I heard Baba yell your name."

So much for having you all to myself. A pipe dream in a house like that.

"The space station heard him yell her name." I looked at you. "Are you freaked out?"

"No, it was kind of cute. It's obvious they love you."

"Whether we like it or not. Right, Alfie?" Anna scooped up a ball that the kids let roll off the grass and kicked it back to them. "Can you believe she bought paper napkins? I begged her to use cloth, but no."

"Anna is the resident earth police," I said. "If she gets her way, both the house and the restaurant will be fully under sustainability practices by the end of the year."

"Not soon enough." Anna tossed the ball the kids kicked back. "I'd like to make it out of the ninth grade without a massive tsunami taking us out."

I rolled my eyes.

"I'm going to go help Eleni. She looks a little overwhelmed." Anna jumped up and jogged across the yard.

You shivered and crossed your arms over your torso, pulling your sleeves over your hands. Reluctantly I stood and offered you my hand. You took it, but a question lingered in your eyes.

"You're freezing. Let's go inside."

When we sat at the counter, Mama immediately assigned you a job. Inside, I was already imagining the *Thanks, But No Thanks* text you were surely sending me that night. Because who invites someone over and puts them to work?

But you not only took her challenge, you met her with one of your own.

"Mrs. Thanasis, how do you make these? They're wonderful!"

You couldn't know this, but asking my mom to show you how to make something was her holy grail. She loved you from that moment on. Seeing you work next to her in the months to come filled me with so much joy, I can't tell you. Watching your forehead crinkle in concentration as she showed you how to clarify butter or your hands practice the motions of kneading bread was like fireworks and a warm bath at the same time.

But that day, on the day we celebrated my eighteenth birthday, Mama commissioned you to put out olives-and-feta platters on the different tables. A small but important welcome to the family.

When it came time to open presents, most of the papous and theos passed me small envelopes.

"Put that toward your college."

"You should start a retirement account. It's never too early."

"Buy your girl something nice. She's too pretty for you."

But Mama shoved three boxes in front of me.

"From Baba and me."

"You bought me presents, Baba?" I teased. He grunted and waved me off, going back to his Greek television and lively discussion with the rest of the men.

I glanced at you, then the packages. They were wrapped in gold paper with big green bows. Mama was never one for fancy ribbons, so my hunch was someone else wrapped them.

A strange sensation flooded my insides. Is it possible to feel dread and excitement at the same time?

"Open them, agapi mou." Mama shooed me toward the packages.

"Is it time?" Anna appeared at my side and shook my arm. She looked at me with her most sarcastic expression. "I wonder what it is."

The dread in my stomach separated from the excitement like olive oil and water in a dressing bottle. I was almost tempted to bounce up and down to mix them again. At least, then, I wouldn't have to face you feeling like this after I opened them.

You and I had just decided I would look at East Coast schools, but the colors of these boxes implied something different. I hadn't said anything to my parents about our plans yet, because I wanted to hear what Coach came up with before I started any fights at home.

And fights there would be.

In my family, we were expected to stay close, physically and emotionally. It's just the way things were. One of my uncles married someone and moved to Colorado a few years back, and instead of waving goodbye as they drove away with the rest of the family, my grandparents cried and yelled "We failed" over and over until my uncle and new aunt were out of sight.

So yeah, telling Mama and Baba I wanted to spend the next four years three thousand miles away was mildly terrifying. But if I could get a sweet enough offer, it'd be impossible for them to say no.

But the gold-and-green boxes on the table in front of me said none of that. They said, *Family tradition is more important than your dreams, Alfie.* They said, *We're letting you go to college and giving you a pass on the family business, but that's progressive enough for a generation.* They said, *You're going to University of San Francisco or nowhere at all.*

"Do you know what they are, Anna?" You motioned her to sit next to you. "Tell me!"

Glancing at you, I took off the bow of the biggest one and ripped through the paper.

"We don't save the paper like you." I shrugged, thinking back to how you unwrapped your sash and crown.

"No judgments." You waved it off with a smile, looking way more comfortable than you did when you first walked through the door.

I hoped you would still feel that way when I opened the box.

Inside lay a neatly folded dark green hoodie with the USF logo across the chest. Anna threw her arms around my neck from behind.

"Don't you love it?" she asked.

I took in your expression from the corner of my eye. Your face was blank, like the way it gets when your squad sits with you at lunch. Shallow thoughts on the surface, but inside, a dark whirl-pool of emotions. I closed my eyes and forced a smile.

"Yes, I love it. Thank you, Mama."

"It's really because of me," Anna whispered into my ear. "I made her drive over there one day and visit the bookstore. She needed to see it wasn't that far away."

Yeah, it was a lot closer than New York, that's for sure.

"Open the rest!" Anna clapped.

I'm sure I don't need to remind you what was in the other packages. A matching baseball cap and lanyard. The basic things any college-bound kid wears the rest of senior year to claim their new life.

After the cake and other sweets made their way around the sleepy partygoers, and families began their goodbyes, you slipped away. I found you sitting on the edge of my bed, the only light in the room streaming from the hallway. Your feet were flat against the floor and your fists planted into the mattress at your sides. You were staring at my desk.

"Hey." I pulled the desk chair out and straddled it so I faced you.

"What about going back east, with me? Was that a lie?" You swallowed and relaxed your facial muscles so your eyebrows spread apart.

"No, of course not."

"Doesn't look that way to me." Your eyes flashed to mine, and heat flared against my neck and ears. You stood and looked out the window onto the street, now emptied of cars. "I mean, obviously you can go wherever you want. We weren't even dating when we applied to schools, so it's not like this is out of the blue or anything. I just thought we had a plan."

I tucked the chair under my desk and wrapped my arms around you. Your body pressed against my chest. Tears stung my eyes as I buried my face into your neck.

"We do. I want to be close to you—that much is true. Mama wants me close by is all. She's voting for San Francisco so I get baseball exposure and they get me on weekends. I haven't said anything to them because I'm waiting to see what Coach and I can figure out. I'll have a better shot at convincing them if I have a good offer in my hands. Please don't worry. I just know we'll be together in New York."

You tucked your arms and head against my chest. Then you pulled away and sat on my bed, this time against the headboard with my pillow in your lap.

"Your family is a lot."

"I tried to tell you." I sat at the foot of the bed, one leg crossed in front of me, the other on the floor.

"I don't mean it in a bad way. I like the energy." You stared out the window. "My family is so . . . sterile next to yours. Bland, even."

"They're not that bad."

"I didn't know families could love each other the way yours does." Your gaze dropped to your lap. "My cousins would never play together like that. We never even see each other."

I said nothing. I have always loved the way my family comes together. The noise and chaos create a rhythm if you listen hard enough. But I've always struggled sharing them with my friends, because their lives were a lot like yours. Sometimes church and family on holidays, but the rest of the time, they go to their own corners of their houses. Live their own lives. Mine was a package deal.

That you saw them the same way I did only made me fall harder for you.

"I love you, Mia." The words were out before I formed them in my head. But that's how I know they were true. My heart spoke before my brain could get in the way.

Your eyes jerked to mine, surprised but happy—maybe curious, too.

"What made you say that?" You scooted closer. I pressed my lips together and shrugged slowly. You folded your hand into mine and leaned in so that I could feel the warmth of your skin on mine. Then my hand was wet, and when I looked, tears streamed down your cheeks and rolled off your chin.

I didn't have to ask why you were crying. I already knew. I could feel it. You radiated it.

"I love you, too, Alfie."

They say love transcends time and place. They say it fills the gaps pain leaves behind. And it does.

It did.

But they don't tell you that sometimes love isn't enough. I saw it on your face in that coffee shop before the world fell apart. You ran away from me so fast. Like you never loved me at all.

Mia

MY NEW FRIEND ALICE TELLS ME THE QUICKEST WAY TO GET TO
Alfie's work is to hop the fence of the baseball field and head south,
so I do. I run toward him as fast as I can over tattered cement in
my ruined Uggs. Anticipation swells in me like a kid realizing it's
Christmas Eve. He is close. Finally, I have a destination. Finally,
I have a path.

I can practically feel him.

There's no one directing traffic on this street. It's dark and
quiet except for the reverberating sounds of student chatter from
the field behind me.

Hastily written signs from people searching for those they
love appear on garages and doors of the houses and businesses
I pass.

*Henry Jenkins, I am at the middle school down the street. Red
Cross Center. Please come.*

*Eliza Woods, meet me at the shelter on Fulton. Love you,
Varun.*

Sign after sign of people calling for their loved ones. If I had
a pen and paper, I'd write one too.

Actually, that's not true. No, I wouldn't. What would I say?
Hey Alfie, I heard you still talk about me. Or *Alfie, meet me at
your work. I promise not to be awkward.*

No. What I have to say has to be done in person.

A few blocks down, an older woman stands in front of a chain-link fence where most of the messages are posted. It's covered in paper pleas in various shades and handwritings.

Thin and barefoot, the woman's wearing pajama bottoms and a long-sleeved shirt. Her hair is white and cut short above her ears. She reads one of the posts, mumbles something, and moves to the next one. Over and over. Instinctively I look for someone else who might be with her. There's no one. I clutch my blanket a little tighter.

As I get closer, she turns in my direction. Her face lights up like she recognizes me.

"Barbara, come and see." She extends her hand, opening and closing it to summon whoever she thinks I am.

"Oh, sorry. I'm . . ." I point to the street corner.

"Look at all the messages they left me." She takes hold of my arm so gently, it's like a bird landing there. I don't have the heart to stop her.

"That's really nice." I pat her hand and try to step away, but she turns us both back to the messages. I point to the corner again, like there's some explanation she'd understand if she'd only look that way. "I should keep going."

"I used to own a nursery right here, the only organic one in the entire city." She ignores my pointing. "You remember, don't you, Barbara?"

My impatience melts into an ache somewhere in my chest. She really is out here alone. Barefoot. Probably cold. Maybe if I go along with her for a minute, she'll go back to wherever she came from, hopefully somewhere safe, and I can keep going. With a longing glance down the street, I reply.

"Sure do. It was lovely."

She lets go of my arm and hobbles around to face me. Smiling, she takes my face in her hands. It's all I can do to stand still. I finally have a direction—know where to look. But she obviously needs help. I shift my gaze anywhere but on her, but her grip is firm. Reluctantly I meet her eyes. My heartbeat quickens.

"You were always so kind." Serenity fills her icy-blue irises. They're so peaceful, even in the middle of a wrecked city with people's desperation hanging on the fence. The softness radiating from her slows my pulse, and I feel myself being drawn in by her.

In a blink, she shuffles back to the wall of posters, running her finger over the names as she whispers them aloud.

My heart longs to keep walking, find Alfie, and say the things I couldn't before. But this woman is confused and probably freezing. I can't leave such a kind soul out here, barefoot in the dark. With resignation, I pull my blanket off my shoulders and drape it around the woman's.

"What's your name?" I close the blanket over her chest and tuck one side under the other.

"I'm Devi, Barbara. You know that."

"Do you know where you live, Devi? I can take you home."

Please let me take you home.

Instead, she points to an unseen place on the other side of the fence.

"Do you remember that giant willow tree right in the middle of the nursery? The roots got so long—the city made us cut it down when they wanted to build. Said they would upset the underground pipes."

"You fit a tree in there?" I looked at the small space between the buildings on either side. Now I know she's confused. I have to get her somewhere safe.

"Well, this wasn't here back then." She motions to the brick two-story on the left, the blanket waving with her hand.

I look up and down the street for some sort of sign of where she might have come from. Based on her dirty but otherwise cared-for feet, she must not be far from home. Across the street about a block over, people in scrubs are ushering wheelchair after wheelchair out of a facility. A glimmer of hope blooms inside me. She might be from there.

There's only one way to find out.

"Devi, let's walk this way." I gently guide her to the corner where we can cross. Although where we do doesn't matter, really. Not in times like these when the street's a relative ghost town. Funny what rules we choose to follow when we don't have to.

When we finally get within shouting distance of the facility, I wave my hand that Devi isn't leaning on.

"Excuse me," I say. "Can you help us?"

A woman in scrubs with tight braids checks her clipboard as someone else counts the people in wheelchairs.

"I'm trying to find out where my friend lives."

"If she's your friend, wouldn't you know where she lives?" The woman continues checking her clipboard.

"We just met," I say, incredulous. This time, I'm not sorry. That causes her to look up. "She was about two blocks that way. I'm hoping to get her someplace safe." I plead with my eyes.

"Sorry, hon, don't recognize her." She clicks her pen, taps it on her clipboard, and goes inside.

"But . . . what do I do?" I say to the closed door. The van door closes too, before I can figure out who to talk to. They drive away, leaving Devi and me to fend for ourselves.

My eyebrows shoot up as I huff out an exasperated breath.

This feels worse than after being dropped off by Raj. At least then, I only had myself to worry about.

I glance at Devi, thinking she'll be just as frustrated as me. Instead, she's looking back at where her tree should be, humming something soft and beautiful. I take a deep breath and let it out slow.

What if she were my grandma? Wouldn't I want me to at least make sure she gets somewhere safe? She could cut her foot or fall. Or worse. A shiver trickles down my spine.

It's just that Alfie is literally blocks away. After all this time. After how far I've come.

He's *right there*. Every atom of my body is being pulled toward him. I think if I wanted, I could grow wings and fly there.

I could leave, but I'd spend the rest of my life wondering what happened to her, and probably having nightmares about the things that could. Just thinking about it makes my insides turn to lead. Resolve finds my feet and plants them next to hers. I have no choice but to finish what I started, so I can keep going.

Except I'm in a relatively strange city with a map I barely know how to read and a cell phone with 10 percent battery life. Probably less.

And the one person with me is living in an alternate San Francisco with her friend Barbara, where willow trees grow between buildings.

Easy-peasy.

Alfie

IN THE MONTHS AFTER MY BIRTHDAY, YOU CARVED A PLACE IN my big, loud family's hearts and at their kitchen table. Easy-peasy, like you say. Mama even let you help her roll dolmades when she prepped for Easter, which is its own miracle. But the best part was how free you looked when you were there. You smiled your real smile and laughed with abandon—my favorite sound in the whole world.

And Opening Day was no different.

As I warmed up on the field with the rest of the team, you and Eleni sat on the highest bleacher behind everyone, her hair pulled into a ponytail just like yours. You held up homemade signs with my jersey number and name in glitter. Anna stood next to you holding a sign that read TURF ISN'T BIODEGRADABLE, trying her hardest not to have fun. Even for her, that was impossible when you were around.

From my first pitch to the last, you screamed the loudest when I struck someone out. And if they got a hit off me, you still clapped. Josuè gave me so much shit for that after. Even Chuck chimed in a little, which is saying something because during games, he's usually all business.

"If she's clappin', you best be tappin'." Josuè chucked the ball to me after a play.

"You're disgusting."

I noticed Simi sitting with you about halfway through the game. Remember the bet you and I had? The one where you said she would ask Josuè out first, and I said it would be him that made the first move? She locked in on him as he played, then looked away every time he glanced at her. It was obvious I'd win.

I guess I did, technically.

Coach took me out of the game at the seventh inning so I could rest my arm. We were ahead by four, so I didn't mind too much, although it would've been cool to have you see me pitch a whole game. But I had to keep my arm in top shape for when the scouts showed.

Sometimes I wish they never had, because then things could've been different. But that's not how life works.

After the game, we ate dinner at my house. You had a permanent place at the table by then, right next to me. And Eleni on the other side, of course. I still can't believe you got her to eat tomatoes. She would've done just about anything to impress you.

I know the feeling.

I never asked, but I always wondered if the way we prayed before eating weirded you out. I know your family prayed all the time, but the way we did it was so different than you were used to. You learned to make the sign of the cross, which Mama loved, by the way, although I don't know if you ever really felt it. It was the only time you became public Mia when you were with us. For just that moment, it was like someone painted you with a hard enamel to protect you from the elements.

Then it was gone as quickly as it showed up.

That night, after dinner when I took you home, your house was dark.

"I think my dad's at some church finance meeting. Lord knows where my mother is." You unlocked the front door and opened it. "Want to come in?" The look in your eye said you had an idea about what we could do.

"Oh yeah, I want to come in." I lifted your hand and kissed the back. You jerked it away and used it to swat mine, fire dancing in your eyes.

"Alfie! Don't be gross."

"What? I like spending time with you." I pasted the most innocent expression I could muster all over my face.

You wanted to go to your room, but I felt better on the couch in the family room. Since we didn't know where your mom was, we didn't know when she would get home. And the last thing I needed was for her to find another reason to bare her teeth at me through her fake, lipsticked smile.

You turned on the TV and lowered the volume to almost nothing. I leaned my head against the back of the couch and watched the shadows dance on the ceiling. You lifted my left arm and snuggled against me. After pitching all afternoon, I was grateful you chose to sit on that side. My right arm was Jell-O.

I tilted my head so my cheek rested on your hair. I don't know what shampoo you used, but I loved the way it smelled. Like coconut and spun sugar. I tried to inhale without you noticing. I couldn't get enough.

When you lifted your face to meet mine, the scene must've changed on the television because all the shadows scattered away. White light braised the already ghostly walls, and I closed my eyes. Your lips brushed mine, lightly at first, then more forcefully.

Your mouth searched mine, and I knew exactly what you were looking for. I pulled you closer. When you straddled my lap and locked your fingers in my hair, I forgot all about the shadows. All that mattered was you and me and the heat between us.

I swept my fingers up your back and down the sides of your neck. You put your hands on top of mine and pushed them down your chest. Your silent permission took my breath away, but I had to make sure.

"Is this okay?" I said between kisses as I grazed your breasts with my fingers.

"Mm-hmm." You moaned into my mouth and I sucked in a breath. You broke away and, for a second, I thought you'd changed your mind.

But then you lifted your shirt over your head, making your long waves fall over your shoulders, eyes full of hunger. Seeing you that way, unafraid and vulnerable, overwhelmed me with emotion.

"At the risk of sounding like every teen boy in every movie, can I tell you something?" My fingers played at the crease above your belly button.

"Are you going to be weird?" You kissed my neck.

"Not weird. Honest."

"Go ahead." You sat up but kept your hands locked with mine. I took them and framed your face.

"I love you, Mia. And you are so beautiful. And I don't know how I got so lucky as to be here with you right now. But I'm really glad I am."

I thought you would say it back. Say something.

Instead, you studied me, your eyes mirroring the shadows on the wall. At last, you stood, your hand reaching for me. My heart skipped exactly five beats.

"Let's go upstairs." Your voice scratched against the silent buzzing in the background. I sat up straight as my eyes involuntarily went to the back door.

"Won't your parents be home soon?"

"Who cares." A mischievous smile crept up one side of your mouth. You laced your fingers through mine and pulled me up.

Just standing so close to your bare skin took my breath away. Your sweet scent the only thing keeping me here on earth. Darkness danced at the edges of my vision, and I almost took a step as you pulled my hand behind you.

To both of our surprise, I pulled back.

I willed my feet to move. One in front of the other. I wanted to make you happy, chase away your shadows once and for all. But I knew in my gut this wasn't the way.

I wasn't ready.

I know you don't believe me, and you think I was being a gentleman or whatever, but it's true.

I wanted our first time to be just us, not some hurried excursion to your bedroom, racing against the parental clock. I mean, we hadn't even talked about it yet.

"Mia, I can't." My voice was sandpaper.

"Come upstairs with me." You hooked your arms around my middle and pressed your hands into my shoulder blades, your warm skin pressing on mine. I almost gave in.

Those two steps backward were the hardest ones I'd ever taken in my life.

Something inside you broke when I lifted your shirt from the couch and held it out for you. Like you thought I was rejecting you. Like I confirmed something you already knew. But you wouldn't let me explain.

"Just leave, then." You started upstairs. "Just go."

I hope you know that I never meant to hurt you. More than anything, I wanted to be with you.

The steps to my truck after that were hard.

But none were as difficult as the steps I had to take after graduation.

Mia

AS DIFFICULT AS THE STEPS ARE FOR HER, I LEAD DEVI THROUGH
the broken mess of the city and around the corner. We look for
signs of activity, hoping to find someone who might know who she
is. On the block ahead, a door is open, and light leaks onto the
sidewalk. My breath catches. I hadn't realized how much I took
light for granted until there wasn't any.

I will never look at a light bulb the same way again.

"Let's go there," I say. "Maybe we'll get lucky."

We shuffle our way to the door and the light, my feet resisting
the urge to go faster. More than once, I have to force myself to
take calm breaths, slow myself down for Devi's sake. Between her
poor feet and wobbly balance, she is the turtle to my hare.

Finally, we arrive.

Inside, the front wall is a giant mirror lined with battery-run
lanterns. The mirror echoes the bare bricks of the other walls. An
empty rack sits in the back. Mats occupy nearly every inch of the
wooden floor. Several people, some in yoga gear, others in suits and
streetwear—obviously post-earthquake ensembles—gather on the
mats closest to the large kerosene heater in the middle of the room.

"Come in, come in." A slender woman with high cheekbones
and long, graying hair welcomes us. She folds her hands over her
heart and bows slightly. "I'm Shauna, and this is my place. Come,
get warm."

Relief floods my body, but the warmth of the room makes my

back and leg muscles ache as they defrost. I didn't realize how cold I was. I glance at Devi's bare feet and am grateful for my fuzzy boots, even if they aren't the best hiking gear.

"Thank you so much," I say. "I'm Mia. This is Devi. I met her outside. Pretty sure she's lost."

"Well, let's get Devi warmed up." Shauna puts her arm around Devi and guides her to a mat near the heater.

I eye the door. I'm so close. I've come all this way, and now I'm stuck a few blocks from the boy I love. But I have to make sure this kind old woman has a safe place for the night. With a sigh, I follow Devi to the mat.

Shauna brings us cups of tea she pours from a large dispenser, which we take gratefully. As we sip, Devi straightens her legs in front of her, and Shauna brings her a pair of soft blue socks. Once Shauna helps to put them on, Devi flexes and points her feet, alternating one with the other.

"Those are pretty," she says.

"Your poor feet." Shauna rubs the tops, I'm guessing for heat. "They're so cold. Do you know where you left your shoes?"

"It was summer when I left." Devi lifts her shoulders as she sips her tea.

Shauna's lips stretch wide. With a nod to me, she excuses herself to tend to someone new walking in.

"Were you going somewhere?" I ask Devi.

"I wanted to check on my tree, see if it was okay." Her gentle eyes find mine, but now there's grief hovering over her like the dust and fog hangs in the air outside.

"I'm sorry it wasn't there."

"You know how that tree got so big?" she asks as if I hadn't said anything.

"Water?" It's all I can think of. She bows her head in an exaggerated nod.

"That, and love." She dots the air with her finger as she says the last word.

I had a teacher in high school with a huge plant in her classroom window. She always said it got so big because it soaked up all the energy left over in the room. Is that what Devi means?

"Plants and trees grow when they're loved, just like people. When you plant them, you have to dig the hole twice as wide and twice as deep, then fill it with rich soil. Give the roots somewhere to go."

"That's good advice." Shauna lowers herself onto the mat next to Devi's and rubs her back over the blanket.

I nod to her, unsure of what to say. I don't really understand why an old tree is so special, but this moment feels important somehow, like we need to listen, bear witness to this kind woman telling her story. So instead of barreling out of here, I compel myself to stay silent. Listen. Take sips of my tea and let it warm me from the inside.

"Trees are a miracle," Devi says. "Especially the willow. And not many people know this, but the roots are just like the branches. What's above, so below."

As she speaks, I conjure an image of a willow tree. Its branches bend and wind in what seem like random directions. I smooth some of my own curls in sympathy. I've never seen actual tree roots except in fragments as they broke through old sidewalks or in high school biology texts. They, too, seem to travel in random curvy patterns. Devi is right. The branches and the roots are the same.

"What the roots take from the earth, the branches give to the sky. And when it rains, the sky gives back."

Shauna and I exchange a look. My whole body tingles, and I can't tell if it's from the warmth of the tea or if it's Devi's story.

"Om shanti," Shauna whispers. Devi closes her eyes and repeats Shauna's words.

"What does that mean?" I ask.

"In simple terms, it's a way to acknowledge the tranquility in connection to the Divine. It means peace." Shauna smiles at Devi, who's repeating the words over and over, her eyes still closed.

"That's beautiful." My eyebrows cinch together. I'm not used to making my own spiritual connections. At home, I was told what to believe, and if I didn't, I should at least be polite enough to fake it. But Shauna's words beg to be understood. I just don't know how to put it all together. "Can I ask what it has to do with willow trees?"

"Try saying the first part with me." Shauna widens her mouth and draws out the word so it sounds more like long vowel sounds ending with a hum. I try to copy what she does. "Notice how the sound travels from the front of your mouth to the back and then the front again? That's the sound of the entire universe."

I draw back, my brain racing for the answer to how the universe has one sound. My mom and her prayer circle pray over each other, letting their words blend into a tangle of sounds. Chin-Sun spoke soft melodies when she prayed, even though she was speaking to the same god. Maybe this is the same. I straighten. "Is it a prayer?"

"Kind of. More like a reminder."

I try to put the sound and the willow together. Front and back and front again. Roots to branches to sky and back again.

Oh.

My skin tingles and the hairs on my arms stand straight. I smile at Shauna, who, in turn, smiles and bows her head.

"You get it," she says.

"Om shanti." Devi pats my hand.

I say the words, and I feel the sounds connect. *Om*—it sounds like a hug. The good kind when someone you trust wraps their arms around you from behind, letting you lean your whole weight against them. I say it again and see the tree, its roots as long and deep as the branches are high and wide. The way Alfie's and my roots are. Just because the branches are broken doesn't mean the tree isn't thriving underground.

I've been crying on and off all night, but the tears spilling down my cheeks feel different as the three of us beam at each other in this moment. A connection, maybe? A release? We cry when we're happy; we shed tears when we're sad. Either way it's the same expression, the same cycle. Shauna's right. Front and back and front again.

"My willow grew so large and so beautiful," Devi says, interrupting my thoughts. "But then the city made us cut it down. Oh sure, they said we could trim the roots back so they wouldn't harm the buildings or break up the sidewalks, but you know what happens when you do that? The trees fall over. What's the use?" She dismisses the idea with a wave.

"That's a beautiful way to look at things," Shauna says. "Your family is lucky to have you."

I should ask where her family is. Try to get her home safely. But I want everything to stop so I can sit with this revelation.

Everything's connected.

I let the words roll around in my mind, touching every part. Melting all the ice that's collected in the corners. I take a deep breath and imagine them floating to Alfie. Settling over him. Hugging him, too. If anyone would understand, it's him. He always got me, even when I didn't want him to.

Trees fall over without strong roots to hold them up. When my family rotted mine, Alfie grew in their place. And I chopped him off, just like what the city wanted to do to Devi's willow.

But he's close, and when I do finally see him, I'll tell him this story and show him how sorry I am that I forced him away.

The idea moves my desire to see him again from simmer to flame, and I realize it's time to go. I smile at Devi, then shift my legs to stretch the warmth into the muscles.

"Shauna, can Devi stay here with you?" I ask. "I have somewhere I need to be. I only wanted . . ." I gesture to Devi, and Shauna nods.

"Of course. We can help her find home." Shauna stands when I do and takes my empty mug. "But are you sure you should go out again? It's dark and pretty chilly. And you're only wearing that sweatshirt."

"I was using the blanket." I gesture to its new home as Devi's shawl. "But she needs it more."

"You're a kind soul, Mia." She bows the way she did when we came in. This time, I lower my chin and feel something pass between us. *Everything's connected.* "Come back if you need to."

I give Devi a hug. She returns it and squeezes my face together with her palms when we part.

"I love you, Barbara. You remember that."

Even though my name isn't Barbara, and even though I most likely won't see Devi again, I take her words into my heart and wear them with honor.

"Thank you, Devi. I love you, too." To my surprise, I mean it.

She begins to untuck the blanket corners on her shoulder, and I put my hand on hers.

"You keep it. It's yours now." I know Chin-Sun would be happy to know her red blanket is giving warmth to someone in need. I smile at the thought.

If everything goes the way I want, I will be warm enough in a matter of minutes.

Alfie

IT'S SO COLD IN THIS FOG AND MIST. I SEE BUILDINGS, BUT they're dark, and you're not there. When I find you, though, we can find warmth together. We will make our own. We always could, except when you turned away from me. In those times, I felt like the sun had decided not to shine.

We didn't talk the entire next day after our fight. To be honest, I didn't know what to say other than that I was sorry. When you didn't text me back, I tried to let it go. Let you ride out the storm in your own way. Then Sunday afternoon, you asked if we were still on for the double date like nothing happened.

At that point, I think I'd gotten used to you brushing things under the rug, pushing them somewhere deep so your pain didn't hurt anyone else. I shouldn't have ignored it either, and I'm still sorry. When I find you, I'll tell you that exact thing.

Baba overheard us talking about our Josuè-and-Simi bet and insisted we plan our meet-cute at the restaurant.

"Why go somewhere else," he said. "I let you and your friends eat for free." He tapped at his temple like I was the dense one for wanting to go somewhere my dad wouldn't be watching everything I did with my friends.

We made sure we got there early and grabbed the table farthest from the kitchen and counter, even though Baba had bat hearing when it came to his livelihood. I got waters for us while we waited.

Self-service was part of the Eat Free package.

You wore your hair down that night, its long waves spilling onto your oversized sweater. Your lips were stained a berry color, which made your eyes electric. I silently wished I'd kept you to myself. But I'll admit, I hoped they'd finally confess to liking each other.

"Should we be doing this?" You shifted in your chair. "I'm not sure we should be doing this."

"We eat with them all the time at school. What's the difference?"

You flashed your *Are you serious?* look.

"What?" I sipped my water to avoid your stare.

"That's entirely different and you know it. We're basically forcing them on a double date without telling them."

"Come on. Simi thinks he's a dreamboat and Josuè will totally be down."

"Please don't ever say *dreamboat* again."

Before I could defend my word choice, Josuè swung open the door and presented himself, arms open, smiling wide. His baseball cap topped his hoodie and jeans, like he'd just come from the batting cages.

Probably should've warned him to wear something nice.

"I'm here, bitches. What's good?" He straddled the chair next to you and tossed a head nod to me. Baba shot me a look from behind the counter.

"Can you not say *bitches* when my dad is here?" I spoke softly and tried to not move my mouth in case Baba could read lips.

"Oh shit—sorry, dude." Josuè covered his mouth with his hand and hunched forward. "My bad."

"Yes, that's much better," you said. I laughed, despite the frown Baba wore as he glared at our table.

"What are we doing tonight, lovebirds?" Josuè rubbed his hands together and waggled his eyebrows. "Interested in exploring your options?"

"I told you this was a bad idea." You sighed.

"What's a bad idea?" Josuè asked.

"We invited Simi, too," I said.

"You did what?" He jumped up, his chair screeching against the floor. "How did you invite her?"

"Mia texted her."

"No, like *how* did you invite her?" He lifted off his cap and combed his hand through his hair. I shrugged.

"They want you to like the girl," Baba yelled from the back. "What's it take with this one, eh?"

I dropped my head onto the table and rolled it back and forth. I wanted to tell him to stay out of it, but there was no telling him anything. You were laughing so hard, you snorted, which made me laugh too. But Josuè was definitely not laughing. In fact, he looked a little green.

"I cannot with you two." He lowered himself into his chair.

"It's just dinner. And maybe a movie." You blotted tears from the corners of your eyes, always so careful not to smudge any makeup.

"No, it isn't. You want me to have dinner with Simi. Like *dinner* dinner. I can't do it."

"Why not?" Your back stiffened. You weren't laughing anymore.

"Because of that right there." He pointed to your frown. "Best friends of the girls who are the girlfriends of my best friends are off-limits. Things don't go well and I'm the monster and my friends side with their girls. No thanks—I like my junk where it is." He grabbed his crotch to emphasize his point.

"Gross." You threw up your hands and blew out a breath. "I'm going to the bathroom."

"Was all that really necessary?" I motioned to his lap once you were gone.

"Making my point is all."

"We're going to eat, talk. See a movie. No one's asking you to swear undying devotion to her or anything. Do it for me, man."

"This is how it starts." He shook his head as he picked up my water and downed it.

"And don't lie. I know you and Simi have been texting off and on since the winter formal." I sip from my own glass. Josuè clicked his tongue.

"Dude, see? It's already happening." He rubbed his eye.

"What's happening?"

"The only way you know that is because Mia told you. And Mia knows because Simi and her tell each other everything."

"What's the big deal if I know?" I asked. Josuè looked around, then leaned in like he was about to reveal a huge secret.

"That girl will ruin my rep, man. She's too good." He leaned back in his chair and dropped air bombs from his hands. I stared blankly at him.

"It's dinner, not an engagement," Baba yelled, then muttered in Greek. I busted out laughing.

"What'd he say?" Josuè whispered. I shrugged.

"Just saying, you better eat whatever he puts in front of you."

"Fine, but if this *dinner* goes downhill, I'm bailing."

After you came back and Simi got there, I ordered a large plate of gyro fries and got us more drinks. Simi looked cute in her green top and jeans. She wore her hair up but not in her usual bun. It was combed into a ponytail that was almost as long as yours.

Josuè grabbed a bottle of hot sauce from the condiment station and opened it over the platter.

"What do you think you're doing with that?" you asked. He froze mid-pour.

"Making this food better," he said.

"My food is perfect." Baba's voice boomed from the register. Did I melt into the floor at all? I feel like I melted into the floor.

"Put it on the side or something. I can't do hot sauce."

"Mia doesn't do spicy." Simi took the bottle from Josuè and poured some onto one of the small plates.

"Makes me all splotchy," you said.

Josuè looked at me, then opened his mouth to say something. I shook my head as quietly as I could. You wouldn't have appreciated his joke—trust me on that.

I think Simi ate more of the hot sauce than Josuè did, and you thought it was cute that they shared a plate, even if they seemed a little awkward doing it.

After we ate, Baba insisted I bus our table, so the three of you waited out front. When I met you outside, you suggested we all walk to the movie theater and see what was playing. I'm sure you already had the times memorized and knew exactly which one we were seeing, but I appreciated the act of spontaneity.

"That's okay." Simi pulled her keys out of her pocket. "I need to get home."

"What? I thought we were hanging out tonight." Josuè's voice was higher than normal. Simi pressed her lips together and nodded.

"Yeah, I can't. Strict parents. What can you do?" She hugged you in that sideways nudge you two always did and said she'd text you later.

Josuè stood there, his mouth hanging open until she drove away.

"Dude. What just happened?" He took off his cap, shook his hair, and put it back on.

"I guess she had to go." You smiled into your phone as your fingers flew over the keyboard.

"So messed up," he said. "I'mma head out too. Don't do anything I wouldn't do . . ." He shot finger guns at us as he walked backward to his car.

I waved and put my arm around you.

"I guess that leaves the two of us," I said. "Do you want to do the movie or something else?"

You slipped your phone into your pocket and wrapped your arms around my neck. You tilted your head up, and before I kissed you, I glanced through the window to check for Baba. All clear.

"We can do something else if you want," you said.

I knew just the thing.

After we settled into our spot at the lake, I spread out the pillows and blankets still behind the seat in the cab of my truck, and you tossed some of the leftover fries Baba made me take in one of Anna's environmentally friendly containers to Ruchard and his friends.

"You think he remembers us?" you asked.

"Well, he chugged over here as soon as we parked, so maybe, yeah." I propped the last of the pillows against the back of the bed and sat down. You climbed in and pulled one of the blankets over us.

"I like this comforter, by the way. Very sweet." Sarcasm dripped off your words.

"Thank you. I thought so too." I batted my eyelashes for effect. "It was Eleni's when she was little. Found it in the garage." I smoothed it up to your chin. Ruchard jumped onto the wall of the truck, quacked, and flew away.

"We are Ruchard's family now." You rested your arm across my stomach. "Someday we will have little grandducks to feed."

"We might already, you don't know. How many ducklings can a duck foster?" I picked up my phone. "I need to do research."

You took it out of my hand and set it behind you.

"Not tonight, you don't."

Something about the way you kissed me was different. More, somehow. I didn't think I could feel more of anything when your lips touched mine. It's like a current streamed from your mouth directly into my heart, and from there, it radiated light through every vein in my body.

I knew I was ready. Ready to be with you completely.

"You okay?" It pained me to stop kissing you, but I had to be sure.

"Oh yeah."

That night, under a sea of stars and my sister's old Strawberry Shortcake comforter, we gave each other everything we had. Your breath became mine. My skin became yours. Your eyes a mirror into my own soul.

I know I fumbled a bit and probably did a thousand things wrong. Elbows too wobbly, knees too pointy. But being with you forever changed me.

After, we lay with our legs intertwined, your head on my shoulder. We traced the outlines of the trees against the midnight sky and listened to the sounds of the water lap the shore. Your smile pressed against my chest.

"I'm glad we did it together, here, like this," I said.

"Definitely more fun than doing it alone." You let out a soft laugh.

"No, that's not what I mean, goof. I mean . . . you know. Losing our virginity together." Heat flushed my neck and threatened to rise to my cheeks.

Your smile faded against my chest as you adjusted your arms and folded them over yourself. I should've pulled you closer. Stopped talking. But I kept going, too embarrassed to stop.

"I can't believe you made me say *virginity*."

"If you can't say it, you shouldn't be doing it." You sat up and pulled on your sweater.

"Neither of us are doing virginity anymore. That's kind of the point." I sat up too, my skin braced against the cold.

"You know what I mean. Besides, it's not even a real thing." You brushed your fingers through your hair, pulling harder than you needed to at the knots.

"What's not a real thing?"

"Virginity. It's part of a patriarchal bullshit construct to make women feel bad about liking sex." You crossed your legs so you were facing me. You'd given up on untangling your hair, and now you were bunching it into a messy pile on top of your head. I flung myself onto the blankets and sighed.

"Why do you always do that?"

"Do what?" You reached for your phone and clicked on something.

"Can't you let me have one romantic moment? I thought girls were supposed to love romance." I sat up again. "I know you do, because you said getting nominated to the court together would be romantic." I pointed at you like I'd just identified the killer in some old cop-show serial.

"It can still be romantic. Let's just call it something that's not an antiquated way of subjugating women."

Then I saw what you were doing. What you always did when you felt yourself getting too close to real feelings. The extended vocabulary was always a clue.

"Okay, no patriarchal construct that subjugates women shall pass these lips again. Pinkie promise?" I looped my finger around yours and squeezed, but your attention was turned toward your lit-up screen.

"Don't pull away from me, Mia. I love you, and I know you love me. This is how I pictured it would be for us. And how it'll be when we go to New York." I looked away. "Not like it would've been at your house, constantly looking over shoulders, wondering if we'd be interrupted. Let's just have this night."

Instead of answering, you typed something and hit send on your phone. The realization that you were talking to someone else at that moment, in our moment, snapped me out of whatever spell was left over.

"Do you have to recount the night to Simi right now? Before it's even over?"

"That was my dad wanting to know when I would be home. Code for *You should be home*, and I was telling him I'm on my way. Sorry." You said the last word like you were anything but. The wind deflated from my lungs.

"No, I'm sorry. Of course. It's late and I should get you home."

Silently, we folded the blankets and stuffed the pillows behind the seats. With barely a glance, we loaded ourselves into the cab and I started the engine.

At the stoplight, I studied your somber expression.

"It's like you can't let yourself be happy," I whispered. It was too quiet for a full voice.

Without speaking, you reached for my hand and squeezed. We sat like that the rest of the way to your house. When I pulled to the curb, you squeezed again.

"You make me happy. I have a hard time expressing it sometimes. I wish it was easier." You pulled your lips into a sad grin, your downturned eyes glassy.

"You can trust me." I kissed your hand. "I love you and you can trust me."

"I love you, too, Alfie. I really do."

And then you opened the door, walked up the driveway, and into your house. I drove home with the windows down, welcoming every bite of the cold winter air.

Mia

I'M STILL THINKING ABOUT DEVI'S WILLOW TREE STORY AS I make my way through the cold winter air, back to where I saw her in the first place. She may not have meant it as a metaphor, but it sure landed as one.

As above, so below. Everything's connected.

My whole life, I've heard that people are made in God's image, and I've always wondered if the opposite isn't true—that God is made in ours. We hurt people when we try to love. We are quick to get angry when we should forgive. But we can love. That's what being human is.

What if we spent our time trying to be more human because that's what being God-like really is?

Devi missed her tree, so she came to visit. The actual one isn't there anymore, but it lives on in her heart. In her broken memories. She may not have a lot of them left, but she will never forget that tree.

I arrive at the wall of notices that Devi pored over earlier. There's so many. Some on full pages of printer paper. Others hastily written on the back of receipts and take-out menus, desperation in every handwritten swirl.

I know how they feel.

Alfie was there for me in every way a person could be there for someone else. And I screwed it up every time.

If he wanted more, I pushed him away. But the worst part?

When he needed to step back, I forced his hand. Especially that night at the lake.

The familiar heat of humiliation burns my cheeks as I relive the time I ruined a perfectly romantic moment.

Even though the air turned cold, we stayed warm under his silly comforter, wound together, legs intertwined, my head pressed against his chest. He tried to say how happy he was that we had our first time together, and I had to turn it into a stupid argument.

I mean, virginity *is* a social construct designed to make women lesser to men somehow, but I didn't have to pick that moment to come down so hard on the side of third-wave feminism. I could've waited until we were at least dressed. My ribs squeeze my lungs as I fold inward.

I may not know exactly what I believe, but sometimes it's easier to identify what I don't. The fact that I made him feel bad about his own beliefs makes me want to climb into a hole, but I never understood how he could just take someone's word on the entire structure of the world. Isn't it important to arrive at our beliefs in our own way? My face contorts as I argue with the air.

I freeze, my muscles slack under the weight of a thousand realizations at once. Alfie has been going to the same church his entire life. He volunteers in the altar, helps the old women bake for their annual festival, even plays with the little kids while the grown-ups drink coffee after church.

What if he simply agrees? Have I been doing to Alfie what my parents did to me? Bile rises in the back of my throat.

Chin-Sun believes in her own way. I saw it in the way she gave me water and a granola bar. Plus, she literally covered me with a blanket. And when she prayed, her voice was so honest, so pure. Nothing like what I heard every night at the dinner table.

Devi believes in people. She said trees need love to grow just like people. She may not know where home is or what season it is, but I know she knows how to love people. She held my face in her frail hands and looked at me with such purity and honest admiration for merely standing there with her. Not because I'd bought her anything, not because I said something nice. She showed me love just because I stopped.

But the thing is, I don't know how to do that. Any of it. I swallow the lump in my throat, but that makes my stomach angrier.

Praying is awkward for me because it feels like I'm talking to myself. Sure, I can give food and water to someone who needs it, but that's just being a good person. If you need a god to tell you to do that, then hell isn't the worst of your problems.

Maybe I can plant a tree, but I doubt I could keep it alive long enough to have to trim back anything. Forget about people.

If I can't handle a simple tree, how can I love anyone?

How can I love Alfie the way he needs to be loved? How can I ask for forgiveness when I've never given it myself?

Maybe this is a mistake. Maybe Simi is right and all I do is run. Run because I can't deal with anything.

Maybe I need to stop and think about this. All of it. I pushed him away for a reason. If Alice is telling the truth, then he might be willing to come back, and what if I run again?

I could fail.

A deep foreboding fills my lungs like black tar. It spills into my chest and fills my legs with a heaviness I can't shake.

I force my feet to carry me to a bus stop bench and collapse, hoping the feeling will shrink back to wherever it came from. Wishing a bus would show up and drive me away from everything.

But it's pitch-black on a cold October night, after the worst earthquake of our lifetime, and there's no bus coming.

And there won't be for a very long time.

Alfie

Hey A-man!

Congratulations, you've been offered a full ride at USF! I just got off the phone with their head coach, and he thinks that if you put your mind to it, you could have a shot at the majors!!

You also have a great offer from that school in Bronxville you wanted me to look into. Keep in mind, however, they are a lower division than USF, which means you won't have as much exposure there.

You should be receiving your official offers soon, so keep your eyes peeled.

Proud of you!

Coach

Alfie

I KNOW YOU'LL THINK IT'S WEIRD, BUT ONE OF MY FAVORITE memories is that night you invited me for dinner, even if there wasn't any actual food—or wouldn't be for hours. I was so excited to tell you the news, but when I got there, you were sitting on the porch wrapped in your big coat and deep thoughts. You finally noticed me as I climbed the stairs to the door. You jumped up and walked right past me.

"Let's get out of here."

"Everything okay?" I tried to peek through the window into the house, but the curtains were drawn with no light behind them.

You said nothing, just walked to your side of my truck and waited. With one more glance to the door, I followed and let you in.

I half expected your dad to come blazing out, screaming at me to get off his lawn or worse, your mom screeching at me to stay away from her daughter. I thought maybe they'd found out about what happened at the lake or maybe you were . . .

I said a little prayer and made the cross as my stomach nearly dropped out of my body.

Closing your door, I ran around to my side and started the engine.

"Are we going anywhere in particular?"

"Anywhere but here." Red blotches clumped together on your neck and cheeks as you hunched into the corner. You stared out the window, your breath creating clouds on the glass.

We drove around town for hours until I couldn't stand the suspense anymore. I pulled over in front of the senior center and put the truck in park.

"Are you okay? Did they find out about us?" I tried my best to keep my voice steady.

"What? No . . . I don't know. It's not that." The blotches on your skin had faded and you were sitting straighter, facing front. "They came home from church, and my mother stormed into the bedroom and slammed the door. Dad never came out of the garage. I tried to ask my mom if we were still having dinner, but she didn't answer." You huffed and rolled your eyes. "I'm fine. I'll figure it out."

The blotches crept up your neck again, so I rubbed your shoulder. I hated that you were so miserable, which made me feel guilty for the relief flooding through my veins. I let myself relax a little, hoping some of it would make its way to you.

"They just completely ignored you?"

"She did. I didn't even try with my dad." You leaned into my hand. "What's the point?"

It was that moment that my stomach generously reminded us that I hadn't eaten since lunch. It let out a loud roar, and I pressed on it hard to make it stop, but no such luck.

I scrunched my face and waited for you to say something. Instead, you stared straight ahead and tucked your lips between your teeth. But you couldn't hold in your laughter. It came out as a loud snort. I laughed until my stomach demanded more attention.

"I'm sorry you didn't get dinner." You tugged softly on my earlobe.

"I'm sorry my stomach is so rude. But hey, teenage boy." I

pointed to myself and shrugged. "Want to go somewhere and get food?"

"How about your house?" Something about the smallness of your voice when you asked told me you needed more from my house than what our kitchen had to offer. I put the truck in drive, made a U-turn, and steered us home.

Dinner was put away by the time we got there.

"Alfie, is that you?" Mama asked as I closed the front door.

Mama and Baba were on the couch watching their Greek TV show while everyone else was probably in their rooms. My parents commandeered the living room every weeknight to watch it. It was the only thing they did together all week, and I liked knowing I would find them in their spot, Baba's head on Mama's lap while she yelled at the blonde in the show making all the wrong decisions.

I checked the time, and they had twenty more minutes before it was over.

"Yeah, and Mia. We were going to get something to eat."

"There's some leftovers." Mama pushed Baba off her lap and stood. "Hello Mia, agapi mou."

I loved that she called you that.

"Hi Mama," you said.

"That's okay, Mama. Watch your show." I nodded to the TV. "We can make eggs."

"Suit yourself." She put her hands up near her shoulders and sat back down.

As we entered the kitchen side of the open space, Baba opened his mouth to say something.

"I'll clean everything up, Baba."

He waved me off and settled into his spot.

"Hi, Mr. Thanasis." You waved. He waved back but said nothing.

"You call her *Mama* and him *Mr. Thanasis*?" I whispered into your ear.

"He never said to call him anything else." You got the eggs out of the fridge while I got the bowl and pan. You sat on the counter next to me as I mixed up the eggs and milk. I made two plates with scrambled eggs, some bread and cheese, and set them on the table.

Mama's show ended, so she woke up Baba, who'd been snoring on her lap, and they went upstairs.

"I have other news, besides my parents being complete jerks." You nibbled on your bread.

"Oh yeah?"

"I got my letter from Sarah Lawrence."

I dropped my fork on the table and stared at your expressionless face.

"Way to bury the lede. What did it say? Did you get in?" I sucked in a breath. "What am I saying? Of course you got in."

You continued to stare.

"Well?"

"Are you finished ranting?" A slow smile stretched across your lips and you bit the bottom one.

Just thinking about when you did that makes me warm inside.

I slid the imaginary zipper on my mouth closed and folded my hands in front of me.

A giggle floated from the stairs.

"Eleni, let them eat." Mama shushed her.

"I want to say hi to Mia," Eleni whined.

"Go to your room and play."

"I'm in sixth grade, Mama. I don't play in my room anymore."

"I'll come read with you when I'm done," you said.

"You heard her. Now go play," Mama said.

Eleni groaned and stomped up the stairs and across the landing, slamming her door behind her. I rolled my eyes.

"Yes, I got in. Partial scholarship."

"I knew you would!" I jumped up and raced around the table to hug you. "This is so great!"

"Have you heard anything?"

"Funny you should ask." I released you and pulled Coach's printed email off the fridge.

"What's this?"

"Read it." I bobbed my eyebrows up and down and rocked on my heels while you did.

"You got in?" Your face stayed neutral. In fact, you didn't sound happy about it at all.

"They want me to play for them. Isn't it great?"

You pinched your lips together as you handed the paper back to me and sat down, poking at your lukewarm eggs.

"Why aren't you excited? This is what we want." I returned to my seat across from you. The table and a whole country between us.

"What he said about USF. And the majors? You can't turn that down. And your mom already got you all that stuff." You gestured toward my room. "It's basically a done deal." You folded your arms over your stomach.

"Hey." I reached across the table and laid down my hand for you to take. You sighed and slowly lifted yours to meet mine. "You know I don't care about that. Baseball is what's getting me to college, not the reason I'm going."

"Really?" You looked up from your plate of cold eggs, and the vulnerability in your eyes broke my heart. How could I want to be anywhere you weren't?

"We are going to New York together." I squeezed your hand as your whole face blossomed into joy.

A tiny "Uh-oh" drifted from the stairs. I rolled my eyes.

"Eleni, go to your room."

"Don't yell at your sister." You smiled as you got up, but it didn't spread farther than your lips.

"Yeah, don't yell at me." Eleni scrambled up the stairs.

"I'm going to read her that story." You kissed the top of my head and followed her up the stairs to her room.

I scooped up my fork and piled the last of my eggs into my mouth. Too excited to chew, I had to gulp half my juice to make them go down. It was really happening. I didn't care if the school was smaller or if their division was lower. In fact, it'd make playing less strenuous, and I could devote more time to my writing—and you, of course. It was actually perfect. We were going to make it perfect.

When you finished reading, I met you at the bottom of the stairs. I opened my arms and you folded yourself into them. I held you like that for a long time, smoothing your hair and kissing the top of your head. We said so much to each other without speaking a word. All our fears and hopes wrapped into that hug. In that moment, we would've done anything for each other. Moved states or mountains.

And that's why that night is one of my favorite memories. I knew you best in those moments, Mia.

And I would go through everything again just to feel the real you one more time.

Mia

I'VE GONE THROUGH SO MUCH, JUST TO SEE YOU ONE MORE TIME.
Now that I'm so close—blocks away—I don't know if I can take the last steps to get there. I'm curled up on a bench, and the phone in my pocket presses into my leg, the metal cold against me.

Besides Simi, Alfie's the only person who loves me for me and not what I do or represent for them. Second on the squad and holder of feet in the pyramid; the perfect daughter with the great GPA and fake smile. No matter how many times he made me laugh or held me so I felt safe, I pushed him away.

Would he still love me like that if he really knew me? Could anyone?

My mom and dad's marriage didn't implode overnight. There were years of erosion. A nail in a tire, slowly leaking air, and the more they tried to drive, the flatter it got. It looks like the tire's full when you go to bed, then flat in the morning when you wake up, but that's not how it really happens.

Every time I pushed Alfie away, I drove the nail deeper into our tire. How can I ask him to help me repair it? How can I ask him to forgive me when I can't forgive myself?

I want to feel softness again. I want to feel safe again.

I pull out my phone and press the on button. I stare at the light as the lock screen comes to life. The battery's at 9 percent. And bars! I suck in a breath.

My fingers immediately search for Alfie's name, then pause

when my brain catches up. I shift against the cold metal bench, my mouth hanging open at my own decision. Alfie is within walking distance, but she's a hundred miles away. I only have a tiny bit of battery left, and I need to make another call.

Trepidation slows my fingers, but they find the right contact buried deep in my call history. Chancing it, I dial the one number I never thought I would.

She answers in two rings.

"Hello?" Mom's voice is raspy and urgent.

I open my mouth to reply but suck in a small breath instead. The cold air stings the roof of my mouth and throat as I swallow it down.

"Mia?"

My back goes rigid. Just one word, my name, out of her lying mouth. All the times she judged what I ate or what I wore or who I talked to come flooding back. All the while lying and cheating herself. I slide the phone from my ear and press end.

I can't.

She ruined everything. Dad's gone. He took his suitcase and money and left me to pick up the pieces alone. She's too preoccupied with saving what little reputation she has left to notice how what she did changed my life forever.

I wonder how long it took her to realize I'd left. The idea that it might not have been immediate clenches my heart. I bite down on a sob, so it comes out a weird guffaw. I shake my head and tell myself not to cry, but the tears come anyway.

I had enough money in my birthday account for a bus ticket to San Francisco and to keep me going until I could find a job. I emptied out my savings, took the clothes I could carry, and left my debit card on my dresser. I wanted nothing from her. I still don't.

After hearing her voice, I know that for sure. Calling was a dumb idea, because this phone's the one thing I still keep from my old life, and she can probably figure out where I am.

I take in several breaths, forcing them out fast, one after the other.

Doesn't matter.

I thought all I needed was to find a job and a place to live, and things would be okay. I hadn't counted on Mother Nature messing everything up. Now there are no jobs. Not even places to live. I bet half the city's homeless for the foreseeable future. All I've wanted this whole time is the chance to tell Alfie how stupid I've been, but I can't bring myself to leave this bench.

Apparently, I'm my dad's daughter after all.

With a sigh, I drop my feet to the ground, hunch my shoulders, and drop my head on the back of the bench. But Mother Nature isn't ready to let go yet. The sky is still dark clouds of dust and ash with no stars in sight.

"Mia?"

I sit up straight. I know that voice.

"Is that you?"

Alfie

THE SKY IS STILL DARK CLOUDS OF DUST AND ASH WITH NO stars in sight. I'm so, so cold. I can't wait to hold you in my arms, Mia. If you would've let me, I'd have scooped you up right there in the coffee shop. Held you close. But you did what you always do. You ran.

I wish you could understand you never need to run from me. Just like that day at school. Like the late spring weather, your moods shifted from hopeful to gloomy for weeks. But the worst day was during Orthodox Holy Week. The day you didn't show until lunch.

Josuè had been trying to get Simi to laugh at his stupid jokes, but the more he tried, the more she ignored him. Chuck had already eaten and was talking with Coach in the corner about his new quest. He'd heard about that Ken Burns documentary and was on fire about the idea that baseball was the continuation of the Civil War and a way into civil rights.

He always seemed to need a cause and, through high school, we were it. He looked after the team. Now we were graduating, and we'd all be going different directions. He never complained about us not needing him next year, but once he saw that film, he had a new way to help people. He spent every lunch in Coach's office trying to learn more about it. I'm not an expert, but it seemed to me he was running from something more than running to help.

I was trying to finish the reading for English, but with Josuè flitting around and Chuck going on about segregation on the field, it was impossible.

I knew something was wrong as soon as you walked in. Puffy rings around your eyes competed with red blotches on your cheeks. You came straight to the table and put your head down.

"Mia, what happened? Are you okay?" I rubbed your back.

"Hey, what's going on?" Simi was there too, in full best-friend mode. She held your hand from across the table. Even Josuè and Chuck got quiet. ·

After a couple minutes, you took a deep breath and sat up, wiping at your eyes. I handed you one of the paper napkins left over from someone's lunch, and you wiped your whole face with it—something I'd never seen you do before.

"I actually left on time." You gestured to your face. "And I had makeup on and everything. As I was backing out of the driveway, I realized I forgot my phone, so I went back in to get it." Your breath hitched.

"Take your time," Simi said.

"My dad was rolling his suitcase out of the bedroom. The big one. And he had two more bags over his shoulders and his suit bag draped over his arm."

"Oh, Mia." I rubbed your back again, but you shifted away. I let my hand drop next to your leg in case you needed it.

"I asked him what was happening, and all he said was . . ." A sob escaped your throat, and fresh tears collected on your cheeks. "All he said was, 'She's your problem now.' And he walked out the back door."

You put your head down again as silent sobs racked your body. I leaned over you, draping my whole self over your back like a shield. Anger boiled in the back of my throat, and I'm sorry, but I had an overwhelming urge to punch Cow Palace Jeff right in the face for making you cry like that.

"Did he say why?" Simi's lips pinched together, and her eyes focused on some replay in her head like she was searching her memory for clues.

"No." You lifted your head and rested your chin on your crossed arms. "I've known something was off, but I didn't think it was a big deal. My mother is a lot, but Dad always seemed into it. I don't know."

I kept rubbing your back because I didn't know what else to do.

Just then, Madi walked in, her own face blotchy and swollen. She stopped at our table and stood across from you, staring. Simi wasn't having it.

"What do you want, Madi?" Simi stood, her normally kind eyes hard and arms crossed.

"Just wondering if Mia and I should decide on matching bed-spreads or not." Madi clutched her books to her chest. "What do you think? Do you want the top or bottom bunk?"

"What are you talking about?" You sat straight, your spine as rigid as your jaw.

"Your mom, my dad. Haven't you heard? We're going to be sisters."

"What is your problem, Madi?" You spit out her name like rotten fruit.

"My problem is that your whore of a mother has been sleeping with my dad for months. Apparently, when your dad found out, he reported it to the bishop. Now everyone's lives are ruined, but hey, at least we'll probably get to share a closet."

You fell back onto the bench, your eyes wild, searching for something inside yourself.

"Keep your voice down," Simi slashed at Madi.

"Why? The whole town knows. And now Mia does too." Madi turned to me. "If she's anything like her mother, you better watch out."

A piercing scream boiled up from inside you and, as it erupted, it took you with it. You stood, arms and back rigid, and you screamed in Madi's face. A primal, mortified sound echoing in the lunchroom on burrito day.

The entire room froze into a shocked tableau.

Madi backed away, her flippant expression turned ghostly. Finally, I knew what to do. I scooped you close to me and ushered you to the parking lot. As I let you go to unlock the door, you clawed at me.

I grabbed your arms, but you fought so hard.

"I don't need you to fight for me. I don't need you to fight for me." You said it over and over until it was a whisper. My heart flew into my throat as you beat it into oblivion. Then you were dragging us both to the ground, to our knees. You still clawed, but your swipes were weaker then, your voice a scratched record in between sobs. "I don't need you. I don't need you."

I realized you were no longer talking to me. You were lost in a place deep inside where your parents wounded you.

"I don't need you."

Once you were still, I lifted you into the cab, clicked on your seat belt, and drove you to the safest place I knew. I was where I needed to be. Where I thought I should be, anyway. I wanted to shield you from all that sadness and rage, but you needed somewhere to put it, and I had room. I let you give it to me.

• • •

I took the long way around town to our usual spot at the back of
the lake. This time, I didn't back in because we stayed in the cab.
By then you'd gone quiet. You stared at the water a long time. I
scooted to the middle part of the seat to get closer, and you put
your head on my shoulder.

"I'm sorry I hit you," you whispered.

"You didn't mean it."

"It was a shitty thing to do."

"I'll call the cops later." I kissed your hair and smoothed it back.

A long, slow breath escaped your racked body, and you relaxed
your full weight against my arm. I raised it and turned toward you
so you could rest against my chest.

"When I was little, I thought my parents were aliens. Did I
ever tell you that before?" You cleared your throat.

"No, I think I would've remembered that."

"I'd be downstairs playing, and I would hear them in their
room making these sounds I didn't understand. I knew it was
their alien language they spoke when I wasn't around. I'd look at
the family portrait on the wall and imagine what they looked like
without their human masks."

"Um, I don't think they were talking." An awkward laugh
escaped my throat.

"I know that now." You nudged me with your shoulder. "Or if
they were talking, it came through the walls jumbled, and I was
too young to figure it out."

"Did it scare you?"

"I don't think so, not really. I mean, my kid brain didn't think
about it that hard. I felt more alone than I did unsafe, if that
makes sense."

"Yeah, it makes sense." I stroked your hair and arms until your shaky breath turned steady and deep.

You were asleep on my shoulder. After a while, my eyes weighed heavy, and I drifted off too, listening to the sounds of your breath against the lapping of the lake.

Then you were shaking me and it was dark. The air turned icy, and steam clouds formed as I exhaled.

"Alfie, wake up. It's so late. I'm in so much trouble."

"Okay, give me a second to get my head together." I jerked myself awake and sat up, scooting behind the wheel. I started the engine and cranked the heater. You held your phone up and the light seared into my vision, causing little white dots to float every time I blinked.

"My mother called me fourteen times. I can't even count the texts." You slid down your seat. "I'm so fucked."

"You didn't do anything wrong. And after the morning you had and the crap at school, I'm sure she'll understand once you explain."

"I'm not explaining anything to her. This is her fault." Your fingers flew over the keyboard on your phone. "I'm telling her I'm on my way and that's it."

I didn't understand why you couldn't tell her what happened. Let her know we fell asleep after so much drama. Sure, she'd be mad because she was worried, but she'd ultimately understand. At least, that's what my mom would've done. Our families were night and day, though, so I stayed quiet, put the truck in drive, and punched the gas.

The lights were off in the front of your house, so we went through the back gate and in through the garage door. You flipped on the light, and your mom was hunched over the kitchen table, cradling a glass of wine. It was the only time I saw her without her makeup and hair done. She looked like a ghost.

"Where have you been?" Her words were slow and deliberate. "You cut school? Out doing who knows what with him? You little slut."

"Mrs. Clemen—" I said. But before I could finish, you put your hand up.

"Stay out of this." Your eyes were almost black.

I took a step behind you and crossed my arms. Sometimes the best shield is the one protecting your back. You stepped closer to her, but not close enough to touch.

"Yes, I cut school. Do you want to know why?" Your voice was molten lava spewing over an icy stream.

"Don't you talk to me like that." Your mom stood but took a second to find her balance. She teetered to the counter and filled her glass. "I am your mother, and you will show me some respect."

I tried thinking about my mother in this situation, if I were to ever talk to her in a way she didn't like. But then, she'd never do what your mom did. This entire exchange was as foreign to me as my family was to you at first. Except I couldn't imagine I would ever grow to love anything like this.

"Respect? That's hilarious. You fucked Pastor Tim and I'm the slut?"

"Mia, let's go upstairs." I tried to guide you gently toward the kitchen and the stairs leading to your room, but you dodged me. You spit out a bitter laugh while my eyes flitted from you to your mom.

"I'll be in my room. Don't bother me." You took my hand, and I could collect air in my lungs again. We could get through it. But instead of leading me upstairs, you took me to the front door.

"You don't want me to stay?" I searched your face in case your mouth and eyes told different stories.

"Not in this mess." You kissed my cheek. "I'll text you later, okay?"

Your eyes confirmed your words and I kissed you back.

"I love you," I said. You nodded and opened the door, but stayed silent. "Wow."

When I shut the door to my truck, my phone buzzed on the seat next to me. It was you.

Wow indeed.

Mia

CHIN-SUN APPEARS FROM THE SHADOWS AND TAKES THE SEAT
next to me, grocery bags crinkling in her arms. Dread takes hold
of my back muscles. The last thing I need is to disappoint more
people. A car rolls north, through the stop sign at the corner, and
turns onto another street.

"Where's your friend?" she asks.

Simi. A lump crowds my throat.

"She found some friends who could help her get in touch with
her family." I don't have the energy—or the nerve—to hold her
gaze. Not after I interrupted Chin-Sun's prayer and embarrassed
my best friend. My eyes travel to the ground in front of us.

"Did you lose your blanket?" She drops the bags by her feet.
She sighs, but it's more of a moan, the kind Alfie's dad makes when
he sits down. My hand goes to my collar.

"Oh, no. I gave it to a woman who needed it more than me."

"I knew you were a good girl." She rests her hand on my knee.

I cringe at the expression.

I've always hated that phrase—*good girl*. Growing up, being a
good girl always meant doing what other people wanted. Ignoring
things I wanted and silencing the things I wanted to say for the
sake of others.

Chin-Sun sits quietly. When I don't respond, she moves her
hand to her lap and folds it with the other. Another car passes by,
headed south this time. A few minutes later, it passes by again,

going the opposite way. I can't take the quiet. I shift on the bench to face her.

"I'm sorry I was rude earlier. Sometimes I have a hard time expressing myself." I tilt my chin down and she holds up a hand.

"I take no offense. I wanted to help, and if my words weren't doing that, then they needed to stop."

I take in a sharp breath. No one has ever said prayer might not be helpful to me before. I was always the bad guy for not wanting to go through the ordeal. Like reliving my good deeds and desires out loud was the worst thing a person could do.

"I've never thought about it like that," I say.

"Anyone who truly wants to help"—she shakes her finger the way grandmas do—"will listen to the person asking and give them what they need. Not what the person helping wants."

A light flickers inside me, and my breath quickens. Help the way people need, not the way you need. Yes. It made total sense. I study her face, smooth with tiny wrinkles around her eyes—the best kind, according to Simi's mom.

"What about people who don't know what kind of help they need?" I ask. Chin-Sun tilts her head toward mine, a sly smile on her lips.

"I suspect you already know the answer to that." She pats my leg. "But there's a fine line, and the only way to know the difference is to listen."

Instead of putting her hand to her ear like I thought she might, she puts it over her heart.

Oh.

"Did you find your friend, the boy?" she asks. I clear the rusty silence from my throat.

"Not exactly." The lump that's taken up residence in my throat grows larger.

She says nothing. Instead, she pulls her folded hands to her chest and rests her chin on top. To my surprise, I want to tell her why I'm stuck here sitting on this bench.

"I found out where he is, but I can't quite make myself go." My head turns south, as if I could see him waiting if I looked hard enough. "He's down that way somewhere, and I'm terrified that if I show up, he won't want to see me. Not really."

"What does *Not really* mean?"

"Beyond the polite *How have you been?* and *Wow, that earthquake, huh?* conversation, he'll make an excuse to have to get back to work and that'll be that. I'll have walked across this entire city searching for him, freezing, surviving on snack food from strangers, for nothing. I'll still have nowhere to live, no job to go to, no one to love me back."

I say those last words, and my throat closes around them. I shove the pain deep into my soul. I deserve to carry the heaviness of their pain with me for a long time. Maybe forever.

"Do you love him?" Her own words are quiet and careful.

"Does it matter? Devi—the woman I gave the blanket to—loved once, and now she's alone. My parents loved each other once, at least I think they did. Now they live to destroy each other. And it's my fault." I can't choke back the pain anymore. Tears slide down my cheeks, leaving icy tracks in their wake.

"What's your fault?"

"My parents. Their divorce. I was always in trouble at church and in Sunday school. My mom was in the pastor's office every five minutes. If I'd been a better person, they'd never have been together so much. They never would've cheated."

"Oh honey, I can't speak for them and why they chose that path, but I know one hundred percent that you are not to blame for anyone cheating on someone else. We are only responsible for our own actions."

I scoff.

"Not in my house. Growing up, respect meant fear, and love meant doing what people expect of you. Love isn't always enough."

"Real love is always enough, my dear." She reaches her arm around my shoulders, and I slowly give in, leaning my head on hers. "What you're describing is intimidation. Real love isn't about feeling. It's about doing. We are called to serve others, make sure they have what they need. You see me outside giving water and blankets to people who need them. That's my way of loving people." She pokes my shoulder with the hand draped over me. "And you giving your blanket to that woman. That's you loving people too."

I think about Devi's sweet smile. Maybe what she remembers of Barbara and her tree is enough for her. Maybe me not running away the second I have an uncomfortable feeling is love too.

My heart wrings out like an old rag.

Maybe I could show up for Alfie. Or for Simi, if she'd still let me. Maybe showing up is enough.

An aftershock rumbles through the ground. Loose bricks from a building across the street tumble onto a parked car below, smashing its front windshield. The sounds of bricks hitting glass and grinding metal turns my stomach.

I sit straight and dry my face with shaky, frozen hands.

"Are you okay?" My voice trembles.

"I'm fine. And you will be too." She smiles, and I smile in return. A real smile. The kind that comes from inside.

The way I smiled with Alfie. All those times he showed up for me. From the camellias to the letter. Maybe it's my turn to do that for him.

"Now, that's a smile."

I study her face and settle in the confidence of her words. She bounces her head in little nods as her lips spread wide. Something breaks inside me, and words rush out of me faster than I can think them. I tell her about Alfie's day of flowers and our first date at the Dickens Fair and how he followed my float around an entire parade to make sure I had fun. I tell her about our kiss that landed on the front page of the town's paper and my mom's cold indifference to it.

I tell her about Madi and how she made sure I felt stupid for wearing a tiara when I wasn't on the court, and the time she humiliated me in the cafeteria by telling everyone about her dad and my mom's affair. And after that, I couldn't look anyone there in the eye anymore. It's why I had to leave.

I tell her how I ended up here, on this bench late at night, with only a sweatshirt and a nearly dead phone. The truth about Simi this time.

My body feels lighter with each name I let go.

Fresh tears threaten my stinging eyes as I finally go quiet. She says nothing. Just wraps her arms around me and lets me shake, my own aftershocks racking my body as I sob.

In the distance, a low rumble explodes into thunder and an alarm screams.

I wipe my nose with my sleeve and turn to look. A cloud

of murky dust mushrooms against the blackened sky like chalk pounded out of erasers.

And my heart—the one part of me I finally am beginning to understand—stops.

However angry Mother Nature was, she's not done yet.

Alfie

FOR DAYS, YOU SULKED LIKE A CLOUD OF MURKY DUST BLACK-
ened your skies. You hadn't heard from your dad at all since the
morning you saw him with his suitcases. You barely spoke to your
mom, and if you did, it was only out of pure necessity.

I hope that's changed.

I was so glad you agreed to come to church with us that week.
You looked stunning in your black skirt and heels. The purple in
your top made your eyes a deep brown.

Holy Week is my absolute favorite holiday, even if we have to
follow a strict fast. True, there's a ton of services and some of them
are really long, but the chanting and stories are so beautiful. It's
like we're walking around in a trance, reliving the stories from so
long ago. I wanted to share it with you.

Sometimes Greek Easter is on a different day than the one
other American Christians celebrate. The Orthodox Church uses
the old calendar and makes sure it's always after Passover. Greeks
are super serious about this because to us, it's the holiest time of
the year. Even more than Christmas.

Plus, we love buying all our Easter candy at 50 percent off.
Everyone wins. And lucky you: you got two Easters! I hoped this
one would be way better than the one you had at home.

When we walked into the church for the first time, your eyes
went everywhere at once, and I got to experience everything for
the first time through you. I took your hand and led you to the

icon of the Theotokos decorated with flowers in the middle of the room.

"We kiss her and say *thank you*." I did my cross and venerated the icon to show you. "You don't have to."

But you did your cross anyway.

"Isn't that kind of germy, everyone's mouths on the same picture?" You scrunched your face into a question.

"We don't talk about that." I winked and your shoulders loosened.

I showed you how to light a candle and where we usually sat. Mama opened the book and pointed where to follow along in English and the pages that explained why things are done in a certain way. I only hoped you weren't overwhelmed.·

I had to go to the altar, but I peeked at you when I could. Anna pointed things out in the book and modeled what to do when the priest came out with the holy water and incense.

Your face was all concentration and keeping up until the prayers to the Holy Mother started.

We prayed to her for assistance and guidance, asking her to help us find peace, to be the mother to all.

I swung the incense in front of Father as he read the prayers, and snuck a look at you. This time, you weren't trying to keep up.

You were inside that place you go, the one where you battle yourself. You stared at the floor, but I knew you saw something else. Tears fell from your eyes onto the pages of the book you held, and you squeezed them shut. Without missing a beat, Mama put her arm around your shoulder.

Seeing you in so much pain and Mama comforting you while you cried as you both prayed to the Virgin Mary, I worried that my heart wasn't big enough to hold all of it. You grieved for your mom while mine tried to make it hurt less. And above all, the Mother of God embraced all of it. All of you. All of us.

The light surrounding you in that moment shone golden, like the halo the Virgin wears in her icon as she holds the Baby Jesus.

You stayed silent on the car ride home. Mama fed us a late Lenten dinner of tomatoes and rice stew, and then I drove you to your house.

"Our church barely even acknowledges Virgin Mary," you said. "Yours has an entire service devoted to her."

"More than one, actually."

"It was beautiful." You inhaled a shaky breath.

"Becoming a convert?" I was grateful to be able to tease you a little.

"I can't say that, but I like the idea of a mother watching over us like her children. There's something safe in that."

I heard the irony in your voice, even if you didn't mean to speak it.

As we pulled up to the curb, your dad was carrying a box down the porch stairs and loading it into his trunk. You nearly jumped out of the truck before I had it parked.

"Dad!" You ran to him and threw your arms around his shoulders.

"Hey." He hugged you back, but he was clearly distracted. "Alfie." He nodded to me as I shut the driver's-side door. I returned the motion but said nothing.

"Are you home?" you asked. "Because you shouldn't forgive her. She ruined everything, and I want to come with you. We should leave her to be alone."

We'd heard through school gossip that Madi's dad was transferred across the country. The entire family moved a week after everything came out. I'd heard the church even paid for them to leave as soon as possible. At that point, your mom had no one.

"Look, Mia," your dad said. "I know you want to go to that school in New York. But after everything that's happened, I just don't think it's wise."

"What? No."

"Listen to me," he said. "I looked it up, and Liberty has a fine journalism program complete with state-of-the-art studios and equipment. With all this disruption, you're going to need the Lord more than ever."

"Dad, I can't go there!" You were practically screaming. "Please!"

"If you want my help, that's where you'll go." He kissed you on the forehead and backed away. "I'll pray for you, honey."

Then he was in his car, backing out of the driveway, and driving away. He honked at the corner, turned right, and disappeared.

"Mi." I stood behind you, waiting for you to react in some way. But you stared at the corner, unable to move forward. "Maybe this is more complicated that we thought. He doesn't seem all that upset, you know? Your mom . . . Have you asked her about what really happened?"

You moved then. You whipped around so fast, I thought time might skip a few seconds.

"I don't need to ask her anything. She knows what she did. I know all I need to." You flipped around and stomped by your mom standing on the porch in a satin robe, holding a half-drunk glass of wine. She grabbed your arm.

"He never loved either of us, you know. Not really."

"That's a lie." You bared your teeth as you said it.

"We were a means to an end. A picture to frame for the office."

"This is your fault." You ripped your arm away from her and disappeared into the house.

"We've all made mistakes." With a glance toward me, she turned and followed you inside, shutting the door and leaving me in the street feeling helpless.

Later that night, Baba knocked on my door and wanted to talk, which as you know, is typically terrifying. If Baba is talking, someone is in trouble. But that night, he sat at my desk and waited until I put down my phone. I'd never seen anyone talk to another person the way your mom talked to you. And to be honest, I was a little more than shocked at the way you talked to her. I didn't know what to say or how to help, so I stared at my screen, waiting to see if you'd text me back, but you were silent.

"You know Mama and I are proud of you—right, Alfie?" he said.

"I know, Baba."

"I don't say it a lot, I know." He raised his arms and turned his head. "It's not easy for me. You do good, you play good, and you made good friends." Emotion blurred his words as he wiped his eyes.

"Baba, you don't have to. I know, thank you." I blinked away my own tears.

"Let me say what I came to say, okay?"

I nodded.

"Your coach . . ." He cleared his throat. "He says you can really play in the big leagues, huh? That's an opportunity not everyone gets. I know you want to write your poetry and books, but just maybe, you could do both." He shrugged in his Baba way.

"I don't know." Talking about all that confused me. I wanted so much to be with you in New York, but it seemed like that might fall apart too. "It would be kind of cool to see what happens."

"Mia is a good girl. Mama and I like her very much." He patted my knee. "She will be so proud of you on a big fancy team while you write those fancy words." He winked, stood up, and closed my door as he left.

I've known my entire life that my dad loved me. He loved all of us more than anything, which is why he worked so hard every day. I know it broke his heart when he realized I didn't want the life he expected me to have. For him to come into my room and tell me how proud he was of not only my abilities but also my choices, it felt . . . bigger than me.

His blessing unlocked something inside me I'd been hiding, even from myself. The more I let myself feel it, the more I wanted to.

But I wouldn't let myself be pulled all the way under. Not until I talked to you.

Alfie

Me: I wish you'd answer me.

You: I'm here.

Me: Aha.

You: Aha?

Me: Yes. Aha.

You: Is that aha like you've discovered who killed the butler in the pantry with the butter knife?

Me: No. Aha!

You: You're glad I'm here?

Me: Yes! The whole aha loses its meaning without the exclamation. Lost in translation, if you will.

You: Okay.

Me: That's all I get? Okay? I'm trying my best to be charming over here. Working up a linguistic sweat.

You: I'm sorry. I'm just not up for charming.

Me: Hey Mi?

You: Yeah.

Me: Do you think we should look at journalism programs closer to home? Maybe San Francisco?

You: Can we talk later?

Me: Of course. I'm at your beck and call. (Did you know it was beck AND call and not beckon call? I learn so much at that public school of ours.)

You: Wow.

Me. It's just that I still have that offer from USF, and if your dad isn't helping . . .

You: I'm going to Sarah Lawrence. I get it if you want to take that offer. It's amazing.

Me: It could be amazing for us both.

You: I'm not staying here.

Me: OK, but can we please talk about all of this soon? I love you and I told you a long time ago, I'd follow you to the end of the world.

Me: Mi?

Me: Wow indeed.

If only I'd known how serious you were, how close I was to losing you. What was coming. I would've done everything differently.

To Mia Clementine,

It has come to our attention that the initial
housing deposit has not been paid and is
now overdue. Please remit payment as soon
as possible. If not paid by the final date, we
cannot guarantee placement in school housing.
If you have any questions, please contact us at
SLHousing@sarahlawrence.edu.

Thank you in advance,

The Finance and Housing Offices Team

Alfie

I STOOD IN THE STREET WAITING FOR YOU SO WE COULD GO TO graduation practice together, but you never showed. At first I thought maybe I hadn't spotted you before because they had us bussed to the university auditorium alphabetically. You were on the *A–L* bus, and I rode the *M–Z*. But when you didn't stand after they called your name for roll, I knew you weren't there.

You didn't miss much, honestly. A couple of guys from the football team ran naked across the stage, and security chased them around the bleachers for a while. Mostly it was pretty boring watching everyone practice standing and sitting at the same time.

You'd think people who survived high school would be better at that.

Chuck and I entertained ourselves by playing paper football. He knew how to fold the paper into a perfect triangle that, when flicked properly, would sail over at least two rows of graduates.

"How's Mia holding up?" he asked.

"She won't respond to any of my texts. And she's not here, so I'm guessing not good." I flicked my football toward your empty chair.

"You don't think she wants to break up, do you?" He flashed me an apologetic grin, then ripped a page from his math notes and began the process of turning it into a flying triangle. "The USF offer is dope, dude."

"She's just pissed at her parents. She'll come around."

"Josuè and I were talking about it, and even he thinks you

should accept. To play on a team where the head coach is already thinking about where you'll go next is not something that happens for everyone." He flicked his triangle at Josuè, who was in the row behind us. He caught it and tipped his chin back.

"Do it, bro," he said.

"You know who was your biggest fan and would be flipping out if he was around to see this for you," Chuck said.

"Bro, are you seriously playing your brother card right now? That's below the belt, man." I shook my head.

"I'm just saying." He lifted a fresh triangle and primed his middle finger behind his thumb; then Coach's voice boomed behind us.

"Thanasis! Since you and your catcher love to play ball so much, you two will stay behind to clean up your mess."

"Yeah, Alfie, stop playing with your balls," Josuè shouted. Everyone around us cracked up. Even Coach turned away with a smile on his face. Chuck folded his last triangle into his pocket and crouched in his chair.

"Thanks, bro," I said.

"Just saying."

After the powers that be threatened us with fines and with-holding our diplomas if we weren't on time the following day, they finally let us go. The sun hung low in the sky as my stomach reminded me it was close to dinner. I took a chance and texted you that I was picking up sushi and ice cream to take to the lake and to be ready in twenty minutes.

When I got there, I texted you, but instead of coming out, you asked me to go around back.

You sat at the table in the yard, the umbrella overhead shad-ing your face. The grass reached my ankles as I walked toward you, and from the look of the weeds in the flower beds, the gardeners hadn't been there for a while. As I approached, you lifted your cheek and I kissed it, although your eyes stayed stationed on the ground. I sat opposite and laid out the sushi on the table.

"Should I put the ice cream in the freezer?" I motioned to the house.

"Put it in the little one in the garage." Your voice hit me like hail on pavement, choppy and hard.

"Are you all right? I was worried when you didn't come to practice."

"I couldn't do it. Be around all those people, knowing they know. And no one's coming to watch me anyway."

"My family will be there." I set everything on the table and dragged my chair next to yours, sliding your California roll closer to you. "You should eat something. Get your strength."

"You sound like your mom." A small smile slid up one side of your face, and a tiny light flickered in my chest.

"She does say that, doesn't she?" I picked up a piece of your roll and handed it to you. Then I picked up one of my own. "To us surviving high school."

You let my hand touch yours in the toast, but you didn't reciprocate. You just put the piece in your mouth and chewed. I followed suit.

After a few chews, I had to spit it out.

"Sorry, that was gross." I downed half my water. "All I can see is my yia-yia sucking the eyeballs out of a fish head." I shivered.

"Why did you get eel, then?" A little more life appeared around your eyes.

"I didn't know what to get, so I asked the guy to give me his favorite. How was I to know he was deranged?"

"Well, thank you for getting me my favorite. Even if you don't like it."

The sun shifted in the sky, and the umbrella's shadow moved with it. Light reflected off your hair, giving it red and gold strands. I reached out to stroke it.

"I will always bring you sushi in your time of need. I love you." I slid my hand down your arm and clasped your fingers. I started to bring your hand to my lips for a kiss, but you pulled away.

"Did you turn down USF's offer?" You stared at the floor.

It was then I noticed the dark circles under your eyes, how pale you'd gotten. Even your hair, as beautiful as it was, lay tangled over your shoulders. I bent down to your line of sight, and you turned your head.

"Can you look at me?" My heart was in my throat. I'd never seen you this way. Not this bad.

"Did you?" You turned and your eyes flashed from fire to ice, searching my face for an answer. I swallowed hard, knowing what I had to say.

"Mi, we should talk about New York now that everything's changed." My voice was a whisper.

A wall clamped down behind your eyes. The thud landed in my heart.

I closed my eyes, sending urgent messages to every molecule in my body to pray that you weren't going to say it. Because it made no sense. Zero. We were everything together. We had a plan.

When I opened my eyes, you were staring at me like a knife had pierced your heart. I shook my head and held my breath, willing you, begging you, not to say it.

"I think we should break up."

"What? Why?" The earth could've opened up and swallowed me whole.

Water gathered in the corners of your eyes, and one tear slid down your cheek. The way heroines always cry in the movies. Stoic and brave while making a sacrifice.

Except what you were sacrificing was me and you.

"I'm leaving soon and you're obviously staying here. And there's no point dragging anything out if it's not going to last." You stood and started wrapping up the leftover food.

My legs shook, but I managed to stand too.

"You don't mean that." I tried touching your arm, but you backed away. "Yeah, things are bad right now, but you have me. And Anna and Eleni and my mom. It will get better. People will forget."

With a sarcastic huff, you hurdled the back stairs and let yourself into the kitchen nook. Tears flowed freely now, for both of us. I swiped at mine as fast as they came.

"You're hurting, and I get it." I followed you. "Let me be here for you." My voice creaked like the wooden floors beneath our feet.

"We're breaking up, Alfie." You leaned against the large oak table in the middle of the room, like you couldn't even hold yourself up while you said that out loud.

"No, you're not thinking straight right now."

"Don't tell me what I'm thinking!" You exploded into a storm of fury and tears. "I know what I'm thinking, and unless you're coming to New York, we're ending this."

"Dammit, Mia, I want to go with you. Of course I do!" Anger salted my voice.

"Really?" You actually seemed shocked. Like I wouldn't move heaven for you if you asked me to. I took a deep breath and wiped my face with my sleeve.

"Why would you even ask? I always want to be with you."

Then your mouth was on mine, briny and wet. Your hands on my neck, crushing me into you. Backing up, you pulled me onto you as you lay on the table. You pressed hard, scraping teeth and scratching skin. I gave as much back until you pushed me off and stood breathless in front of me.

My head spun as I tried to keep up. First we were breaking up. Then you were kissing me. I opened my mouth and closed it again. You stood against the wall, chest heaving.

I took a long breath and sat up. I ran my hands through my hair and waited until you'd look at me. It was probably only a minute, but those seconds passed like an eternity.

"We need to think about things. Make a plan. Look at programs around here that you can afford." I rubbed my bruised lips together and wiped the tears staining my face.

"What?" Your voice was harsh and broken at the same time.

"Be realistic, Mi."

The way you looked at me felt foreign, like you were noticing me for the first time. Like that day with the golf cart. Your look you reserved for strangers.

Fresh tears stung my eyes. I wiped at them, but you pushed my hands away from my face, daring me to try again. I lifted them only to have you push them away again. Then you stared me down while your hands ripped at my belt.

"Stop." I put my hands on yours.

You threw my hands off and tried again. I stepped backward so I was almost out the door.

"Mia, I said stop!" I blew out a half-panicked breath. "What are you doing?"

"You said you wanted to be with me. So be with me." Defiance flared in your eyes, daring me to prove you right.

"That's not what I meant and you know it."

"Then get out. If you won't be with me when I need you, then I don't need you!"

"Don't do this." I couldn't move. I'd never seen you like this. So obviously not yourself.

"Get out!" You screamed it over and over until I backed out the door and shut it behind me. I went straight to my truck, passing the sushi and ice cream, letting it rot in the sun.

Once the engine was started, I cranked the air and pulled out my phone.

I know you need time, and I'm going to give it to you. But we can't end like this. Not after everything. You owe me at least that.

I saw you one more time, but I wish I hadn't. Because what happened almost broke me.

Mia

AFTER I STOP HICCUPPING AND SHAKING, CHIN-SUN ASKS IF I think a prayer might help. I'm hesitant, but I say yes.

She's on her feet, eyes closed, mouth muttering. This prayer isn't like the one she said earlier. It's more intense, darker. A familiar dread pulls at my insides as she prays. It almost breaks me.

Muffled shouting echoes off the broken buildings. She pauses for a moment and offers her hand.

"Pray with me? Only if you're comfortable."

I don't mind. I get it, I really do. Don't like something? Pray about it. Someone's bugging you? Give it to God. It's something that's never worked for me and something that's been forced on me in every aspect of my life.

I can't reconcile how psychology says I own my thoughts and feelings, yet I'm supposed to give them to some magical being who will morph them into thoughts someone else believes I should think or feel.

"I'm okay with just listening to you. I appreciate you for it, though." I offer a smile, although it's dark enough now that I'm not sure she can see it.

The breeze grows into a wind that shifts direction. Ash and smoke linger under my nose. The sound of another brick crashes into metal, probably the hood of the now-ruined car. It makes me jump.

"Did you ever believe?" Her weight shifts on the bench next to mine as she sits again.

"I don't know about *believe*, but there was this one time, at my boyfriend's church." I think back to the Holy Week service Alfie took me to. The one with prayers to the Virgin Mary. Hearing all those people ask for her to intercede, show compassion for their shortcomings. There was a humbleness about it I'd never felt before. "But it wasn't real. It was all a metaphor."

Sirens wail behind us more than a few blocks away. I try to not think about them and why they're going off, but my blood flows faster anyway. They grow louder as Chin-Sun contemplates what I said, her expression serious. I blow out a breath.

"That's the quiet part." She squeezes my hand, then pats it in that grandma way. "Your heart heard the truth. People have a hard time saying the quiet part out loud, and that's okay. That's why we have other ways of speaking. Of saying what we really mean. The truth always lies within the metaphor. And the metaphor speaks directly to this." She presses my hand into my chest, directly over my heart.

Listen.

"But what if I get it wrong?" My voice shakes, but it's the kind of tremble that happens when truth stands in front of you, demanding to be understood.

"Hear with your heart, and there is no such thing." She picks up her bags. They crinkle as she adjusts them on her hips. "Ask yourself if a teenage girl can make her mother have an affair. Or make her father end his own marriage. See what your heart says."

When I look at it like that, it seems almost silly of me to think I had any say in why my parents do anything. I was so busy worrying about how they messed up my life that I never thought about how messed up their lives were too. I can't remember a dinner where Mom didn't nag about something or Dad didn't make

Mom's contributions seem small. Like she should be grateful she was allowed to live in his house and cook and clean for him. No wonder they tried so hard to make everything look perfect all the time.

It was anything but.

I stand and follow Chin-Sun as she ambles toward home.

"Thank you," I say. I mean it. The kind of thank-you that's real, where a soul sees another. She winks.

"Start walking and listen. You'll know which way to go."

I hug her goodbye one last time and head south, one footstep at a time.

I close my eyes and listen.

All this time I hid the real me from everyone, even myself. I thought I was real with Alfie. And, of course, Simi. But even then, there were things too painful to face. I was too afraid that people wouldn't see what I was supposed to be, but everyone found out anyway. Alfie and Simi didn't care. They loved me anyway. I just didn't love myself. Not the way they deserve.

Or the way I do.

Hand on my heart, I listen harder.

Footsteps on pavement.

The whirling wail of sirens.

Cinder crashing on cement somewhere not too far away.

I hear it.

Loving someone isn't a feeling. It's about showing how you feel. How you show up.

I know what I need to do.

I open my eyes and walk faster. Faster and faster until I'm almost running.

Toward Alfie. Toward love.

Alfie

Josuè: Listen up bitches, the longest night of the year is coming up and y'all are going to show up at my place to celebrate the fact that we fucking made it

Josuè: Leave all your drama shit at home and let's party until we don't remember any of it anyway

Josuè: Mia, I won't take no for an answer

Simi: She'll be there

Josuè: You're coming, too, right?

Simi: Are you finally asking me out on a proper date?

Chuck: 👀

Josuè: Damn, woman way to out me, but yeah. Let's do it

Simi: Sounds fun!

Chuck: Hell yeah bro I'm there

Mia: Okay

Alfie: You know me. I'll be there.

It took you three days to reply. I couldn't respond until you did because if I said I was going and you didn't show, I knew it would've been my fault.

So I waited.

Sometimes those three little dots would appear under your name and then disappear just as fast. You'd judge me so hard if you knew I kept opening the group text to see if you were answering. It was the only connection I had to you that week, so go ahead and roll your eyes if you want. I'd do it again.

Just maybe not be as pathetic about it.

Besides, I wanted to try to convince you that we had time to figure things out. I wanted to bring you the camellia I picked from the last of the spring bloom, even though its edges were rusted with the promise of a hot summer.

I told you once that I loved camellias because they defy the winter—they are beauty in the midst of earth's despair. To me, they are hope incarnate.

That's why the rusty parts didn't matter.

I did everything I could to keep that flower fresh for you. Wrapped it in wax paper and stored it in the fridge. Misted the edges and hand-soaked the stem.

I try to forget where it landed that night, after what happened. All that work, for nothing.

All that hope, rusting in the dirt.

Mia

I RUN PAST THE WAR-TORN STOREFRONTS TO THE PANHANDLE, the broken pieces of metal and glass rusting in the dirt. In the park, I jump fallen branches and tipped-over trees. I dodge abandoned fruit carts and recycling bins left on the sidewalk. This time, I don't wait for the frat guys to tell the cars to stop. They honk, but they're going slow enough for me to weave my way through to the other side.

I can finally hear it. The voice I've silenced so many years, pushing it away, convincing myself it doesn't matter. And the more I listen, the louder it gets.

I stop running when I see a small alley in between two taller buildings. I duck into the dark, cover my mouth, and scream. I scream from somewhere low and primal in my body. Over and over. With every breath and push and shriek, I hear myself. And it's going to be okay.

When I'm done, I keep running toward the mess.

A couple of blocks ahead, emergency red and blue lights whirl and yellow arrows slide across the backs of police cars. Right where I need to go.

I slow down. The fuzz inside the heels of my boots is all but gone now, and my ankles sting from the seams rubbing against the tender spots underneath the bones. I stop in front of a large cathedral that practically takes up the entire block. Its steps lead to two large, wooden doors that remind me of the ones at Alfie's church.

After the service for the Virgin, I went back with his family for the Holy Friday one. At that one, they take the icon of Jesus down from the altar and place it in a tomb decorated with flowers from top to bottom. The entire congregation, led by the priest and all the altar boys, walks a funeral pilgrimage around the outside of the church. When they reach the doors, they lift the tomb high over their heads so as the people reenter the church, it's like they're walking into the tomb too. It's supposed to be a metaphorical sealing of the tomb that doesn't open until Easter morning.

Today I feel like I'm the tomb, and the earthquake shook open the part of me I'd sealed away. I'm alive and I love Alfie and I'm coming. I'll be there soon.

I shove my toes as far forward into my boots as I can and run toward the lights. I'll figure out what to do when I get there.

As I approach, a police officer puts up his hand. His bulk looms like a shadow between two police cars.

"This area's off-limits, ma'am." He rests his hands on his belt. "Too dangerous."

"I have to get in there. My friend . . ." My heart drops into my stomach. I can't have come this far to only come this far.

"Is being looked after by search and rescue." He softens the bark in his voice. "I'm sorry, but there's a lot of damage here. It's best you go back the way you came and wait for news."

His words take the breath right out of me, and all of a sudden I'm looking at him down a long tunnel. I take deep breaths and blink until my vision returns to normal and search for any place I might get in. I need to see for myself.

Behind him, the corner building tilts into the street, its entire bottom floor crumpled into a pile of oversized Legos. It leans so far, the second-story corner window lies dented and smashed in the middle of the road. The house to its right is nothing but scraps. Its broken roof covering the insides like a cake frosted too soon. The building behind it sits perfectly fine. Fire hoses snake through the bike lanes as firefighters call out for survivors.

Every inch of me hopes Alfie is one of them.

Alfie

YOU KNOW THAT PART IN HAMILTON WHERE ANGELICA SINGS "I remember that night" over and over? I swear that's been playing in my head since, well, that night. Because Angelica and I have something in common—regret.

I was late getting to Josuè's party because I had to pick up Simi. You should've been the one to bring her. She needed you to help psych her up. She was so nervous about seeing Josuè in a date kind of way, and I couldn't give her the kind of support she needed from you, her best friend. But you'd already cut yourself off from everyone.

It'd been a week since graduation, the day you told me you didn't want to be with me anymore. I knew you didn't mean it. I knew it then, and I know it now.

Before you go and get all *A woman knows her own mind*, I don't mean it that way. You weren't yourself. Simi saw it. I saw it. Everyone did, except you.

You were too busy unraveling all the work you'd done to get where you wanted to go.

We only wanted to help you see, and you punished us for it. But more than us, you punished yourself. And that's why I say you didn't mean it. You pushed everyone who loved you away.

"Thanks for the ride, Alfie."

As I backed up my truck and parked next to the levee, Simi took in the bonfire from where you normally sat. She twisted her palms in circles against each other.

I turned off the motor, and the early summer heat pressed the cool recycled air out of the cab. A heaviness settled in my lungs, and I sucked in a breath in protest. I wasn't going to let us end like this. Not after the bangers and mash at the Dickens Fair, the kiss at the light parade, the nights at the lake.

We deserved better.

"You ready for this?" Simi unlatched her seat belt and took a deep breath of her own.

"There's only one way to find out."

Cupping the camellia I brought for you, I took a last breath of the chilled air. As we climbed out of the truck, someone shouted my name from behind. I turned toward the levee and gave a generic wave to the shadows on the ledge. One thing about the country—there's no streetlights to keep out the pitch black when the sun goes down.

Simi and I made our way through the handful of people lingering on the outskirts of the property toward the large, hollowed-out firepit in the middle of the freshly cleared field.

"I don't see Josuè." Simi's eyes darted from one group to the next. "Do you think he changed his mind?"

"Relax." I squeezed her arm. "After he finally got you to say yes? He's probably getting something from the house."

She nodded but didn't say anything. She needed her best friend, not me. She needed you, Mia.

We both needed you.

My heart twisted into something strange and unrecognizable in that moment. How could I be so hurt, so hopeful, so angry, and so in love all at the same time?

"I don't see Mia either." Simi gave me a gentle smile like she could see everything going on inside.

"Her car's over there." I nodded to the driveway on the other side of the field. "She's around."

Voices laughed and shouted from the levee. People from school scattered around the open space while others leaned against the big wooden fence rails along the property line. A couple of guys from the team played beer pong on the patio. Woodsmoke swirled through the early summer air.

We made our way to the firepit, where Chuck was staring into the flames, lost in thought and holding a full Solo cup of beer. Josuè's dad was a *Don't ask, don't tell* kind of parent. When he had a party, his mom and dad turned in early.

"Hey." I patted Chuck on the back, and he blinked back to reality.

"You made it." He smiled.

"Have you seen Josuè?" Simi asked.

"Hi, Simi," he said.

"Sorry, hi." Her face reddened. "I guess I'm nervous."

"Yeah, you're sort of jumping into the deep end dating Josuè, aren't you?" Chuck asked.

"Dude, way to calm her down." I smacked his arm.

"I'm just saying . . ."

"It's okay." Simi's rosy hue turned putrid, and she shivered despite the warmth of the blazing fire.

"He's a good guy. I'm playing around." Chuck nodded toward the fence by the driveway. "He was over there the last time I saw him."

"Have you seen Mia?" I asked. Chuck faced me.

"Are you sure you want to see her?"

"What kind of question is that?" I narrowed my eyes. "Of course I want to see her."

"I guess I'm asking if you think she wants to see you." His voice dripped with the same tone he used on the field, patient and way too condescending for my rapidly growing irritation. "Maybe you should give her some space."

"She's had a week to figure things out. We need to talk."

"You need to talk."

"Dude. Yeah, I need to talk. To her," I said. Someone threw a log onto the fire, sending sparks into the air. Chuck sucked his teeth and shook his head. "We need to sort this out before the entire summer is over." Before you left for Sarah Lawrence, but I didn't say that.

"You two will work it out." Simi stepped closer, offering a reassuring smile.

"Maybe you need to think about more than just yourself," Chuck said. "Maybe you aren't the only one with problems."

I drew in a breath like he'd punched me in the gut. Chuck never talked like that. He was the calm one, even when it pissed me off.

"You okay, man?" I softened my voice. Chuck ran his hand through his hair.

"My brother would've been sixteen today." He stared into the flames.

"Shit, I'm sorry." I stared into the flames too. Supergood friend, right? I'd been so caught up in me and you, I forgot about the anniversary of his brother's death. At least this explained his sudden need to jump into help mode again. "Seizures suck ass, man."

"They fucking do."

"Yes, they fucking do," Simi said.

Chuck and I both turned to her. You know she hardly ever cusses. Simi pointed to Chuck's cup.

"Are you going to drink that? Because you've been holding it a long time and you haven't touched it. But if you want it, you should totally have it." She blew out a breath, closed her mouth, and waited.

Chuck raised his eyebrows and handed her the cup, his mouth twitching into a grin, despite the grim subject. Simi took the cup and downed half in two gulps. After a breath, she downed the rest.

I was always impressed by the amount of food she could put away. It shouldn't have surprised me she could drink like that too.

A few more people found their way to the firepit. A guy from the team sat in one of the Adirondacks and pulled his girlfriend onto his lap.

"Mia's over there," he said.

"Yeah, with Josuè." His girlfriend giggled, and he shot her a warning look.

At first, I didn't understand why she was laughing, but then I got her meaning.

"I'll see if I can find them." I knew that girl was wrong, but I wanted Simi to stay behind just in case.

"Um, no. I'm coming with you." Simi pursed her lips and looked the girlfriend up and down.

My head agreed, but the knot in my gut said something different.

As we followed the path from the patio to the barn, the heat from the fire evaporated and the air turned more October than June. I shivered and wished I would've brought the sweatshirt Mama put by the door.

Simi turned the corner before I did and froze. A few steps later, I saw why.

The image still comes to me in the most inconvenient times. Brushing my teeth. In the middle of a lecture.

It's always you pressed against Josuè. Josuè pressed into the wall. Your mouth on his. His mouth on yours.

Over and over.

Sometimes it's fast. Sometimes it's a freeze-frame. Mostly it's just there.

For some reason, it's only that part. Not the rest.

You kept kissing him. It was like watching a foreign film without subtitles. I couldn't get what was happening. I couldn't wrap my mind around what my eyes were taking in.

But then you slid your hand down his side and past his belt. He pushed you away.

And I couldn't breathe.

Simi dropped her cup. It rattled over the cement, which got your attention. Josuè freaked out, started saying it wasn't his fault. He didn't do anything. Hands dragging down his face, feet turning his body in circles.

But you stood there. Arms crossed as your best friend gasped. For a moment, when you saw Simi there, your eyes widened. There was panic in your expression, but only for that split second. Then you swallowed and went stone-faced.

And I couldn't take in enough air to get past the stone on my chest.

Josuè ran toward me, begging me to believe he didn't do anything. I stepped around him so you would have to look at me.

"Why?" It's all I could croak out.

Simi silently scooped her cup into her hand and slunk away.

You didn't move. You held your head high. So stoic. So sure you'd done exactly what you came to do.

I followed Simi to the truck, but Josuè caught up and jerked my arm hard, turning me to face him.

"Look, Alfie. You're my friend, I would never . . ." He licked his dry lips. "Mia was buzzed and asked me to take her to the bathroom. Next thing I know, she's on me, pushing me against the barn."

"Looks like you were there awhile," I said through gritted teeth.

"Nah, it was just for a minute. I didn't know what was happening. She, just like, went for it." He looked at his crotch. "Dude, I freaked."

I turned to walk away, but he held on to my arm. The stone on my chest was gone, and a swarm of angry bees replaced it. I closed my eyes and took a breath to calm down.

"I gotta tell you something I've never told anyone," he said. "Please, man, listen. All that player crap? That ain't me, man."

I scoffed and stared straight ahead.

"It's true, though. My dad . . . He thinks that's me. He used to always be on me about girls and living my best life before I was trapped by some knocked-up girl, but that ain't me. I told him I had sex just to get him off my back, and it kind of grew from there."

The place you'd been standing was empty. You were gone. I flicked my eyes over Josuè.

"What do you mean, 'that ain't you'?" I air-quoted the last part.

"I think I want to be a priest." He folded his arms over his middle. "I'm a virgin, man. A fucking virgin."

I couldn't help but laugh at his choice of words. Probably a good thing since it helped calm the bees.

"I swear on my catcher's gear I would never do anything to hurt you." He held his hands up. "And neither would Mia. She was drunk and didn't know what she was doing."

I sighed. "I believe you, man. But she knew exactly what she was doing."

Josuè sighed a huge breath of relief and held out his hand.

I reached for it, but something inside me snapped. The bees went wild. My hand scrunched into a fist and flew at his jaw. I hit it so hard, my knuckles cracked. He landed on the ground with a thud.

"That's for not pushing her off sooner." Shaking out my fist, I turned to leave and walked straight into you.

You had tears in your eyes, even though you were trying hard to look sure of yourself. Arms folded and head still held high. But you didn't fool me.

"I know what you did," I said. "I know exactly what you did." And then tears rolled down my cheeks as my fist burned and my heart broke. "But now you finally get what you want."

I walked away after that, so I don't know what you did next. But I can guess.

You forget I know you, Mia. Every tic, every gesture, every tone in your voice. You wanted me to see that so I would want to break up with you. You nearly killed me that night, even though I know you probably didn't even like kissing him. But it worked. It was enough.

As usual, you got what you went for.

Simi and I drove home in silence except for a sniffle here or a choked sob there. When I pulled up to her driveway, she turned to me and patted my sore hand.

"I'm so sorry, Alfie." Then she got out, walked to her porch, opened the door, and went inside.

"I'm sorry too," I said to my empty truck.

Mia

I SAY "SORRY" TO THE POLICE OFFICER AND BACK AWAY, UNABLE to take my eyes off the sideways house.

I've seen toppled buildings and fires, cracked sidewalks and broken asphalt, the entire way here. But I never thought about what this place would look like. I knew the dorms at USF might be in trouble, but when it came to seeing Alfie again, my mind painted a scene unbroken, whole, like I wanted us to be again.

The night I made sure Alfie would stay away from me feels like a hundred years ago.

I was on my second, maybe third, beer by the time Alfie's headlights grazed the back pastures of Josuè's property. Alfie backed up his car to the levee, letting his engine idle and the beams of his headlights bore into the throng of baseball players and the others at the shortest-night-of-the-year party. I imagined him sitting in the darkened safety of his driver's seat behind the veil of the car lamps–turned–interrogation tool, watching me try to balance on the wooden fence that marked a practice ring for the horses. Working up his nerve to try to talk me out of breaking up.

Let him look. I was having enough trouble discerning the fence from one of those mechanical bulls they let you ride at the rodeo. Not that I'd ever ridden one. Too many variables. Too many directions, too fast. Just like that damned fence. Or at least that's how it felt.

I'd already done a shot by then too. Something blue and bitter, and probably stolen out of some unsuspecting parents' cabinet. Whatever it was, it didn't matter as long as it got the job done. Considering this was only the third time I'd tasted alcohol—outside of communion at Alfie's church, that is—it was definitely doing something.

Alfie needed to understand that he'd be better off in San Francisco, building a life for him and his family. One where my drama or I couldn't screw any of it up. And if that was going to happen, I would need the liquid courage to help pull it off. Even if I had no idea how.

Josuè climbed the post I was grasping, straddled the next section of fence, and faced me. I shifted my blurred focus to him and concentrated on his lips. It's easier to tell if people are being honest if you watch their lips. The slightest twitch or smirk, and you know. I don't even know when I started doing it. But after a few beers and bitter blue stuff, it wasn't as easy. I fought the urge to lean closer for a better read.

"What's your boy doing out there?" He nodded to Alfie's truck. "He's bringing Simi, right? Wonder what they're talking about."

"He's not my boy. Not anymore."

But the truth was, they were talking about me. I knew it. Simi was probably trying to explain why I broke up with him and Alfie was explaining why he wouldn't accept it. A fight between me and him with my best friend-since-forever as proxy. She could always say things better than me, make people somehow understand. I'd asked her to try, to get him to let me go. She didn't want to. Said I was being stupid, but I begged.

I couldn't let him throw his dreams away to move across the country with me. For what? A smaller team at a more expensive school? After my dad left and my mother decided her scarlet letter was an act of bravery for true love, I saw my future laid out in front of me—a road map to a hellish existence if things stayed the same. Alfie, as usual, took the noble route. He said he wanted to be with me, make sure I was okay. There was no way I could let that happen.

College was a time of change and growth. I mean, all the high-school-sweetheart turkey dumps over countless Thanksgiving breaks proved that. What if we grew apart and he spent the rest of his life hating me for being so selfish? What if he was sorry he gave up a huge opportunity for me and I crashed and burned? No way. I had to make him see we were better apart. Even if that meant breaking his beautiful heart.

"He will always be your guy. Everyone knows that," Josuè said. I ignored his comment.

"They're probably locked in some nerdy argument about science versus poetry." The words felt clunky in my mouth. He put his hand on my shoulder and I leaned into it, grateful for the help balancing.

"You okay there, Clementine?"

I nodded, but my head felt heavy, like my chin dropped faster to my chest than it should. He peered into my eyes, but I stayed focused on his mouth, catching up on his words.

"You need some water. Let's walk over to the cooler. You can walk, right?" He hopped down while I swung my leg over and slid belly to fence post to the ground. Josuè's arm found its way around my waist as we walked toward the small barn on the other side of the path.

"What about Simi? Don't you want to see her?" I asked. "Isn't this a date?"

"Yep. But I'm a fan of all the gals, you know that." He puckered his lips, but he couldn't escape the tiny curve upward at the corner. See? Watch the mouth and no one can keep anything from you.

"You like her," I sing.

"Shhh, you'll ruin my reputation." He propped me against the wooden wall and cracked open a bottle of water and handed it to me. "Drink this. You'll feel better."

The water was icy cold, and my body shivered against the warm summer air. I tilted my head against what was probably oak and closed my eyes, letting the world spin. Maybe if it shuffled everything around a bit, things would get easier.

"Hey, you okay, Clementine?" He gripped my shoulders and jolted me back to reality. I opened my eyes wide, blinking a few times to focus over his shoulder.

Alfie walked straight toward us, kicking my adrenaline into action.

"Don't go passing out on me. My parents will shit a brick," Josuè said.

Apparently, adrenaline is a funny thing. It gave me enough energy to stand up straight and balance on my own, but not enough clarity to avoid what I thought was a brilliant plan cooking up in my brain. I knew exactly how to end things for good with Alfie.

As I concentrated on Josuè's lips forming those last words, I stood on my toes and leaned. My face crashed against his, our lips smashing together. He was the last person in the entire school I would consider kissing, ever. His lips felt wrong, out of sync and empty. I couldn't think about how this wasn't Alfie. I just needed it to last long enough for him to see.

I was counting on Josuè's player personality making him seek out some action before his *Bros before hoes* code would kick in. What I didn't count on was who else would see.

When Josuè finally pushed me away, I didn't look at him. I didn't have to see his face to know how he'd react, even if my brain was still fuzzy from the alcohol. Over his shoulder, as Alfie stood there, Simi gaped, mouth open, her eyes reflecting our life-long friendship. Broken, just like everything else.

Josuè would fix it with her. He would explain it was my fault. That I was drunk and didn't know what I was doing. She would forgive him, even if she never spoke to me again.

Because I did know what I was doing. And I knew Alfie would see we were over for sure. I'd done what I came here to do, even if it was in a way I instantly regretted.

Simi was a casualty I hadn't considered, although after everything, I deserved to lose her and more. The blue alcohol churning in my bloodstream confirmed it.

I grab the collar of Simi's sweatshirt that's protected me all night and inhale what's left of her earthy vanilla scent. She could've never spoken to me again or worse. She could've thrown it all back in my face, but that's not who she is.

She's my Simi. I'm pretty sure she's made of forgiveness and light and all the things in that poem about sweet little girls. And I'd put good money on her probably having all the stuff little boys are made of too.

The next day, I went to her to apologize. Her mom let me in, but her door was closed, so I texted her from outside in the hall.

Mia: Hey, can I come over?

Simi: I'm not home, sorry.

Mia: Oh, your mom said you were. I just want to tell you I'm sorry.

Simi: Okay, you said it.

Mia: I want to say it to your face. You deserve that much.

Simi: Maybe when I get home. I'll text you.

That's when I knocked on her door.

Simi: You're outside, aren't you?

Mia: Sort of ¯_(ツ)_/¯

She opened the door, and I did my best impression of a steely gaze, but it didn't last long. As soon as I saw her, tears exploded down my face. Then she was crying too. She's like that—compassion first, because whatever's next can wait.

"You liked him so much," I said.

"Well, you know we've been texting since the golf cart fiasco. We kind of got over the flirting thing a while ago. Turns out, he's not that good at it." She shrugged. "He told me about wanting to be a priest earlier. Let's just say we make better friends."

We hugged and collapsed on her bed. I told her everything—how I didn't plan to kiss anyone, especially Josuè. How I drank too much and couldn't think straight. She asked why I didn't talk to her about it, and I said I didn't want her to talk me out of the breakup.

I knew I'd screwed up when Alfie punched Josuè. He's not the kind of person who punches anything, especially people.

I had two people who loved me for me, and I was too blind to see it. And too stubborn to hear my own heart crying out. I hope one day Simi will let me apologize. Really tell her how sorry I am, not just that lame *Don't hate me* crap.

I collapse on the stairs of the church and bury my face in my hands. My raw heels burn against the backs of my boots.

The Haight district is a block or so behind where the police officers were standing. Where the sideways house and broken buildings are. If the record store is in the same shape, Alfie could be really hurt.

I force the thought from my mind and try to picture him next to the firefighters and rescue crews, calling out to others, being the hero he always was, at least to me.

Either way, I need to find him.

Taking deep breaths, I force my pulse to slow from racing to pounding, and the thumps in my chest soften. This is not the time for panic. Or tears. I stand and survey the street. I could try getting past the cop, but then I'd have to deal with the firefighters who, no doubt, heard him tell me to leave.

It's best if I circle around to find another way in. It'll be dangerous, and there are still fires popping up and aftershocks rocking the ground, which could cause more falling buildings and smashed cars. But the boy I love is in there, and now that I know we belong together, I need our happily ever after to start as soon as possible.

Alfie

I'M GLAD SIMI GAVE YOU MY NOTE. I WANTED TO GIVE IT TO YOU personally, but after Josuè's party, I couldn't bring myself to try. I wasn't sure we were going to get our happily ever after.

Sometimes I wish I'd never written it. Sometimes I hoped you ripped it up instead of reading it. Because after everything that happened, all you did to get me to give up, how pathetic can a guy be, right? If you'd never seen it, you could move on. Figure stuff out and finally be happy. Because that's what I want for you, Mia. To be happy.

When I find you, I'll explain what I was trying to say earlier, on the phone. It'll be better in person, anyway.

I'm trying really hard, but it's so dark and so cold. I might close my eyes and rest—wait until morning. It might be best. But if I never see you again, at least know how I felt. How I feel. And that I'm okay.

As long as you are too.

Mia

THE CLOSER I GET, THE MORE I WORRY. IT'S COLD AND DARK, and there is so much in between us. My phone is at 3 percent, but I try Alfie's number anyway. Instead of ringing, it clicks over to an annoying beep. I hold it at my side, limp north to the next block, and turn left.

I wish I'd stayed at the coffee shop instead of running away like I did. When I check again, the battery falls to 2 percent, so I power it down and tuck it away. I'll wait until I'm closer to try again. The last thing I need is to be completely without it.

I pass a school, then houses. Finally, I arrive at the next block. I turn left, but farther down Ashbury, that crossroad is blocked off too. I'm not getting in that way.

I continue down the street, faster now. The commercial buildings become houses.

A mass of bricks covers the sidewalk, and half of a large tree has toppled onto a car, denting the hood and smashing the windows.

I didn't know how awful broken windshield glass could smell—putrid, like death and decay washed in onion. The fresh wood where the tree cracked in half sweetened the air, but not enough.

Someone planted that tree. Dug the hole, maybe the same way Devi dug hers. They placed the seedling in the ground and covered it with rich soil. Maybe they talked to it, telling it how big it would be one day. And now it's ripped in half.

But the roots are still in the ground. They don't move and sway like the branches. They stay firmly in the soil, pressure from above and below keeping them in place.

I don't feel sorry for the tree, because it will grow again. As long as the roots stay in the ground, the tree will live again.

My feet go faster.

Maybe that's why people are so fragile. Our roots aren't embedded anywhere. Ours travel with the people we love, wherever they go.

Lights flash a few streets down, but there are enough houses here that I can slip through one of the yards.

A woman sits on the steps of a twisted building, trying to calm her crying baby. She shushes and rocks her and smooths the top of her head, but the baby screams anyway.

A crackle pops above them, and one of the sideways window frames smashes into the ground. The baby wails, and the mother clutches the tiny body to her chest. I should tell her to go somewhere safe, but I don't stop.

I focus on the ground, hopping over bricks and other debris.

The house on the corner still stands, but enormous cracks splinter the plaster in large chunks. Counting on the flashing lights ahead to shield me, I slip into the tiny space between this house and the next. It's so narrow, I have to turn sideways to get past the garbage cans by the garage door. This space is extra dark as still-standing treetops hover over the area.

Farther into the yard, the long walkway opens up to a small patio, which is now at a forty-five-degree angle, fallen planters everywhere. The windows are dark too, and there's not enough light from above to see my way out.

I take out my phone, hold it in front of me, and bow my head.

I talk, but not to my parents' god, and not to Alfie's, either. I talk to the one telling my inner voice what to say. The one who loves unconditionally without rules or judgments.

I ask for strength and courage, and maybe a percent or two added to my phone's battery wouldn't hurt. Just acknowledging that I need those things makes me feel them come alive inside me.

When I open my eyes, I see clearer, like the dust and smoke and ash have parted a little, letting starlight and the moon peek in. Maybe my eyes adjusted to the dark. I don't have to climb the fence at the end of the yard because it's leaning so far into the next. I scale its surface and jump over a planter box on the other side. My heels slip inside my boots, wet now from what's probably blood. But I shove the pain away.

This pain is temporary.

At the corner, I sneak a look at the police at the intersection, and they're looking the other direction.

I scuttle across the dark road and eventually come to a large commercial building. As I move down the cement walkway at its side, I'm forced to stop. Brick after brick pile into a huge mound, like a child dumped out their blocks and left them in the middle of the floor.

A sudden memory rushes into my mind. A bear hunt book I loved back in kindergarten. *Can't go under it. Can't go over it. Got to go through it.*

The happy memory gives me the strength I need to push forward.

As quickly and carefully as I can, I climb on all fours across the heap of ruined building. I reach the top, and a brick shifts underneath the one I'm holding on to. That starts a few more cascading onto the sidewalk. Soon I'm sliding headfirst into a new pile in front of me. Covering my head, I squeeze my eyes shut and hope for the best.

I roll over the pile, the bricks' sharp corners slicing my back and the blunt sides bruising my legs and arms.

When everything stops moving, I open my eyes and crawl out of the mess.

But nothing prepares me for what I see.

Mia

HAZY AIR FILLS MY LUNGS AS I TRY TO BREATHE, AND I CHOKE on the ash. A restaurant in between two clothing stores sparks smoke and flame, some reaching the blackened sky. The immense heat burns my eyes and heats my skin. I pull my sleeves over my hands for protection as my pulse races. People line up and pass buckets of water to throw on the edges of the flames to keep it from spreading. Firefighters race on foot to the scene, dragging heavy spools of hose with them. There's no way a truck could make it inside. Others scoop up the trailing hoses and run with the uniformed—they move together like a Chinese dragon without the costume.

To my left, a man in a green safety vest throws bricks and broken furniture from what's left of the building. He calls for survivors, but I can barely hear him over the roar of the fire and the crashing of stone and wood on asphalt.

One of the clothing stores leans precariously forward, threatening to reduce its size from three stories to one. Some men scavenge the wreckage for wooden beams to prop it up, shoving them hard against the walls and kicking them into place on the sidewalk. One of the guys goes still and cocks his head to the left. My eyes widen. Then he's shouting and waving, and I suck in my breath. The man in the green vest runs toward him, and they dive into one of the lower windows.

Alfie wouldn't be in there. Would he?

Stepping forward to see better, I catch my foot in a large crack in the road and twist my ankle. I roll with it and land on my side, but I'm able to pull my boot free. A hot pain shoots from my ankle to my knee, and my face contorts with the pain. I hobble to my feet anyway. Seconds later, the man is climbing out of the window, holding someone's legs. All the blood in my body rushes to my screaming feet. The green-vest guy follows quickly with his arms looped through those of the barely conscious person they're carrying out. They lay him on the sidewalk.

Not Alfie.

I bend forward, putting my hands on my knees, and breathe, holding most of my weight on my good leg. A hand grasps my shoulder, and I nearly fall over. A strong grip keeps me from meeting the asphalt one more time.

"Are you all right?" Another man in a green vest and an old fire helmet faces me. He shoots me a quick glance.

"I'm fine," I say, shaking off the clothing-store panic. "I'm looking for a vinyl store. Do you know where it is?"

What sounds like a jet flying above silences everything else, and the street rolls like a shaken-out blanket. I grab for the man's arms, gulping down the scream threatening to break free, and together, we surf the aftershock until the street is still again.

A car alarm shrieks a block over. A tree tumbles into a store window to my right. I jerk to the left out of instinct, hopping on one foot. The man steadies me. As I turn toward the crash, I see it. The sign for the vinyl store.

My pulse is in my ears, louder than any drumline. The man says something.

"What?" I know I'm yelling, but I don't care. I watch his lips as they move.

"You'd think those things would shake less." He lets go and laughs bitterly.

"Oh. Yeah." My voice is an afterthought as I stare at the sign.

It reads FLY VINYL AND OTHER JAMS, except the *J* is broken off the last word. The pole the sign sits on leans to the right. My eyes move to where the store should be, but only half of it is there. I blink and look again.

Maybe it's shadows. Maybe it's the black spots playing at the corners of my vision. Maybe the glow from the growing fire is playing tricks. Putting one foot in front of the other, I move up the street, praying the shadows move.

At the end of the block, they do.

With shaking hands, I pull out my phone. Somehow, there's still 2 percent left. I dial his number. It rings. No answer.

The door to the store is closed, but only the bottom half still holds its glass. The entire building bends in on itself, purple bricks piled on purple bricks. Like an old man without his dentures. Someone's crying, and then I realize it's me.

The back half stands relatively intact.

Maybe Alfie's there. Trapped in a back office.

Maybe he was in the bathroom or supply closet or break room. Maybe he'd stepped out for a break.

Please God let him be anywhere that isn't the actual store.

I limp closer.

Or on the other side, outside, where I can't see. Maybe he's trying to save the records so his boss will thank him and give him a raise for caring so much. He's like that. Taking care of everyone.

He deserves a raise. And he'll get one when this is all over.

An October breeze swirls the ash and smoke in the air into tiny spirals lit by the orange glow of the flames behind me. I glance at my phone.

One percent. I dial again. It rings. I hold my breath.

My foot lands on a purple brick in the middle of the street. I pick it up—I don't know why. Like putting it with the others will magically put everything back the way it's supposed to be. Alfie inside, behind the counter, listening to some weird indie band. And me jingling the bell over the door as I enter, a weary smile on my face, a shocked but happy one on his.

I drop the brick onto the ground in front of the store. It lands with a thud.

The right side of the store, the one I couldn't see from where I was, looks like a ruined Rube Goldberg machine made from dominoes. Except the dominoes are purple bricks and roof shingles and window frames and broken glass.

"Alfie?" I barely croak out his name. I clear my throat, but it burns from thirst and pollution. "Alfie?" It's louder this time.

I press the green button on my phone, but I don't bring it to my ear. Dropping my hand to my side, I close my eyes and listen.

Listen the way Chin-Sun taught me to do.

A faint song plays from under the dominoes. I choke on a sob. It's the first song we danced to at the winter formal, some rock ballad I said was stupid but secretly downloaded as soon as I got home and played on repeat.

I guess he did too. He made it his ringtone.

I step closer, carefully checking where I place my feet through my tears.

It gets louder, then stops.

No. Come back.

I press dial again, but my screen is black.

I half scream, half sob, my whole body trembling.

"Alfie!" I yell his name over and over, but there's no response.

Mia

MY HANDS FIND BRICK AFTER BRICK. I THROW THEM ONTO THE sidewalk, beside me, into the empty space in the street. Anywhere but where they stood a few hours ago. I throw chunks of roof, plaster, shattered records, whatever my grip lands on. I yell his name the whole time I'm pulling debris from the pile.

His phone is there, so he's got to be too. It's still alive, so . . . I can't even think the last part. My brain gets stuck on *alive*, and that's the only word echoing in my head.

The green-vest guy from earlier is here, his hand between my shoulder blades. I keep pulling and throwing.

"Slow down," the man says.

"Alfie!" My voice croaks from the smoke and ash.

"You might make the rest of the wall slide if you pick the wrong brick. Haven't you ever played Jenga?"

This makes me pause, and my eyes pass over wherever one brink touches another. He's right. The risk is too great. A fresh sob bubbles up. I face the man.

"Please, you have to help. Someone is under there. I heard . . . I heard him." Breathing hard, I point with a shaky hand to the spot where the music played a moment ago. He turns to the others and cups his mouth with his hands.

"Hey, we've got someone!" He circles his arm over and over, waving to get their attention as relief fills my lungs. More hands mean we can find him faster. Two guys jog as safely as possible to where we stand and inspect the rubble, hands on hips and squinted expressions.

"Where's the body?"

I flinch.

"Sorry, I mean the survivor. It's been a long night already." He rubs his nose with the back of his hand as the green-vest guy and I point to the spot. "If you go from the outside in, it should stay stable. Just don't pull anything out from underneath anything else."

I nod, eyes wide and every hair on my body alert. We move en masse to our new digging point. Three of us pull and throw while the other points to possible danger zones. Soon more people are next to me, passing bricks and ruined merchandise to others who make piles and shout Alfie's name.

I shout too sometimes, but mostly I listen. I want to be the one who hears him yell for help.

My body is heavy and clumsy now, and my hand slips off a brick and over something sharp. I jerk it back and clamp my other hand around the cut, but blood oozes through my fingers. A woman in one of the green vests points to a tent across the way. I don't remember it being there before. But under it, supplies sit on tables, and people in white shirts silently watch us dig.

"You can get that looked at over there."

"I'm fine." I bend to pick up more, but she stops me.

"You can come back after you get it wrapped up. It won't help anyone if you bleed all over everything."

I roll my eyes, but she's right. I know it.

I let one of the white shirts stop the bleeding and clean out the cut with saline. They tell me they're med students from the university and have set up stations all over the area. One of them hands me a water, which I down way too fast. My stomach rejects it, and I can't tell if I need to burp or throw up. Once my hand is bandaged, I hop up, landing on my sore ankle. Forgot all about that.

One of the women in the white shirts asks if she can look at it, but I say no. I'm afraid I'll never get my boot on again if I take it off.

The people digging all stop at once and stare. I run-hop to where they're working and look too.

A tiny black rectangle is lodged between two bricks. Someone with long arms and longer legs reaches over the rubble and wrestles it loose. A shattered screen glints in the orange glow as he turns it toward us.

A choked noise rises from my gut and escapes my lips. Everyone turns from the discovery and stares at me, but I don't care. Adrenaline floods my body, and I immediately forget everything—the pain radiating from my ankle, the cold gnawing at my skin, the smoky air burning my eyes and lungs. Everything but that phone. My eyes dart from one worn face to another.

"Someone give me their phone. Please!" I beg, choking back sobs.

An older woman hands me hers. Trembling, I flip it open and manage to dial Alfie's number. I press call and wait.

The cracked screen lights up as the rock ballad plays.

My legs give out and I drop to my knees. The man next to me catches me so I land soft.

"That's his phone. He's there." I point. "Please." My chest is so tight, I think my heart might burst into a million pieces. One piece for everything I would give to make sure he's all right.

Please let him be okay.

I sit paralyzed as the group digs again with a new energy. Not a minute later, someone yells for everyone to stop.

"We've got a hand." He barks directions at a few people and tells the rest to back away. I push myself to standing and stare, too afraid to look, but too nervous to look away.

In minutes, the area around Alfie's head and shoulders are cleared of the broken building remnants, but no one moves him.

The world flips sideways, and a wave of nausea whips through me.

"It could be too dangerous. We need a medic to look at him first."

They finish uncovering the rest of him and make a decent clearing next to him. His eyes are closed, his dark hair gray from the dust. My eyes fixate on his chest, begging for any movement. I press my lips together, holding in breath and tears and hope.

His shirt rises slightly as his chest expands. Only when it shrinks do I exhale too. Tears of joy and sorrow mix as they run down my cheeks.

"Can I?" I point to him lying on the ground. The man nods, and I drag my exhausted body to Alfie and sit as close as I dare.

I brush the building crumbs off his face with my fingers as gently as I can. My eyes search his beautiful skin, cut and bruised by the debris. The stubble he lets grow these days. For some reason, I smile. More than anything, I want to curl into him. Make it like those nights at the lake. I ache for that peace.

I found him. A cautious feeling of relief loosens my chest and lungs.

Peeling off Simi's hoodie, I roll it up and place it under his head without lifting it too much, afraid of hurting him. I take his hand in mine. It's warm. I shut out the noise coming from all sides and focus on his chest. It moves up and down as he breathes, and my lips stretch into a grin for the first time in a while.

Maybe we could have that peace again.

"I'm here, Alfie." I speak low and soft, close to his ear. "It's Mia. I love you and I'm so, so sorry." I lean closer, and warmth blooms between us. I smile into it, imagining it forming a bubble around us. "Can you wake up, please? I'm here."

I don't hold my breath. My muscles don't tense. He's here and I'm with him. And I can't stop looking at his beautiful face.

His full but parched lips spread wide. He clears his throat, but his eyes stay closed.

"I was just talking to you." His voice is a midnight desert. I blink.

"You were?" Real relief floods my body. "Were you dreaming?" About me? A sob erupts from my lips, and tears streak my dirt-stained cheeks. I smooth his hair away from his eyes and wipe away more dust. I can't stop touching him.

His eyes blink open and shut as he adjusts his vision. When they settle on me, he smiles for real. Electricity ignites in my veins, making my heart soar. He slides his hand from under mine and cups it around my face, his thumb wiping away tears. I lean into his hand and close my eyes, vowing to never forget how his skin feels against mine.

"Hey, Mia?"

"Yes?" I open my eyes and look into his.

"How?" His words are choppy, breathless. "What about New York?"

"We had a deal, remember?"

His eyes search mine. When he finds the answer, they crinkle around the edges.

"End of the world." He coughs.

"You said you'd follow me. Turns out I was the one who needed to make the trip." I smile through my tears. "Solid plan." He nods, then closes his eyes. The muscles in his face go slack, and his hand falls to his side.

Alfie and Mia

SOMEONE TAPS MY SHOULDER. THE WOMAN IN THE WHITE shirt who bandaged my hand.

"Let me in there." She's already on her knees as I slide backward to give her room. My heart races. My eyes glued to her every move.

She flashes a penlight in his eyes, which rouses him, and he comes to. I release my breath and hang my head. She presses on his stomach and he flinches.

I flinch too.

"That tender?" she asks, her hand already pressing somewhere else. "How about this?"

Alfie grimaces and she sits back on her knees. Her hands find each end of the stethoscope around her neck and hang there. I look from her to Alfie and back, eager for any information.

"Help should be here soon." She looks at me. "Keep him awake until the paramedics arrive." She lowers her head without breaking eye contact, and my heart sinks.

I know.

I know paramedics are overwhelmed, and the streets are blocked by fires and ruined buildings. I know the med students helping out can only do so much.

I wrap my arms around my waist, shaking my head against the argument in my mind.

Alfie is strong. He's an athlete. Young. He can make it.

My breath catches, and the one that follows is shaky. So is the one after that. But I straighten my spine and force my face to relax. For Alfie.

When she moves on to the next building, I scoot in close to him and face the street so that my thigh is next to his cheek. He lifts his head to place it in my lap but can't. Pain flashes across his features, sharpening them into a grimace. I feel it too, like knife wounds to the gut.

I lie down, facing him, his hand tucked into my chest, my heart in my throat. The ground is ice next to my bare skin.

"Hey," I whisper.

"Hey." He smiles.

"Alfie, I need to tell you." My pulse races, and a cool sweat forms on my face. His smile dims, and I want it back. But I need to say this. I came all this way. I take in a breath and blow it out slowly, steadying the nerves prickling my skin. "I'm so sorry for everything. About that night. At the party."

Words pour from my lips.

"You were right. I should've waited, talked to you instead of pushing everyone away. And I don't know why I kissed, you know." I risk glancing at him. His brows are drawn together the way they do when he's thinking. I have to keep going or I'll lose my nerve.

"All this time I've been angry at my parents for forcing me to live like them, believe the things they do, and then punishing or shaming me when I couldn't. But tonight I realized I was doing the same thing to you. Well, not shaming, but kind of judging, thinking you went along with your family and their beliefs. I never really considered that you chose them. And I—"

"Stop."

My mouth freezes in an O shape as my next words die in my

throat. My heart sinks. He doesn't want to hear this. Of course he doesn't. I inhale a shaky breath and focus on his chest, unable to meet his eyes. Waves of humiliation threaten to crash through me.

"I know." He shifts his shoulders and turns his head. My eyes flick to his, every fiber of me a question.

"You know?"

"I know you." His lips turn up at the corners, and suddenly the ground doesn't feel so cold. My embarrassment recedes like waves to the sea. I look at our clasped hands, but he lifts them and gently pushes my chin until our eyes meet again. "All of that's in the past." His words are breathy, but there's light in his eyes.

Warmth spreads from my torso into my limbs. I was wrong before, when I said I'd walked to the ends of the earth first. He does it for me all the time. With forgiveness. And love. Fresh tears spring to the corners of my eyes, and I let them fall.

I want to say that after tonight, last summer feels like another lifetime. But it wasn't, and I need him to see how wrong I was.

"It was a terrible thing to do, even if I thought it was for a good reason. I wanted to take it back as soon as it happened, but I was humiliated." A rush of heat floods my cheeks at the memory. "Then this morning, when I saw you with Alice, I freaked out."

"Alice?" Confusion rattles in his voice.

"She's the reason I knew where to find you."

"How . . . did you find her?" Laughter danced through his words now. He coughs and I suck in my breath. I don't exhale until he does too. When I'm sure he's okay, I continue.

"I went to your dorm. Well, not your dorm because it was evacuated. I went to the baseball field because someone told me you might be there, and I saw her." I smile at the memory. "I mean, a baseball field had to be a sign, right?"

"Wait, slow down." He rolls his head so our foreheads touch. "You went to the school?"

My throat thickens, and I have to swallow to speak.

"Simi gave me a map." I frown. "Actually, that wasn't really helpful because I'm not that great at reading them." The frustration and panic of being lost and alone strikes my memories. "And I had to save my phone battery. Basically, I asked a lot of people for directions." I roll my eyes. He searches them for understanding, looking at me the way only he can. My heartbeat quickens. I want to dive into his deep brown irises and stay there forever.

He arches his back, and his expression contorts. I freeze for a moment, too scared to move. Closing his eyes, he takes a slow breath. His shoulders relax. I look around for the woman in the white shirt, but she's nowhere. Only green vests digging and shouting.

I force my exploding nerves to settle and my expression into something soothing. I need to distract him until help arrives.

"Oh, and wait until I tell you about the people I met." The smile comes easier when I think of Devi and Chin-Sun. Even Risha. Their own beautiful smiles. "The most incredible people."

His body shakes with silent laughter.

"Oh, that hurts." He groans. My stomach tightens.

"Lie still." I smooth his hair. "Don't talk. Help will be here soon."

"That end-of-the-world stuff?" He coughs out his words.

"Shh, I know. But then the world tried to swallow us whole." I run my fingers down his cheek, electric shocks exploding between my fingertips and his skin. "When the earthquake hit, you were all I could think of. I knew I had to be with you, tell you that I love you. I never stopped."

"I know."

We're both quiet for a while, hearts happy and full of his *I know* and all it means. But then it occurs to me that he might not know all of it. Everything that happened with school.

"After what happened with my parents, my dad made good on his promise and refused to pay for school. And I couldn't look at my mom anymore, so the minute my birthday came around, I boarded a bus to Simi's. I had no plans to find you. I wanted you to live your life. Be happy. You deserve that."

"Oh, Mia." His voice is full of the past, but there's a tinge of something else. I wait. "Everyone deserves that."

"I didn't really know that then."

"That's what I was trying to tell you." He adjusts his head and lets out a soft grunt. "Life is more than who gets crowned prom king or who kissed who at the bonfire. Or even what school you go to, if you go at all."

I recoil a little.

"High school is so small. The world contains so much more."

I must blanch, because he reaches his hand and strokes my cheek. A wave of guilt washes over me. He literally was buried under a collapsed building, and he's trying to comfort me. I cover his hand with mine and lead it to his stomach so he's more comfortable. His expression eases.

"All we need is . . ."

". . . to show up for each other." I finish his sentence. A warm grin spreads across his face.

I can't help it. I brush my lips against his. But gently so I don't cause any more hurt.

He lifts his head and kisses me back. My heart melts into a puddle, but I feel like I could fly.

"I love you," I say.

"I love you, Mia. More than anything." He turns his head to the sky and coughs. Tiny specks of spit fly from his mouth and splatter on his cheeks and chin. Some land on me, too. "Sorry. That came out of nowhere."

"You're fine. It's fine." I wipe my hand over his cheek and move to do the same to mine. Instead, I freeze, and stare.

Tiny lines of red are smeared across my fingers and palm. Blood. Fresh jolts of panic stop my heart. I'm not a doctor, but I know coughing up blood is never a good thing. I tell myself it's not bad. Probably from a cut on his lip. Or maybe he bit his tongue. The adrenaline surging through my veins knows I'm lying to myself. For the millionth time, I take a deep breath. I can't show him how scared I am. After everything, he deserves my strength.

As calmly as I can, I tell Alfie to be still and rest. I sit up and my eyes dart around the area, looking for anyone in a white shirt.

Sirens wail in the distance behind us, maybe three or four blocks away. But who knows how fast they can get through. I run my cleaner hand up and down his arm for warmth.

"Mia, you know I could never be happy without you." His words are choppy and his breath labored. My heart clenches. I don't stop him. I'm selfish. I want to hear all of this. But I watch his mouth carefully for more blood. "I'm like that last camellia. The one I brought, that night. Rusted and withered, but fighting like hell to hang on just to see you one more time."

His last words dig their way into my body and bury themselves in my soul. My lips flatten into a straight line. This will not be the last time. We found each other and we will stay together.

"I saw you drop it," I admit, my voice thick with tears. "When you left, I went back for it. Something about kissing the wrong guy sobers a girl up fast."

"I like to imagine you did." His eyes close, and my breath catches. I rub his arm a little faster. They open, and I can breathe again.

"I pressed it in a book. The Bible your mom gave me, actually." I look at the ground. "Seemed right."

When I look back, Alfie's eyes glisten with tears.

Alfie and Mia

SIRENS ARE CLOSER NOW. ALFIE SHIVERS NEXT TO ME, SO I gently take the sweatshirt under his head and wrap it around his torso.

Settling next to him for body heat, I squeeze his hand. I close my eyes and mentally send him all my body heat. He hasn't coughed up any more blood. I tell myself it was a one-time thing, but the possibility lingers like a heavy stone. I shove it into the back of my mind.

When his shivers slow, I study the purple bricks all around us. So many broken pieces. A building so full of memories, happiness, nostalgia, brought down by a faulty foundation. I snuggle closer to Alfie, grateful ours is stronger.

"Maybe the next time the world ends, we could do something different," I say.

"Like what?" His words are rusty and slow.

"Maybe plant a tree? I don't know."

"Trees live in dirt. You know that, right?" A small smile traces his lips.

"I met someone who showed me how important they are." I smile too, remembering Devi and her kind eyes. When Alfie doesn't speak for a few minutes, I'm suddenly alert. I rub his arm again. "Hanging in there?"

He nods.

"Besides the stomachache, and the whole building-collapsing-on-me thing, lying here with you looking at stars is pretty great. Reminds me of the lake."

"Stars? There are stars?" I'm surprised to feel lightness flowing through me. I let myself welcome it. I look up, and sure enough, the breeze cleared patches of the sky, so a few stars shine above. It feels like the whole world opened up just for us. My chest swells. "There are! This is the first time I've seen them all night. There's been so much junk in the air, I couldn't see anything." I look to him and back. "There's so many, even in those little places between the clouds. Too bad it can't be this dark every night. Who needs electricity anyway?"

"Right? We make enough on our own." He winks, and my heart skips its next three beats.

The paramedics finally arrive. They let me ride with him to the hospital.

"You should be seen too," the female medic tells me. I don't respond. I focus on Alfie, hoping that if I send him all my energy, the paramedics will as well.

The nurse makes me wait in a chair outside his room while they remove his dirty clothes and get him hooked up to machines and IVs. Chewing on the skin around my nail, I watch the minute hand on the wall clock. Even it seems to be affected by the heavy pull of gravity.

After what feels like hours, he's ready, and they let me see him.

I enter his room slowly, as quietly as I can. Everyone around me is loud, hurried, slamming drawers and charts into cubbies. I'm choosing to be quiet. For Alfie. So he can rest.

His room is bright with overhead lights. I turn them off.

When he sees me, he reaches for my hand. I give it to him.

"We can pretend we're still looking at the stars," I say.

"I wish we were." He rubs his thumb over mine the way he used to. A tiny part of my shredded heart heals with every touch. As the machines beep, he adds, "I'm sorry about New York. That was your dream."

"I don't know." So much has happened since then. A strange calm floats into my chest. "Maybe it's for the best."

"Why do you say that?"

I think back over the last few months. How I hated my dad for leaving. How I blamed my mom for everything. How I shoved everyone away and everything deep inside.

"I had my foot so hard on the gas," I say. "Always pushing, always running toward something. I never really took the time to figure out if it's what I wanted. I was bound to crash." I rest my forehead on our threaded hands.

"Better to do it around people who can help pick up the pieces?"

I think about his words and who I'd had to help me figure things out. Simi was always there, except when I made her leave. And of course, Alfie. But no one else. Not really. Not when it counted.

My parents' last fight crashes into my memory. Their faces distorted with anger, jealousy. Dad letting Mom take it out on me. How untethered it made me feel.

I'm more than surprised to realize that I'd felt unsafe long before the earthquake and all that came with it. Something deep inside me settles, like roots taking hold.

Alfie's eyes close, and his breaths become slow and even. I let him sleep, but I don't let go of his hand.

Alfie has always been surrounded by tons of people who love and support him—his team, Chuck and Josuè, his church, and above all, his family. He probably can't comprehend depending on one or two people.

But if tonight has taught me anything, it's that people can come together, help one another. Chin-Sun is right—loving is doing, not feeling. I read somewhere once that people are really good at acute sympathy, but they're terrible at long-term empathy. I'm going to be better at that.

For me, and for Alfie. For everyone.

The steady feeling spreads from my hips to my lower back. Closing my eyes, I straighten my posture and practice Shauna's words in my mind. *Om shanti.* I let the calmness settle around me, not realizing the long moments that pass by, more focused on Alfie resting next to me. His quiet breathing.

"Hey." His soft voice jolts me out of my thoughts, and I open my eyes. His warm smile radiates through me.

I dust his hair from his eyes. "How you feeling?"

"Better. Still, the overall experience is probably a three out of ten. Would not recommend."

"A three, huh?"

"Only because you showed up at the end." His face blossoms into a sleepy smile. I roll my eyes but can't help grinning, too. When he looks at me that way, I'm sunshine and camellia blooms on the inside. I think of all the mornings to come when I get to wake up to that sleepy smile. Warm satisfaction settles over me. "How about you? How's your ankle?"

"Oh, it'll be fine." I ignore the sharp reminder stabbing my foot and hamstring. I'm fairly certain I'll have to cut my boot to get it off my foot, but I'm not about to spend time anywhere else but right here. "I can get it looked at later if it still hurts."

"Mm-hmm." His eyes narrow as mine widen.

"I will, promise." I kiss his hand and rest my cheek on it.

"Should you call your mom?"

"I tried calling earlier." An oily feeling slips down my neck as the memory of her panicked voice comes to the surface. "I didn't know what to say."

"How about hello?"

Now it's my turn to narrow my eyes. But he's not wrong. I'm not entirely sure of the rules about what happens after a deadly natural disaster, but checking in with family is one of them. Even if you haven't talked to them in a while. Something about the world ending makes people run back to the familiar.

Plus the thought of talking to her now, after everything that's happened, feels right. In my gut. Exactly where Chin-Sun said to trust.

A nurse comes in and checks his IV. Her scrubs are wrinkled, her hair pulled up in a messy bun. Purple rims her eyes.

"How we doing in here? Need anything?"

"I could use a trip to the bathroom," Alfie says.

"That's a good sign!" Her voice is too perky, too loud—it makes us both cringe. She must be on autopilot after a night like this. Despite the assault to my ears, I smile.

"All that fluid they're pumping into you. It's working," I say. A lightness blossoms in my chest, and I breathe a full, clean breath.

"Let's get you a urinal," the nurse says.

"On that note," I say, "I think I'll step out and let you have some privacy." I kiss his hand, then scoot my chair back.

"Did you ever ask your mom why everything happened the way it did? You could, when you call her. Just an idea."

"A building falls on you and you think you get to tell people what to do now?" I tease.

He shrugs.

"Wow," I say.

"Wow indeed."

When I get to the doorway, I turn back and smile.

"We've got this," he says.

I nod, excited for the future we finally get to have, and the nurse slides the curtain closed.

Alfie

THE SECOND YOU LEFT TO CALL YOUR MOM, I WANTED YOU back. Here, next to me. I know it was my idea that you call, and you need to. It might be selfish, but it's been so long since I've been able to see you, touch you. Love you.

I can hear you talking to the nurse in the hall, asking about phones. Rust coats your voice from the polluted air, but it's the most beautiful sound I've ever heard. I close my eyes and listen. She's asking you if you're the one who saved "the guy from the Haight," and you're too humble to take credit. But Mia, what you did is incredible. How you walked across the entire city to find me—in Uggs, no less—blows me away.

I'm almost glad I can't have pain meds yet, because then I wouldn't be able to feel the sheer euphoria about to burst from my chest, thinking about how you found me.

I'm so tired, but I won't sleep. I don't want to miss a minute with you. I have to close my eyes, but I'm still listening.

Machines beep, some louder than others. Footsteps vibrate past the curtain that separates me from everyone else. They're like ghosts, trapped to wander the halls here, forever unseen. A child is crying somewhere, but there's laughter, too. The nurses, I think.

In here, though, in this sanitized dormlike space, quiet blankets the room. Maybe it's the lull of the blood pressure machine's puffs and release every few minutes. Or the milk-blue colors on the wall that give it a sense of peace.

People always say chaos and peace are opposites, and I guess that's true. But they can only exist together. A tension of opposites that makes them mean something. A hurricane can't exist without its eye. Healing can't exist without the hurt.

I was at work when you called me. Of course I picked up. I hadn't stopped thinking about you since I saw you earlier. To be honest, I didn't really believe you were there. Not at first. I see you everywhere. A glimpse of your hair on the train, your favorite jacket across campus, but it's never you.

The girl at the coffee bar talking to the manager couldn't be you. Until she was.

Mia, my heart. It couldn't decide whether it should soar or sink. I felt like that first time you came into Baba's restaurant—all of a sudden, I was an awkward kid with nowhere to hide. Then you were barreling toward me soaked in coffee, and I froze. I actually started to open my arms, thinking you'd run into them, like that movie where the couple runs to each other on the beach. Except this wasn't in slow motion. This was real time, or maybe even fast-forward.

You ran right past me, shoving through the crowd at the door. You were so close, I could smell your shampoo.

And then you were gone.

Alice pulled my arm all the way through the line. She ordered for me, shoved a cup of something in my hand, but I couldn't taste it. The rest of the day, I was a zombie, playing my part.

Until you called.

I know I answered fast. My phone never left my hand after the coffee shop, hoping your name might show up on its screen. When it did, my heart knew exactly what to do. It soared, Mia, straight into the sky.

I think that might be what saved me, after the quake. Knowing my heart rose so high, tethering me to the stars until you found me.

It's beating so fast right now, just thinking that I get to spend the rest of my life giving it to you. My eyes burn from the tears flowing from them, but I don't care.

We get our forever. And I'll never be happier about anything else.

Mia

A DIFFERENT NURSE STARES AT A FILE AT THE HUGE STATION in the middle of the emergency room. I stand on the other side of the counter and try to paste a polite smile across my face.

"Excuse me, is there a phone I can use?" I ask. Without looking up, she gestures with a half wave to her left.

"There's a phone bank out that door."

"Oh, okay. Thank you." My voice feels small. Standing at these types of counters always makes me feel too young, too inexperienced, too conspicuous. I clear my throat. "Do you know how they work?"

Super inexperienced.

She looks up, and the lines in her forehead soften as she takes me in. I must look a fright. Tangled hair, dirt smudges everywhere, tear stains on my cheeks. I press my hands to my sides to keep from smoothing out my frizz. She leans back in her chair.

"You're the girl who came in with the guy they found in the Haight, right? You dug him out of the rubble?"

"There were a lot of people helping." My skin grows hot. The last thing I want is to be cast as some sort of hero. People are always looking for others to put on pedestals in times like these. That's the problem, actually. We make helping people special when it should be second nature. "I've never used a phone bank before. Do I need money or a credit card?" I swallow, hoping she says no, because I have none of the above.

She considers me for a few seconds, then opens a drawer. She pulls out a cell phone and hands it to me.

"Let me help you, then. Use mine. Just bring it back up here when you're done." She nods to a hallway on the opposite side of the room. "It's quieter over there."

"Thank you." I take her phone, grateful and humbled. I'm so raw, her kindness almost breaks me open again.

I follow her directions and limp down the hall. Halfway there, I cross the entrance to the waiting room. So many people. Some waiting to be seen. Some just waiting.

Simi is there, through the window on the other side of the door, handing out sandwiches to the people waiting. My stomach drops. She's there offering them comfort. I close my eyes and feel my heart grow heavy.

Our argument seems silly now. Not because we fought, but because of what we fought about. She was right. About the party. My breaking up with Alfie. Even my resistance to Chin-Sun. My classic MO is to run away as soon as things get difficult.

But I'm not going to do that anymore. Not with Alfie. My mom. Or her. I know now that the only way anything gets better is by showing up and figuring things out. I take a deep breath, open my eyes, and look for her.

I don't need to. She's right there, on the other side of the glass, looking back at me. Her face is dark, burdened with everything that's happened. She doesn't smile her Simi smile or even move to acknowledge that I'm here.

It's like she's waiting for me to run away. Prove her right. I lift my hand in a small wave and she does the same. My heart reaches out to hers, and a tiny crack forms in her mask of neutrality. Her lips curl into a slight smile.

Slowly, I open the door to all the noise and chaos filling the room. She starts to walk toward me, but I put up a hand telling her to stay there.

This time, I'm coming to her.

I stand with her, in front of the screwed-down plastic chairs. She puts down her basket of food and folds her arms. I study the floor next to her feet.

"Are you here with Safa?" My voice is barely above a whisper.

"Yes." It's only one word, but she wields it like a weapon. It lands like one too. I nod. "Did you find Alfie? Is that why you're here?" I nod again, and her face grows softer.

"Simi, I'm sorry."

She stiffens.

"Really sorry. For all of it. You were right. I was running. I see that now." I meet her eyes. Her bottom lip pushes forward as she draws her beautifully full eyebrows together.

I take a chance and reach for her hand. She lets me, and my shoulders sink from my ears.

"I've learned so much tonight. I want to tell you all about it, but I need to call my mom first."

She jerks her head back, and I let out a soft laugh.

"Can you meet me in Alfie's room, in the ER bay? When you're done?" I point to where it is. Her eyes narrow and her lips slide into a daring grin.

"Just let them try to stop me."

I throw my arms around her and squeeze until she begs for breath. But she squeezes me back just as hard. When we let go, we're both a little breathless.

"Thank you," she says. I lower my head and smile.

"I love you, Simi. I promise I won't run away anymore."

"I love you, too."

We hug one more time, and she promises to find us when she's done. I hobble back to the hallway with a lightness filling my chest. I've at least repaired two relationships tonight. I hope I can repair one more.

I find a quiet part of the hallway and press the numbers to my mom's phone with a shaky hand. Bracing myself against the smooth, rounded corner, I press send.

"Mia?" She answers before it hardly rings. "Is that you?"

"Mom?" I close my eyes. I thought I would hate hearing her voice, the shrill *Everything's fine* tone she always fakes. But her voice is thick with tears and worry. After everything that's happened, hearing her sound so scared because of me slices me into a thousand pieces. Her voice is raw, honest. Home. "It's me."

"Oh, Mia. Are you all right? Where are you? Is this a San Francisco number? The area code . . . Oh my gosh, the earthquake!"

"I'm okay, Simi's okay." Emotion wells in my throat and winds its way around my tongue.

"Thank God." Relief breathes through her words. A sob breaks free, and suddenly we're both crying. "I've been so worried. So glad you're all right. I've missed you so much." Her sentences are short and wet.

I take several quick breaths and swallow to make room for my own words.

"I missed you, too." My body reels from surprise, but the words settle in my core, and I know they're true.

"Oh, Mia."

"I'm at the hospital, with Alfie. He was hurt." I brace myself for her typical cold response, unfeeling as usual when I bring him up.

"Simi's here too. She's not hurt. Just helping." I add in the last part to soften the blow. I press myself into the wall and close my eyes.

"Oh no." There's genuine concern in her voice. "Good to hear about Simi. But how badly is he hurt? Will he be okay?"

My eyes pop open. Maybe all that's happened has changed her, too. The band around my chest breaks, and I'm crying again.

"I can call his mother if you'd like. Give her the information so she can get to him."

"Um, yeah, that would be great." The ice around the mom-shaped place in my heart thaws a tiny bit more. "I can give you her number."

"I have it." She pauses. My heart skips. "We've been talking since . . ." She trails off.

Since I left. The words she doesn't say land with a thud at my feet.

"Oh. Can I ask why?" I can't stop myself from asking, even though the usual warning bells sound in my head. I keep waiting for the Maryanne Clementine I know to come back and remind me of all the mistakes I've made. She might even think I came to the city to chase after him. The familiar dread creeps back.

"It occurred to me, when you . . . left, that maybe I didn't know you as well as I thought. I wanted to know the part of you that Alfie's family loved so much. I think I was jealous, but I get it now. They're great people." There's sunshine in her voice, a dawn breaking through the storm that is—was—our relationship. I can feel it, all the way over here, a hundred miles away. I raise my face and let it melt away the rest of the icy parts between us.

Then a spark of realization hits me. I guess I didn't know my mom as well as I thought I did either. It occurs to me that I judged her as harshly as she did me.

"Mom?"

"Yes?" Her response is so open, so full of hope, it breaks my heart that it took an earthquake to let us talk. Real, judgment-free talk. I take another step into her sunshine.

"Maybe when this is all over, you can tell me what happened? I mean why? I don't think I know your side of the story."

"I would love nothing more."

I'm crying again, but this time they're springtime tears, cleansing and hopeful.

I give her Alfie's information the best I can and promise to call if there are any changes. I've cried so much, I have to dry off the phone when we hang up. My insides are empty and full at the same time. I didn't know how badly I missed her. My mom. It finally feels like the dust may actually settle.

On my way back to the nurses' station, a loud voice echoes through the curved white halls.

"Code Blue. 10C. Code Blue."

Mia

10C. ALFIE'S ROOM.

Code Blue.

I bolt toward his room. My leg screams in pain, but I don't listen. My heart is in my throat. I'm running as fast as I can. I round the corner and almost crash into the large desk in the middle of the room. Simi arrives just after me.

A hurricane surges through my body.

Alfie's room is stuffed with masked people in blue and green scrubs, a sea of arms and hands reaching and grabbing in all directions. Through the glass wall, I see someone push his bed flat and yank his pillow from under his head. I fight to keep from gagging.

"Don't look," Simi says. But I do.

I'm here. I inhale icy shards that make my whole body shake. I swallow the sobs erupting from my throat and exhale through the tears. I'm showing up. I won't turn away. Someone rips off his blanket and shoves his gown to his waist. His bruised skin pale under the fluorescent lights.

They move his arms to his sides. His beautiful arms. I want to close my eyes and imagine them around me. Safe and warm. I don't. I stay present.

A deep voice orders adrenaline, and another body injects his IV with a clear liquid. The perky nurse from earlier climbs on top of him and pushes so hard on his chest, I hear the snap ten feet away.

A part of me breaks too.

Please don't hurt him.

Simi's hand is on mine. She squeezes. She's giving me strength to keep standing.

They pump his chest with rigid arms. They force air and pump again.

I breathe the same shaky rhythm.

A doctor asks for paddles.

"Clear!" Alfie's entire body jerks.

I jolt upright.

Flashes of Alfie in the golf cart burst into my mind, his shocked face falling with relief when he realizes I'm okay.

The doctor shouts a number. "Clear!"

Then it's Alfie on the pitching mound, crisp uniform and his full-force smile, waving to me in the stands.

"Clear!"

At the lake, his razor-sharp jaw twitching, eyes wide, as I feed our duck.

The doctor shouts another number and rubs the paddles together.

Air seeps from my lungs and I have to gasp to fill them. I want to give it all to Alfie.

"Clear! Come on, kid."

His full lips on mine as I fall into his arms from the homecoming float.

The beeps turn into one continuous sound. My exhales turn into moans.

Someone yells "Clear!" again. His body lurches.

Alfie in that bed. Smiling and hopeful for what's to come.

I didn't know what a flatline sounded like before today. It

really is flat. A solid sound drawn out for eternity. It's lighter than I thought it would be too.

"Time of death . . ."

I stop listening. I slide down the front of the desk's Formica surface and watch each pair of hands exit his room. Simi is next to me, her arms heavy on my shoulders. I lean on her just as much.

I feel like my heart left my body. Floated to the stars and is hovering there. Watching from a distance. It's like all my nerve endings short-circuited, and now everything sounds and feels like I'm underwater.

The nurse who lent me her phone kneels in front of me.

"You can go in to say goodbye, if you want."

Of course I want to. But how? How do you say goodbye to a part of yourself? That's what Alfie is. He is the best part of me. Because he has my heart.

He is my heart.

I'm here. Staying present for everything. But what happens when everything is too much? We aren't made to take in so much at once.

I close my eyes and let myself sink to the bottom of the lake inside me, where it's quiet and no one is asking me to move or speak.

Because if I do, then it's real.

I push myself further into the deep.

It can't be real.

Simi's hand squeezes mine, and I'm back in the hallway, its pungent, sour-sweet smell turning my stomach. I take in her normally warm tone, blanched under a twisted expression. Her eyes ask the same question as the nurse. She's right. I need to keep my promise. Even if it hurts.

"You can do this," she says. I inhale through my nose and push myself up. She stands too, but stays in the hall. Her sobs echo off the walls.

Fat tears choke my nose and throat and sting my eyes as I inch toward his room. Something breaks open inside me, and the lake takes me. With every step, I sink further. This time, I fight. I push my foot forward, and it feels like I'm fighting and kicking to get to the surface. I gasp for air, but it's only sand and dirt that I breathe in. Every step, I get closer until I'm there.

My chest heaves as I suck in big gulps of air. Coughing out the snot and sand. Wiping the salt from my eyes until I can see.

He's there. But he's not.

Not really.

His room is littered with deflated gloves and plastic vials. A disconnected breathing tube juts out of his mouth. Medical tape pulls at his cheeks.

I lay my head on his chest. It's so still. He's solid and soft at the same time. Warm where we touch.

My tears pool on his stomach and drip down his side. The waters inside me recede. Or maybe I've cried it all out.

Mia

ALFIE'S DEATH WAS SUDDEN, UNEXPECTED. AN OVERLOOKED blood clot come loose. There was nothing anyone could have done, they said. The lab techs were overwhelmed with CT and MRI orders, and Alfie seemed all right. Cheery, even.

It just happens like this sometimes, they said.

They said . . .

Mia and Simi

I FINALLY GET MY ANKLE LOOKED AT, AND I WAS RIGHT: THEY do need to cut off my boots. They were ruined anyway. I find a place to sit outside the main doors. A pew-shaped thing the color of a tombstone, dedicated to someone named Hugh Toland. I push my palms into the hard stone bench and let the cold seep into my bones.

Pulling out my phone, I flip it over and over in my hands. How much faster could I have found Alfie if only I'd remembered to keep it charged? How much more time might I have had with him?

I slouch forward, resting my elbows on my knees. Shutting my eyes, I focus on the icy trails winding up my back and out to my limbs and push down the tornado of emotions swirling inside me until all that's left is emptiness. I let its dark chill spread to every one of my limbs.

After a while, a warm presence appears to my left. I open my eyes, and Simi is there. Her long hair braided behind her back. Mouth pulled down at the corners. Worry in her eyes.

I can't look in them right now. If I do, I'm going to dissolve into nothing right here on Mr. Toland's memorial. I turn my phone screen side up. "I met this older woman tonight," I say. My voice shatters the silence and shocks us both.

"Oh yeah?"

"She was looking for a tree she planted, like, a million years ago." I keep thinking if my phone was working, there might've been a text from him. Something that would tell me what he was thinking. What he was feeling. I press the power button on the side of my phone, but nothing happens. "At first, I thought she was lost, but she knew right where she was."

"Was she?" Her tone is slow, deliberate. It grates down my spine.

"I think she has dementia. She kept calling me Barbara." I chew on my lip and press the power button again, harder this time. "I ran into Chin-Sun again too."

"Oh wow."

"She's pretty cool, once you get to know her." I keep trying. The more I press, the harder I press, the bigger the balloon taking up space in my lungs gets. I can feel Simi watching me carefully. Studying me.

"Mia." Her hand presses against my thigh. I ignore it.

I have to see if there's anything. I have to know that he tried to call me back. Or sent a message. Why didn't I think to check earlier? Why didn't I call earlier? My nostrils flare and I pinch my mouth shut. I smash the power button hard against the side of the phone. Over and over again.

"Mia, stop." Simi reaches for the phone, but I jerk it away. "It's not going to turn on. Remember there's no battery." Cracks appear at the edges of her calm demeanor. She's losing her patience.

I don't care. I need to know.

"Mia, stop." She lets out an exasperated sigh. "Give it to me. Mia, it's not going to work. It's . . ." She sucks in the last word, but it's too late. I know she didn't mean it, but it doesn't matter. I heard it.

I felt it. A poison dart shot straight into my throat.

I recoil from her, my chest heaving, my hands clutching my phone to the place where her poison permeates my bloodstream. With every heartbeat, that word drives itself further inside me until it finds its target.

Her eyes are huge moons staring at me. Her lips forming a tiny circle like she could suck out the poison from there.

I say it. I say the word she left off.

"Dead."

Something dark rises from deep inside me. Something primal. Low and thick. Guttural.

I open my mouth and it pours from me, taking everything with it. I don't care who hears or sees. I collapse into a heap. Simi's arms wrap around me tight, holding the pieces of me breaking off together. I roll my head onto her lap, sobbing and heaving, fists beating my legs.

"Why is this happening?" I choke out the words. "After everything we went through. I found him. He was so happy. We were going to be happy."

"I know." Simi's own voice is husky and wet.

"It's not right. Not fair. He was fine and now he's gone." I want to rage, throw rocks at every star until they all fall out of the sky. So everyone can feel this pitch-black hole of nothing in my heart.

I cry and scream into her lap. Her own tears fall onto my face and slide down my neck.

"I'm so, so sorry." She says that over and over until I stop sobbing. She smooths my hair away from my face. I turn into her leg because that's what I was doing for him. She rubs my back until there are no more tears left to shed.

Morning dawns, gray and silent. The sun sneaks in under the

haze, almost as an apology. Even it knows that feeling like this should only happen in the dark.

At some point, exhausted and spent, we gather the strength to go inside. There's paperwork to fill out. Parents arriving to help. Next steps to plan.

Mia

A FEW WEEKS LATER, SIMI DRIVES ME AND ANNA TO THE BACK-side of the high school's baseball field. We sit quietly as Simi navigates the dirt road in Alfie's truck, which his parents let us use for this task. Sitting in the cab, smelling his scent and remembering how his hands draped over the steering wheel was almost too much.

Anna sniffs every now and then. Simi clears her throat. I close my eyes and try to soak in as much of him as I can. Even though we're all experiencing this in different ways, we're connected through the silent contemplation of what we'd planned. Coach gave us permission and let us use the service road to get as close as possible since I'm still using crutches to get around.

I'd done more to my ankle than sprain it that night. I'd amassed several hairline fractures in my foot too. I don't mind the crutches, though, even if they do make my arms sore. In some ways, they're the last direct link to that night. To Alfie.

After the dust settled, Simi's school released a safety report that said the dorms would be closed permanently. They gave students the option of finding housing on their own with a stipend or finishing the semester online. Simi chose the latter option, since we were used to it from our early high school days. Plus, I think she felt safer at home for now, after everything that happened. Even if she wouldn't admit it.

I came home too. But just for a visit. Just long enough to settle some things.

When she shuts off the engine, we all climb out of the cab. I open the tailgate and take out the shovels and lean them against the tire well. Anna lifts the heavy bags of dirt out and stacks them on the ground. Simi climbs in and drags the large wooden planter to the edge of the bed. It takes all three of us to lower it to the ground.

"We should've brought a dolly," Simi says, visually measuring how far we need to slide it to the spot we picked.

"We can do this." Anna's face is full of determination. She and Alfie have the same eyes, and they narrow in the same way when they're challenged. Emotion swirls inside me, and I have to stop myself from touching her face.

Anna and Simi drag the supplies to our designated spot at the backside of the field, a straight line to the pitcher's mound. They have to do the heavy lifting since I still have the crutches. I do what I can to help, but mostly I'm just here.

The mounds of folded dish towels Alfie's mom taped to the top of my crutches don't take away all the armpit pinching, so I take a break against the tailgate. Both times I've seen her since, I don't think she sat down once. She wouldn't stop fussing over my leg or filling everyone's glasses or coffee cups. Making sure everyone is eating. Everyone but her. She can't talk about it yet. But really, how do you speak the ugliest words out loud?

I lean the crutches against the back of the truck and take in the area. There are a few trees already lining the fence and spotting the area beyond. This one will be the first willow, though.

Simi hops onto the tailgate beside me. We've been together almost every minute since that night. Like it used to be. But also in a brand-new way that seems easier. I study one of the trees at the edge of the fence. It's tall—oak, I think.

"You see that branch?" I pointed to one growing out and to the left. Simi nods. "Did you know that once a branch grows in a certain direction, it's impossible to change its route? Only a new one growing out of the trunk can go another way."

"I did not." Simi pretends to inspect my scalp. "Are you sure you didn't get hit on the head or anything?"

I push her hand away and laugh. The sound of my laughter is different now. Quieter, more sure. Something inside me shifted that night, but ultimately in a good way.

"Mia?" she asks. "I'm glad we're doing this."

I think of Devi looking for her tree. Loving the way the branches curled everywhere. Even loving the parts she couldn't see, safe in the knowledge that the roots were working just as hard. Maybe even harder.

Alfie's no longer here with me, but that doesn't mean he's gone. Not all the way. He's in the way the new moon never tires of starting anew. He's in the way the ducks argue over stale popcorn at the lake. In late-night stargazing sessions. In renditions of "Take Me Out to the Ballgame" and the seventh-inning stretch.

But most of all, he's here, inside me. Like all those camellias he loved so much. Defying the winter gray. Showing up when everything else turned to rust. That's the best thing about him. And it's all mine.

"Yeah, I'm glad too."

Simi rests her head on my shoulder, and I lay my head on hers. I'm determined to stay strong for her, like she's always been for me. It's about time.

"When's the next time you're going to the Gurdwara?" I ask.

"Probably tomorrow. They're making soup. Why?"

"Thought I might tag along, see if I can help."

"Okay, now I know you hit your head." She laughs. "I mean, of course you can come."

I think Alfie would like that too.

"Are you two going to plant this tree or what?" Anna leans on the handle of one of the shovels, its blade halfway in the dirt. "The environment needs all the oxygen help it can get."

"Coming!" I start to prop the crutches under my arms, but Simi puts her hand over mine.

"Mia?"

"Hmm?"

"I'm going to miss him a lot."

"Me too."

For just a moment, I close my eyes. I imagine Alfie laughing on the pitcher's mound. At the lake, snuggled under a Strawberry Shortcake comforter, afraid of a harmless duck. Introducing a customer to a new band in the vinyl store. At the coffee shop, joking with Alice, saying "That's where it's AT."

He was in all those places and more.

And now he's getting his own willow tree. Where his roots can spread as far and wide as he wants.

We dig until we get Devi's measurements perfect—twice as wide and just as deep. By the time we do, the sun is high and we are covered in sweat and dirt.

Mom shows up just in time with ice-cold water and snacks. She even brings a few candy bars with her fresh fruit assortment and doesn't make any weird faces when Simi and I split the biggest one. Anna goes for the chocolate-covered peanuts.

Mom helps us loosen the tree from its planter and lower it into the ground. I insist on being the one to shovel the dirt back into the hole. Dropping my crutches, I scrape dirt and let it fall over the roots. Anna pours the rich soil we brought into the hole, and I mix it with my own pile.

I turn the blade over and over, each shovel-full a Band-Aid over my heart. I thought it would be too much. Too like burying him all over again. To my surprise, it's like starting over, in a way. A chance to bury the most secret, best part of him—the part of him that will forever be with me—but know that something beautiful will come from it.

As we smooth the dirt and stamp it down, we all help water the freshly turned earth with our tears. Even Mom cries.

When it's over, Anna and Simi pack up the truck and wait for me there. I lower myself to the harder ground near our willow and watch its branches sway in the autumn breeze. Mom sits next to me and puts her hand over mine.

"This will be so nice when it grows some," she says. "I can just picture a cute little couple sitting in its shade eating lunch or watching a game."

The image of some other couple sitting under Alfie's tree twists like a stake to the heart. I pinch my lips as hot tears prick my eyes.

"Oh now." Mom wraps her arms around me and draws me close. "Isn't that why you planted it? So life could go on?"

The bitterness welling up inside me dissolves in an instant. The tears stay, though.

"You're right, I know." I sigh. "It's just, after the earthquake, I met this really sweet older woman who told me a story about how she planted a tree just like this one. She loved it so much that she never forgot it. Not even after her mind betrayed her. She was out that night to make sure it was safe." I wipe my nose. "I never got to tell him about her. About Devi—that's her name. I guess this was my way."

Mom nods, her own face full of emotion.

I pull out my phone and stare at the tiny crust of paper peeking out from the case. I flick it gently back and forth. It's so worn now, I'm afraid that the corner will fall off.

"Have you read that yet?" Mom clears her own grief from her throat. "Since that night?"

I shake my head.

"You know love doesn't go away just because someone isn't here. Your friend Devi knew that, which is why she went searching for her tree."

A sob breaks free from my chest. I nod.

"Look at what you've done here, Mia. You've given your story, Alfie's story, roots. And now you both get to reach toward the stars." She kisses my cheek, then leaves me with his words.

Sometime after I hear her engine start and her tires scrape against the dirt road, I peel off my phone case and gingerly unfold his letter.

Alfie

Dear Mia,

You're the love of my life.

And I know you love me, even if you won't say it anymore. Don't cry over this, my beautiful Mia. Our love was never meant to last forever. We were never marathon people.

We raged and clawed at each other until the friction between us became molten—stone turned liquid. Then we poured into each other, molding ourselves to fit each other's curves and edges perfectly. Until the itch to rage appeared again.

But that world crumbled, like so many do.

I need to let you go because that's what you said you wanted.

But know this. If you speak my name, I will be there. I will keep you in my heart always. All you ever need to do is think of me, and I'll be there.

I'll be the shimmer on the horizon. The waters that become clouds that nourish the earth. The breeze that moves through your hair. If you listen, you'll hear me tell you how beautiful you are. And how much I love you.

I don't want this, but for you I will fade into the background.

One day, you will love again.

You deserve it, Mia. You deserve everything, especially a forever, even if it's not with me.

Because even if our love isn't eternal, it's definitely one for the ages.

Love,

Alfie

Epilogue

Dear Alfie,

It's been a year since the earthquake. That was one of the worst nights of my life, but you know that. It's also one of the best because of the time I got to spend with you.

I know now what you were trying to tell me. What was different than what you said in your letter. We *are* marathon people. We have to be. Even smoke and ash get new life in something else. That's the point. People go through things, and they get hurt. But then they get up, shave off the rough edges, and figure out new ways to show up.

The trick is to keep showing up. You taught me that. Well, you and a couple of amazing women I met that night.

I've been home to visit Mom a few times. Things are different with her now. Better. I don't know if we'll ever be close, but we can both say we understand each other better now.

We can try to love each other in a way that matters.

Tonight's the anniversary of the night the city fell. The media calls it the San Andreas Quickening, but most people think that's a stupid name. I call it what it was, the thing that took you away from me.

I'm taking night classes at the community college, working toward an English degree. I tried taking a journalism class but ended up dropping it. The thing is, I'm not sure that's the way I want to bear witness to the world anymore. I'm finally realizing I can't rush through life just to get to the next thing—I'm keeping the promise I made to you. I'm showing up and doing my best to experience the good stuff in life.

Simi is on track to finish premed a year early and is eyeing a program at your old school. She'll probably be chief of staff somewhere by the time she's thirty. For now, we get to live together as official roommates. She's still as great as she's always been. We have quite a few plants around our apartment, but my favorite is our camellia bush growing on our patio. I sit in front of it when I meditate. I'm sure you can guess why.

I know, I said *meditate*. Don't worry. I keep
showing up, keep taking chances, and keep
trusting that the people I love will be there.
Before that night, I never thought I could
have that for myself. I always believed I
didn't deserve that kind of love because
no one taught me how. All it took was an
earthquake.

The whole neighborhood is commemorating
the night by letting go of wish paper. Some
wanted to do the lanterns, but they're bad for
the environment, so we chose this instead.
Anna would be so proud.

Your mom and I talk once a week. She even
sent me a whole book of her recipes, a
miracle in and of itself. I send her pictures
of my failed attempts, but I keep trying. I go
back on Holy Fridays and sit with her for the
service, holding her hand. She lights a candle
for you every week. The big ones in front of
the Virgin Mary.

They're asking us to get ready for the big
send-off, so I have to wrap this up. In a
moment, I'm going to roll this paper into a
cone. Then I'm going to light it and send it into
the universe. Then it'll be with you forever, just
like you're with me.

I'm going to play that song we danced to, the one you saved on your phone and didn't tell me about. I'll remember how your lips felt on mine. I'll hear your voice in the breeze and see your face in the stars.

You're my past, Alfie, but I'm going to be the future for both of us.

I love you forever,

Mia

ACKNOWLEDGMENTS

If you've made it this far, first of all, thank you. Thank you for reading and spending time with Mia and Alfie. And here's a tissue. Don't worry, I have extra. I knew we'd need them after going through so many of my own while I was writing this book.

I started drafting this story after hearing the song "If the World Was Ending" by JP Saxe and Julia Michaels. We were in the beginnings of the pandemic, when everything and most everyone was locked down. I couldn't get the idea out of my head of two people who, when faced with the potential ending of the world, figured out what was truly important and risked everything to find each other.

The heart of the story started out as an examination of the Orpheus and Eurydice myth and how grief is really an exploration of the Underworld. Looking back over the two years it took to make this book a reality, I see how we were all forced to make that journey in some way. Collectively, we had to take the same trip Orpheus did. The part of the myth that's so overlooked, however, is what happens after Orpheus looks back and Eurydice is thrown back into Hades. He loses confidence that his love is there and turns to make sure she's following him. When he gives up his faith, Orpheus is left to step back into the world alone. His story stops there, but ours has to continue.

Like so many people during the first two years of the pandemic, I lost family members. I was very much in Orpheus's place, unsure of how to continue without that love propelling me forward. Writing Mia's trek to find Alfie helped me learn that the journey of finding and claiming the love we have for people is healing, and grief is simply—or perhaps not so simply—the unexpressed love we have left over. If we let them, over time, those feelings become fuel that helps us live more fully in their honor, and in our own. What Orpheus learns at the threshold between the underworld and the world in which he lives is that Eurydice never truly leaves him. He will carry her with him as long as he lives. Just as Mia carries Alfie. If you're struggling with grief, dear reader, I hope you find that strength to carry those you lost too.

A huge thank-you to my agent, Mollie Glick. You saw the potential in Mia and Alfie and provided the avenue toward publication. I literally couldn't have done this without you. The energy you exude while representing your clients inspires me. The entire team at CAA has been nothing but supportive, and I'm beyond grateful to you all.

To the team at Simon & Schuster Children's, thank you for loving this story as much as I do. Nicole Ellul, editor extraordinaire, you knew how to capture Alfie's poetic heart and exactly how to elevate Mia to be her best (and emotional) self. Working with you, I've learned so much about writing and myself! It's a joy to be your partner in storytelling. Jen Strada, your eagle eye made sure this book was polished to its absolute best, and I'm grateful.

Thank you to Jess Cruickshank for the gorgeous cover design. You captured the essence of the story in one picture, and I'll be forever in awe of your talent.

The initial spark of this story came from hearing "If the World Was Ending" just about every time I got into the car, which means I owe JP Saxe and Julia Michaels a huge thank-you for writing and recording this lovely song. I hope I did your music-baby justice.

I would not be the writer I am without my writing community. Lisa Schmid, Laura Taylor Namey, Allison Bitz, Kelly Devos, Kate Foster, Chris Baron, Jenna Evans Welch, Jacqueline Firkins, your encouragement and friendship means the world to me. Michelle Hazen and Margaret Torres, you're the best sprinting partners on both sides of the Mississippi (ugh, time zones). I had the best time writing alongside you, not to mention incorporating some truly inspiring challenges into the story. I can't believe the hippopotamus made it. Heather Demetrios, the world's best writing coach, friend, and undercover depth psychologist, your guidance and support is on every page of this book. I'm beyond grateful for you and your scab-picking (I promise it's not as gross as it sounds).

I'm not super big on using the word *family* to describe groups of people in my life, but I make an exception with my cohort at Pacifica Graduate Institute. Kiese Hill, Hannah Irish, Dr. Marissa Aro, Veronica Long, your comradery and commiseration have been invaluable to me. Randall Victoria Ulyate, PhD, the universe has spoken and we are forever sisters. You should've been a Virgo, but I won't hold that against you. Thank you for always listening to my wild ideas and being the most laid-back travel pal ever.

Eliza Turrill, we started as critique partners, but now I'm so glad I can call you a friend. Your feedback encourages me to keep going and keep digging so I can be a better writer. You have the best bedside manner, and I love that you keep me on my toes.

Dante Medema, writing partner, plot doctor, friend, and forever sister. Thank you for encouraging (browbeating) me to stop working on my dissertation and write this book. You were right, but don't get used to me admitting that. I love that we get to share this writerly journey. There's no one I'd rather plot books with.

Oh, and sorry about turning your oldest child into a myth junkie. She's going to be just like me when she grows up.

John, words cannot express how grateful I am for you and your unyielding support. You married a banker who wore suits and drank five-dollar coffees and ended up married to a writer who wears the same sweater for weeks at a time and stress-eats chips and Red Vines while on deadline. You gave me room to fulfill my dreams, and I love you for it. Megan, my beautiful daughter, thank you for putting up with the same songs playing over and over in the car and listening to me ramble on about fictional people while I'm working on a new project. I'm so proud to be your mom. Matthew, even though you're a better writer than me, I'm still proud to be your mom. I love your spirit. Thank you for making things interesting.

Finally, I'd like to acknowledge the family I lost while writing this book. Supergramps, the lockdown prevented us from seeing each other much of the last year of your life, but I'm so glad we were able to be together the day before you left this world. This place is better because you were in it. Through your generosity, you helped hundreds of kids—most of all, me. Dad, your death was a surprise, and I'm still not quite used to your absence. I miss your jokes, even the bad ones. But I remember them all and will happily pass them on to your grandchildren. Vickie, the best stepmom a girl could ask for, when I told you the plot of this book, you told me to get out. That's when I knew I might be onto something. Thank you for supporting me unconditionally, all of you.